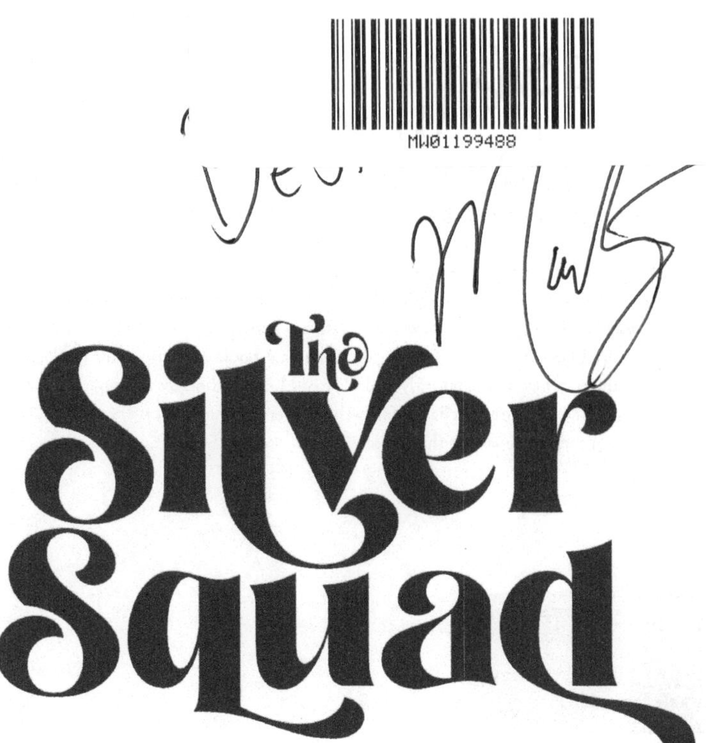

REBELS WITH WRINKLES

MARTY ESSEN

Copyright © 2025 by Marty Essen

This is a work of fiction. The names, characters, organizations, places, events, and incidents are either products of the author's imagination or are used fictitiously. Any resemblance to actual events, locales, organizations, or persons, living or dead, is entirely coincidental.

All rights reserved. No part of this publication may be reproduced or transmitted in any form or by any means, electronic or mechanical, including photocopying, recording, or any information storage and retrieval system, without written permission from the author, except for inclusion of brief quotations in a review. Additionally, e-book versions of this publication are licensed for the purchasing reader only and may not be resold or given away to other people (unless additional copies are purchased for each recipient). Thank you for respecting the hard work the author put into creating this book.

Published by:

Encante Press, LLC
Victor, MT
Books@EncantePress.com
SAN: 850-4326

Cover design by: Laura Duffy, Laura Duffy Design
Interior layout by: Deborah Bradseth, DB Cover Design

Publisher's Cataloging-in-Publication Data

Names: Essen, Marty, author.
Title: The silver squad : rebels with wrinkles / Marty Essen.
Description: Victor, MT : Encante Press, 2025. | Summary: Barry and Beth, once high school sweethearts, reunite at age seventy and go on a road trip across America.
Identifiers: LCCN 2024909498 | ISBN 9781734430394 (pbk.) | ISBN 9781734430387 (epub)
Subjects: LCSH: Love in old age – Fiction. | Vigilantism – Fiction. | Older people – Travel – Fiction. | Animal welfare – Fiction. | Homeless persons – Protection – Fiction. | BISAC: FICTION / Romance / Later in Life. | FICTION / Romance / Action & Adventure. | FICTION / Crime.
Classification: LCC PS3605.S64 2024 | DDC 813 E--dc23
LC record available at https://lccn.loc.gov/2024909498

10 9 8 7 6 5 4 3 2 1

Also by Marty Essen:

Cool Creatures, Hot Planet: Exploring the Seven Continents

Endangered Edens: Exploring the Arctic National Wildlife Refuge, Costa Rica, the Everglades, and Puerto Rico

Time Is Irreverent

Time Is Irreverent 2: Jesus Christ, Not Again!

Time Is Irreverent 3: Gone for 16 Seconds

Time Is Irreverent: Ooh, It's a Trilogy! (Books 1-3)

Hits, Heathens, and Hippos: Stories from an Agent, Activist, and Adventurer

Doctor Refurb

CONTENTS

For:

Warren Spawn

and

Cherie Spawn

CHAPTER 1

Barry

Barry swore that he'd never even consider moving out of his house, yet here he was, touring a spanking new apartment in the spanking new Blue Loon Village senior living center. "Assisted living!" he huffed, looking into the pale blue eyes of his oval-faced daughter. "I don't need any assistance."

Jill ran her hand along the polished granite counter that divided the kitchen from the living room. "Not yet. But that's what's wonderful about this place. It's all here. You would start in an independent living apartment, and later, only if necessary, seamlessly graduate to assisted living, memory care, and even nursing care."

"Graduate! Doesn't graduating require forward progress?"

"You know what I mean. The point is that you can stay in one place through all stages of senior life."

"What's wrong with living in my own home for the stage I'm in now?"

"We've talked about this before, Dad. Since Mom died, all you've done is eat, sleep, and watch TV. What's the point of owning an entire two-story house if you seldom leave your chair? And here you can make some friends your own age."

"I have plenty of friends."

"Who?"

"Bill and—"

"Bill died last year," she interrupted.

He looked away. "Oh . . . yeah."

"And selling your house, while prices are high, is not only wise, but it will also give you enough money to live here for the rest of your life. Besides, we both know that you'd find fault in any apartment where others had previously lived." She stepped around the counter, and with moves reminiscent of a car show model, swept her hand from one side of the flawless white living room to the other. "This is all brand new. You'll never be grossed out, thinking you found a pubic hair that wasn't yours in the shower and have to engage in one of your cleaning fits."

"I don't have cleaning fits," he protested.

"Yes, you do. Remember our last big family Thanksgiving, when you found that fingernail clipping next to the phone in the kitchen?"

"So?"

"You all but put on a hazmat suit to pick it up. Then you spent the rest of the afternoon surreptitiously looking at everyone's hands."

He scowled. "I did not!"

"And you couldn't let it go. You became Barry Swanson, fingernail detective!"

"That's ridiculous!"

"Oh yeah? Then how'd you figure out that the clipping was Harry's?"

"It wasn't Harry's. It was his date's. Whatever his name was. You could see it—"

"Aha!" Jill interrupted.

"That's . . ." He reconsidered and shrugged. "Okay, maybe I went a little overboard that time. But what does that have to do with cleaning fits?"

"Mom told me that after everyone went home, you went through a quarter bottle of Mr. Clean, scrubbing the phone and everything around it."

"I went through a tablespoon of it—tops."

"And that's not a cleaning fit?"

"No!"

Jill closed her eyes for a moment. Upon opening them, she proposed, "How 'bout this? If I agree that you don't have cleaning fits, will you agree to keep an open mind about living here? Try it for a year. If you're miserable after that, I promise to help you find another place to live."

Barry ran his fingers through his abundant gray hair. "I've never been able to say no to either you or your mother. So I guess there's no point in further resistance. But if living among the multitudes isn't for me, I'm gonna hold you to your promise—and the next place might be a secluded cabin near the Canadian border."

She rose up on tiptoes and kissed his cheek. "Thank you. I know you're gonna love it here!"

* * *

Eight weeks later, Barry did what he had done every day since his wife, Marilyn, had died. He eased into his old leather recliner—perfectly broken in to fit his wiry body—only this time, for the first time, he did so in his spanking new apartment. He squinted. As much as he approved of the general cleanliness of the place, the white walls were too bright. Way too bright. He wondered if the management would object if he painted them a different color. Perhaps storm cloud gray.

He pushed out of his chair, shoved it closer to the picture window, and angled it so he could look down at the new residents entering the building. This was the grand opening week at the Blue Loon Village, which meant that pretty much everyone who was going to live here in the near future was moving in within a few days of each other. In fact, the only reason he could move into his apartment on such short notice was that Jill had put him on the reservation list many months earlier, without his knowledge. Much to Barry's dismay, she had even arranged for him to be on the first floor, next to the model apartment he'd toured earlier.

He put a stop to that when he grumbled to the facility's director, Samantha, at his pre-move-in orientation. "That location is for socialites or the nearly dead. My God, it's only two doors down from the dining room!"

The pudgy, thirtyish-looking brunette responded to Barry by gazing across her desk, flashing a big-toothed smile, and speaking with a lilt one might use when training a puppy, "I would think a handsome man like you would want to be where the action is." She looked at her computer screen and tapped a few keys. "All the apartments are rented, but several of the residents assigned to the top floor—that's four . . . floors . . . up—are on the waiting list for the lowest level. Let me see if I can make a switch." She tapped a few more keys and hit enter. "There! You're now on the fourth floor, in the far corner, facing the front of the building."

Barry hated it when younger people talked to him as if he were a puppy. He wasn't a cuddly golden retriever, nor had age regressed his mind to that of a child. Nevertheless, since Samantha came through for him, he kept his feelings to himself. After all, he might need another favor from her in the future.

Now, as Barry continued watching from above, he felt a sense of satisfaction. If he was going to live out the rest of his life here, at least he had secured the apartment in the best location. And while he was curious about the kinds of people who were moving in, it didn't mean that he actually wanted to meet any of them. Being tucked away in a secluded corner would help him achieve his goal of avoiding contact with the other residents as much as possible. If he wanted to talk to a human, Marilyn's ashes, in an urn on the coffee table, would suffice.

Animals were a whole other matter. Samantha had provided him with a list of Blue Loon Village rules, and at the top of that list was a rule prohibiting residents from having dogs or cats. At least he was able to bring along Gertrude, his leopard gecko. Had she not been able to join him, it would have been a deal-breaker.

Barry thought about that list as he pushed up from his recliner and walked over to a small terrarium, which sat on a stand. He opened the lid, placed the seven-inch-long, black-spotted lizard on his shoulder, and returned to his recliner.

"Rules," he muttered to Gertrude as he looked down at two teenage boys, helping another resident move in. "When I was a child, I had to follow rules. Now I have to follow them again. If I'm gonna go out the same way I came in, the least life could do is give me all the benefits of youth, too."

CHAPTER 2

Beth

Over the next few days, Barry got into the habit of arriving at the dining room as close to the end of the meal service time as possible, selecting a table as far away from others as he could, and, above all, avoiding eye contact with everyone. He realized that he'd turned into the curmudgeon he swore in his youth he wouldn't become, but back then he never imagined what it would be like to lose his wife so early in his golden years and end up in a senior living apartment.

At most meals, he worked on his life versus death list, never writing anything down, since he planned to continue living for the time being. Mainly, he just wanted to reassure himself that he had something to look forward to and wasn't a burden to others. Failing at that, well, a headfirst dive from his fourth-floor balcony would probably do the trick.

Right now, however, his most compelling reason to live was his daughter, Jill, and his son, Harry. Sure, both of his children had drifted away into their own lives and relationships, but drifting isn't permanent, and he wouldn't subject them to the pain of losing both parents in such a short amount of time.

And then there was Gertrude. Giving proper care to a gecko

isn't for everyone. He certainly couldn't entrust an amateur with that task. At dinner, midway through his first week, he contemplated the numbers: he was seventy and Gertrude was five. Even though some geckos live into their twenties, more than likely she had closer to ten good years left. He could have ten good years left, too. Then he thought about his wife, Marilyn, and his friend, Bill, beating him to the grave and grew less confident about his life expectancy.

"Gertrude could outlive me!" he shouted to the empty chair on the opposite side of the table. When others in the dining room swiveled their heads in his direction, he pointed to his ear and mouthed, "I'm on the phone."

He finished his phantom call and hurried upstairs to his apartment. Grabbing a pen and paper from the counter, he made a detailed list, which he titled "For the Care and Feeding of Gertrude." With that in hand, he walked from room to room, gathered up all the cash he could find—about two hundred dollars—sealed everything into an envelope, and taped it to the side of her terrarium.

* * *

Barry continued to add tweaks to his routine, and by midway into the second week, he was fully into the rhythm of senior living—at least his version of it. To avoid having to socialize in the elevator, each morning he'd take the stairs down to the first floor. From there, he'd ignore the day's activities written in colorful markers on a dry erase board outside the dining room, walk through the serving line, eat, and repeat the process for lunch and dinner. Once, he even took the stairs back up to his room. That, however, was a onetime adventure, which convinced him that all the huffing and puffing and creaking of his knees was worse than the prospect of having to endure the small talk and social activity invites known to haunt the elevator.

His isolation efforts were largely successful until a woman's voice interrupted his quiet lunch. "Do we know each other?"

Her question startled him, nearly causing him to choke on the piece of meat he was chewing. Glancing up, he met the gaze of a slender, gray-haired woman, her delicate features adorned with a playful smile that danced upon her lips. She appeared to be about his age, but then pretty much everyone he saw these days appeared to be about his age. "I'm sorry. I don't think so."

"That's a shame," she said. "Back in high school, I dated a guy who bobbed his head when he chewed, just like you do."

"I bob my head when I chew?"

"You didn't know that?"

"No, but thanks. Now I'll spend the rest of my life—however short that is—being self-conscious about it."

She extended her hand, holding her thumb and forefinger a fraction of an inch apart. "It's very subtle. Nothing to be self-conscious about—really. I always thought it was endearing when my old boyfriend did it, and I assure you it's the same for you, too." Her eyes flitted to the ceiling and back. "Well, enjoy the rest of your lunch. And thanks for sparking an old memory. I hadn't thought about Barry in years."

"Barry? That's *my* name. Wait a minute." He squinted. "Are you Beth Potter?"

"Yes!"

Doing his best to toss aside more than a week's worth of curmudgeonliness, Barry reached down to grab whatever youthful vigor he could find as he pushed himself up to join Beth in a warm embrace. "Oh, my God! How long has it been?"

"Since the summer after we finished high school."

"That can't be. We must've seen each other at least once since then."

She stepped back and shook her head. "Not that I can recall. Although at our age, you can never be too sure."

He chuckled and, with a sweep of his hand, gestured for her to join him at the table. "How true."

Taking the seat opposite him, Beth brushed a few crumbs off the place mat before asking, "So have you lived in Minnesota all this time?"

"No. After college, I started working in radio, and like most people in the business, I moved around quite a bit. Only when I got hired by a radio station in Denver did I find some stability. I adored my coworkers, the mountains, and pretty much everything else about Colorado, and stayed there with my wife until we both retired, and she talked me into returning to Minnesota to be closer to our two children."

"Is your wife here with you?"

Barry looked down and talked to his plate. "No. She died last year—rather suddenly."

Beth reached across the table and squeezed his hand. "I'm so sorry."

He returned her squeeze and glanced up. "How 'bout you? Wasn't it your dream to escape Chisholm, move someplace warm, and never endure another Minnesota winter?"

"It was. But, you know . . . best-laid plans. I moved to New York. Got married; got divorced. Then I moved to New Mexico. What a change that was! I started in the Student Affairs department at Southern New Mexico University and worked my way up to become the dean of students. That's where I met my second husband, Jeremy. He was a professor at the same college, and we lasted for nearly twenty-three years, until I caught him with a busty graduate assistant's lips around his cock. I took a lower-level job the following school year at the University of Minnesota, just to get as far away from him as possible. There, I worked my way up all over again, stayed until I retired, and yadda yadda yadda, here I am!"

"Any children?"

She focused on the wall beyond his left shoulder and said, "Jeremy and I tried for a while, but it didn't happen."

"I'm sorry."

"That's okay. Having college students around me year after year filled the void."

Barry attempted to eat his last piece of meat without delaying the rhythm of their conversation. When he realized chewing faster increased his head bobbing, he slowed down and concentrated on swallowing as soon as he could safely do so. Upon his success, he said, "I have to confess that even though we knew each other casually, practically since the first grade, I don't remember many details about our time together, other than that we didn't begin dating until our senior year and never formally broke up. After high school, we chose different colleges. You went your way, and I went mine."

"Yeah, specific details are missing for me too. But now that we're getting reacquainted, I bet a bunch of old memories will come flooding back for both of us in the coming days." She rapped the table with an open hand. "Oh! Here's one detail I still remember vividly. We were both politically active and pledged that we wouldn't be like our parents. We were gonna make a difference and change the world."

"Well, did you?"

Her lips curved into a faint smile. "I don't think anyone can work as long as I did in the field of education and not influence some lives. But did I change the world? I don't think so. How 'bout you?"

Barry balled up his paper napkin and launched it toward the nearest wastebasket. He missed badly. "I spent my entire career working at radio stations—doing everything from spinning records to advertising sales to general management—but unless something I played from Bruce Springsteen changed someone's life, my impact on the world was minimal."

Beth pointed to the napkin. "Are you gonna pick that up? This is a retirement complex. Someone could trip."

"On a napkin?"

She shrugged.

He pushed away from the table and stared down at the napkin. Could he pick it up without looking like a stiff old man? He glanced back at Beth.

She winked.

He leaned over, powering through the catch in his hips, and grasped the napkin with one hand while resisting the urge to push on his back with the other. Then, without so much as a grunt—at least one that Beth could hear—he straightened and arched a shot into the wastebasket.

"Still trying to show off after all these years?" she asked.

His face flushed. "I guess so."

She stood. "After all that effort, I hate to ask you to sit again. Do you wanna meet back here for dinner?"

His heart fluttered. Whether it did so in remembrance of adolescent love or as a warning that he was too old to go there again was debatable. So he simply answered, "Five-thirty?"

"It's a date!" She offered an exaggerated wave and glided for the main door.

Barry watched Beth disappear before ambling toward the elevator, wondering how she had managed to age so much more gracefully than he did.

He was still pondering that question after returning to his apartment and settling into his recliner, with Gertrude on his shoulder. "It hardly seems fair," he said to the gecko. "Women spend the first two-thirds of their lives being the more attractive sex, but at some point the roles are supposed to switch, with women losing some of their attractiveness and men becoming more distinguished. I don't feel distinguished at all. I feel old."

He closed his eyes, hoping to recall forgotten memories of his teenage romance with Beth, and fell asleep.

* * *

Barry awoke in a panic. He hadn't meant to fall asleep with Gertrude on his shoulder, and now she was missing. Other than tropical fish, the Blue Loon Village had a no pets policy. He'd only managed to get his gecko approved by arguing that the apartment's policy was a form of speciesism. After all, one form of animal contained within a glass enclosure was the same as any other. He hadn't mentioned that Gertrude liked to ride on his shoulder.

His current situation—the result of augmenting his clever argument with what he considered to be a little harmless rule bending—meant that he was fully reclined in his chair, afraid to move, because Gertrude could be underneath among the springs and bars of the recliner mechanism.

With a soft voice, he called out, "Gertrude? Come here, Gertrude." He knew that responding to calls wasn't a gecko feature, but he had to try it, anyway.

He swept the room with his eyes, hoping to spot Gertrude on a lamp, a table, or a curtain. With her nowhere in sight, he attempted to sit up, but even the slightest movement caused the footrest to drop and the back to rise. Any of those actions could separate Gertrude's body from a leg, a tail, or a head.

A glance at the clock next to the television only increased Barry's stress. He had been asleep for almost two hours, and the iced tea he had with lunch was pining for an exit.

After checking his pockets for his cell phone and finding nothing, he felt around the edges of the chair cushion and scanned the room again. Eventually he spotted the phone on the coffee table in front of the couch, well out of reach.

If he were younger, he might have been strong enough to push down on the armrests and lift himself high enough to swing out of the chair without contracting it. He tried the move anyway, confirming that he was too unsteady to follow through.

He tittered as he envisioned a newspaper article, documenting his demise: *Seventy-year-old man starves to death after becoming trapped in his recliner.*

Almost worse than starving to death was that if he wanted to maintain his sixty-seven-year-long streak of not wetting his pants, he had to reach the bathroom soon. As he saw it, he had two options: sit up and risk killing Gertrude or roll over the side and risk breaking a hip. He opted for the latter, aborting his first attempt when the chair started to close. A reassessment of the maneuver told him rolling would only work if he kept his body perfectly straight. He tried again and crashed hip-first onto the floor.

"Owww!" he bellowed.

He lay there for a few minutes, trying to determine if he'd broken a hip. When the dissipating pain confirmed he was okay, he rolled onto his back and swiveled his head right and left. There she was—his beloved gecko—perched atop a book on the bottom shelf of his coffee table. He clambered to his feet by grabbing the chair arm with one hand and pushing on the floor with the other. After exhaling a quiet sigh of relief, he shuffled over, scooped up Gertrude, placed her on his shoulder, and raced to the bathroom. The sigh that followed was much louder.

CHAPTER 3

The Goth Septuagenarian Revenger

Before leaving his apartment, Barry shaved, brushed his hair, inspected his nostrils for protruding nose hairs, and put on a shirt that looked nice but not too dressy. He arrived in the dining room at precisely five-thirty, sat at his usual table, and waited.

Beth arrived ten minutes later. She too had fixed herself up, having squeezed herself into a little black dress, her gray hair teased high with a streak of black, her eyes rimmed with dark makeup, and her fingernails polished black.

"Goth?" Barry asked, as he stood to pull out a chair for his old flame. "Is it even legal for a person older than fifty to go goth?"

She settled into her chair and said, "Don't you remember how much fun we had when we drove to the Twin Cities for the State Hockey Tournament and snuck into a bar to see Siouxsie and the Banshees? When my parents found that picture of us all dressed up in front of the stage, we got into so much trouble. But it was worth it! I thought about that today, on the way to my hair appointment, and told my stylist to go for it." She pursed her black-cherry lips into a mock pout. "You don't like it."

He squinted. "I'm just worried that someone on the staff here will think you're dead and try to stuff you into a body bag."

Beth glared at him as she stood. "This is why we never lasted as a couple. You have no sense of fun!"

"I'm kidding! You're stunning. Please sit down. Rather than someone on the staff stuffing you into a body bag, it's far more likely that my heart will skip too many beats from looking at you, and I'll go into cardiac arrest."

"That's better," she said, returning to her chair.

"And I am certainly capable of fun."

She tilted her head. "Oh, yeah? Tell me about it."

"I . . . I. I think we should go through the food line while there's still a decent selection."

She winked. "I'll let you off the hook this time."

As they loaded their plates, Barry thought about Beth's comment. Did he really have no sense of fun? His father was the person in the family who never had any fun, and he had vowed not to be like him.

When they returned to their table he asked, "How do I change that?"

"Change what?"

"My apparent inability to have fun."

She thought for a moment before answering, "You raise a little hell."

"How do I do that?"

"You . . . we, get the hell outta here."

"We just moved in!"

"Voluntarily?"

He sliced open his baked potato before answering, "Technically, yes. But I was talked into it."

"It was kind of the same for me too. I could've resisted, but I felt pressure from my younger sister to take advantage of this brand-new facility, where I could live out my golden years and . . . well, as she said, it was so logical. Deep down, I suspected she just wanted the peace of mind of knowing that once I moved in, I was good until the day I died." She glanced at her plate and stabbed a cherry tomato with her fork. "And I was going through a bit of depression at the time."

"Did you ever see *Harold and Maude?"*

"Of course. I think most people our age saw that movie."

"I always thought Maude's decision to indulge in a lifestyle of carefree fun before ending it all on her eightieth birthday was laudable."

"I loved that movie, but I don't think I could kill myself. Besides, for us that's only ten years away!" She ate her tomato and thought for a moment. "On the other hand, Maude enjoying a little carefree fun isn't all that much different from my suggestion that we raise a little hell. Have you ever considered that the older we get the more untouchable we become? We could be senior citizen vigilantes, doing what we would've never had the guts to do if we were young. And if we ever got caught, what's the worst they could do to us? Lock us in a jail cell and feed us three bland meals a day for the rest of our lives? Hell, if we develop Alzheimer's, we might not even notice any difference from where we're living now."

Barry laughed. "You still haven't given up on us changing the world, have you?"

She looked up from her plate, with hope-filled eyes. "We still have time."

"Okay, I can see the fun in discussing this, but you can't be serious. We're old. What could we possibly do? Rob a Chick-fil-A and give the money to the poor?"

"I'm serious. And robbing something small and giving to the poor isn't a bad way to start. It would allow us to find out if we have the fortitude to do something naughty before we advance to something monumental."

His mouth gaped open. "Monumental!"

"We can't change the world as small-time robbers, but what if we um . . . *did something* to a corrupt billionaire or politician?" She took a bite of her lasagna.

"How 'bout a corrupt televangelist?" Barry asked.

She quickly swallowed. "Now you're thinking!"

He shook his head. "This is crazy. Even if we take it slow—"

"Slow?" she interrupted. "Either one of us could croak at any minute! Going slow is for the young."

"Either one of us could live for another twenty years, too. . . . Though, admittedly, I don't have any plans that extend further out than tomorrow, and I find it kind of depressing to imagine twenty more years of that."

"Exactly! How alive are you if you have no plans for the future and aren't doing something to give your life purpose?" She pointed to the corner of Barry's mouth. "You've got some salad dressing there."

He wiped a napkin across his lips and said, "Okay. Assuming I go along with you on this. What do we do next?"

"We brainstorm until we find a cause that will be exciting enough to inspire your sense of fun while being fulfilling enough to quench my desire to change the world—even if it's only a tiny corner of it."

"What if I want to change the world, too?"

"All the better. Because you can be damn sure I'm gonna join you in the fun."

* * *

Later that evening, Barry returned to his recliner, with Gertrude perched on his chest. "What've I gotten myself into?" he asked the gecko. "I thought Beth might make a good twilight-years companion, and possibly even a companion with benefits, but I never expected she'd be the Goth Septuagenarian Revenger."

The gecko was speechless.

"Sorry. I know *septuagenarian* is a big word for someone whose first language isn't English. I didn't know it either until I saw it on a card for my seventieth birthday and had to look it up."

Gertrude tilted her head, still silent.

Soon the first-again date high Barry felt after walking Beth to her apartment and giving her a quick goodnight kiss wore off, and he began to feel sleepy. This time, however, the memory of losing Gertrude earlier in the day forced him to his feet. He carried his reptile friend over to the terrarium and shut her inside.

With that worry out of the way, Barry backed into his chair and stretched out. As he began to doze, a thought sprang him upright. "Beth is right!" he blurted toward the terrarium. "I don't have a sense of fun. And as if to prove her point, all I've been doing since I kissed her goodnight is attempt to talk myself out of everything we discussed over dinner. Look at us here, accomplishing nothing. We need to get out of this apartment and raise some hell while we still can."

Gertrude didn't object.

CHAPTER 4

A Fast Car and Coffee

"I'm in!" Barry announced when he joined Beth for breakfast at what was becoming their regular table.

"I knew you would be," she said.

Barry took a moment to arrange his silverware and napkin before looking up and asking, "Who's our first target?"

"Does that mean I get to be the leader?" Beth asked, sucking in a spoonful of oatmeal.

"Well, you are the Goth Septuagenarian Revenger. Aren't you?"

She covered her mouth to avoid spraying oatmeal, composed herself, and said, "I love it! But what shall we call you?"

"No nicknames for me. Thank you very much."

"We'll see about that. And no, I don't have a target yet. We have to get organized first, and learn some things about each other, too. For instance, do you have a car and a current driver's license?"

"Yes, on both. How 'bout you?"

"I have both too, but my car is just a little four-cylinder Honda Civic. It would make a terrible getaway car."

"Mine's not much better." He picked apart his caramel roll and tossed a piece into his mouth. "I'm open to trading mine in for an upgrade, however."

"We also need a lair. Your place or mine?"

"My place, definitely. Gertrude doesn't enjoy being left alone for long."

"Gertrude?"

"My leopard gecko."

"Oh, come on! A gecko couldn't care less about human companionship."

He shot her an impish look of offense. "She's my emotional support lizard."

Beth laughed. "Is she going to accompany us on our capers too?"

"I don't see why not. Who knows? Someday she might come in handy."

"Fine. But if you're driving the getaway car, I'm riding shotgun. The gecko gets the back seat."

"Agreed."

* * *

Despite Beth's claim that they couldn't take it slow, lest they croak, the two septuagenarians—neither of whom had anything more than a speeding ticket on their record—found it more time consuming than expected to become vigilantes.

While Beth worked on compiling a list of possible targets and acquiring basic vigilante accessories, such as a pair of burner phones, a stun gun, and zip ties, Barry worked on acquiring a getaway car. He doubted a fast car would be necessary. After all, they weren't going to rob a bank or anything. Still, it was better to have a fast car and not need it than to get caught in a situation where they needed additional speed and the car couldn't deliver.

He began his search by visiting multiple inner-city car lots, where salesmen ignored his requests for something fast and ushered him to conservative four-door sedans that were more suitable for someone his age. Only when he stopped at a suburban lot did he find what he was looking for. There, an attractive, fiftyish-looking saleswoman flashed a seductive smile and said, "I have just the car for you. It has only forty-one thousand miles on it; it's never been driven in the winter; and it'll do zero to sixty in four point six seconds, with a top speed of 146."

Barry was realistic enough to recognize that he no longer had the reflexes to drive anywhere close to 146 miles per hour. Still, once he laid his eyes on the glossy, black, 2011 Ford Mustang GT, he knew the only way to calm his racing heart was to buy it.

He negotiated a price, which included trading in his old car, plus fourteen thousand dollars. He suspected he was paying too much, but the saleswoman had been so knowledgeable and helpful that he'd found it difficult to put up much of a fight. Besides, he was using money he had set aside for an exotic vacation on a warm island with his wife. Since that vacation was no longer possible, an exciting adventure with an old flame in a hot car seemed like the next best thing.

* * *

As soon as Barry returned to the Blue Loon Village, he rang Beth's doorbell and escorted her to the parking lot.

"What do ya think?" he asked.

"A Mustang? Didn't you drive a beat-up old Mustang when we were dating?"

He nodded. "This one's much better."

She playfully shaded her eyes to exaggerate her opinion of the sun reflecting off its hood. "I appreciate the nostalgia, but couldn't you have found something a little more unassuming?"

"Sure, if I listened to all the salesmen who wanted to sell me old-fogy-mobiles. I'm no car expert, but I think, in general, fast cars are supposed to look fast. That's the whole point."

"I'm just giving you shit."

"How's your side of our project going?"

She opened the passenger side door and spoke over the roof, "Take me for a ride in your hot new car, and I'll tell you."

They buckled in, and as they departed the parking lot, Beth said, "Nice! What year is it?"

"It's a 2011."

"That old? It looks almost brand new."

Barry cast a quick glance her way and quipped, "The previous owner was a little old lady who only drove it to church on Sundays."

Beth chortled and adjusted the tilt of her seat before speaking in a serious tone, "I was growing frustrated creating a list of people deserving of our vigilante services, so I set it aside and went shopping for supplies. When I returned, I rode up the elevator with a woman who turned out to be the granddaughter of Nadine, the lady who lives next door to me. She was wearing oversized sunglasses and had a scarf around her neck. I knew immediately what that was all about and pried some information out of my neighbor after her granddaughter left. The woman's name is Megan, and her husband is a regular abuser who has threatened to disappear with their two children if she divorces him or reports him to the police. We need to arrange an involuntary meeting with that man to scare the shit out of him. Our success won't change the entire world, but it sure as hell will change the world for Megan."

"Are you suggesting we kidnap him? That's a felony!"

"Only if we get caught."

The light ahead turned red. Barry eased the car to a stop, closed his eyes, and bounced his forehead against the steering wheel. "I thought we were gonna start with something small."

"We could croak at any time! Wouldn't you feel terrible if you died, knowing you could've saved Megan from a lifetime of abuse?"

"No. I'd be dead."

She narrowed her eyes. "You *know* what I mean."

"Yes, of course, I'd feel terrible. But how do two seventy-year-old people scare the shit out of a man who's likely in his twenties or thirties and certainly more physically fit than we are?"

"I haven't figured that out yet, but as the brains of this organization, it's up to me to solve that problem."

He laughed. "Are you sure you're smarter than I am?"

"You know what I mean," she repeated.

"And we're now an *organization?* With just two people? If we're gonna be an organization, shouldn't we recruit others to join us?"

"That's not a bad idea. We have an entire retirement complex full of people new to living here. While some of those people require daily assistance, others, like us, are still self-sufficient. I'm sure we can find some recruits who'd rather accomplish something instead of sitting around waiting to croak."

"I wish you wouldn't call it *croaking.*"

"Would you prefer *expire?*"

"No! That makes us sound like we're cartons of milk. Just a simple *die* or *pass away* is adequate."

A car horn blared.

Beth chuckled. "I think the light's been green for a while. The driver of the car behind us probably thinks we've passed away."

* * *

Upon returning to the Blue Loon Village, Barry and Beth got to work on planning their first caper. They both agreed to place their highest priority on not getting caught. That meant holding off on new recruits for now and taking the precautions any competent criminal would take. For instance, when Beth researched burner phones, she learned that authorities could still track them if they made calls on those phones while their registered smartphones were also turned on and nearby. As a workaround, they could switch their smartphones to airplane-mode-Wi-Fi-only when they needed them for non-calling features, such as the camera or a reading app.

Also, as part of keeping their activities secret, they agreed not to tell Nadine about their plans for her granddaughter's husband. That was the easy part. Well, that, and Beth finagling an invitation over to Nadine's apartment for coffee and cookies.

The hard part was acquiring additional information about Megan without making Nadine suspicious. In some ways, it helped that Nadine was likely experiencing the early stages of Alzheimer's disease. Whenever she bristled about too many inquisitive questions, Beth simply changed the subject for a while, and all was well.

As they sat talking on the couch, one of Beth's questions produced Megan's last name, Anderson. But in Minnesota, only the last name Johnson is more popular than the last name Anderson. With so many possibilities, and the husband's first name still unknown, she couldn't just look up Megan's address on the internet. So instead, Beth pushed up from the couch and strolled around Nadine's living room, pretending to admire various photos and trinkets, while hoping to spot an envelope or anything else with Megan's address on it. That's when she noticed a tattered old address book on the table next to the television. If anything in the apartment contained Megan's address, that was it.

She returned to the couch and finished her coffee, knowing that Nadine would soon ask, "Can I refill your cup?"

"Oh, that would be wonderful," Beth replied. "Do you mind if I use your bathroom while you do that? I'm afraid the first cup went right through me."

"Of course." Nadine pointed. "It's the second door on the right."

Beth already knew that, since every one-bedroom apartment at the Blue Loon Village featured a similar layout. She kept that information to herself and instead delayed until Nadine was on her way to the kitchen. Then she grabbed the address book and hurried to the bathroom, where she flipped through the pages until finding

Megan's address and photographing it with her smartphone.

Before returning to the living room, Beth hid the address book under her sweater. A wise precaution, since Nadine was already waiting for her with a fresh cup of coffee and a refilled plate of cookies.

Beth spent the next forty-five minutes patiently listening as Nadine filled her in on all the latest Blue Loon Village gossip. Only when Nadine returned to the kitchen with the empty plate did Beth have the opportunity to slide the address book back where she found it and come up with an excuse to say goodbye.

CHAPTER 5

Surveillance

With supplies purchased, a getaway car all gassed up, and a name and address in hand, the two old flames had everything ready for their first caper, except for the surveillance.

After Barry volunteered for that duty, Beth walked with him out to the Blue Loon Village parking lot and said, "Since you don't have any surveillance experience, are you sure you don't want to read up on the subject first?"

"Oh, come on. How difficult can it be? All I have to do is find the house and verify when the husband comes and goes. It'll be easy-peasy!"

"Be careful!"

"Of course." He pushed the unlock button on the key fob and pulled open the Mustang's door.

"Oh, and try to get a photo of both Megan and her husband. I thought it strange that Nadine listed only Megan, not her husband, in her address book. There could be many reasons for that, but it's possible I photographed an old address from before the two got married. It would be embarrassing to go to the wrong house and accuse the wrong man of being a wife-beater."

"That would get us off to an inauspicious start, wouldn't it?"

He gave Beth a little wave before shutting the door and starting the car.

Barry owned a smartphone and could have used a maps app to lead him to Megan Anderson's house, but he had purchased a Garmin GPS navigator long before he gave up his flip phone for a smartphone. Since his GPS always got him to where he needed to go, he saw no reason to switch devices. Therefore, he entered Megan's address into his GPS and was pleased to learn the drive would only take twenty-two minutes, getting him there around the time when people commonly arrive home from work. He made it without the GPS-lady's voice nagging him to make a legal U-turn even once.

The house Barry needed to watch was in the middle of a block in a quiet residential neighborhood in Northeast Minneapolis. Most of the houses there were smallish bungalows and Tudors, much older than the residents who occupied them. It was the type of neighborhood that attracts families who can't afford a house in a posh location yet desire a place where their children can play outside without constant supervision.

After parking across the street from Megan's barn-red bungalow, Barry watched for ten or so minutes before realizing that surveillance was a boring job and wishing he'd brought Gertrude along. That's when it occurred to him that he'd hardly spent any time getting to know his new used Mustang. If he multitasked, he could watch the house while learning the function of every knob, button, and light in his car.

Feeling pleased to have discovered an efficient use of his time, Barry would look over to the house, learn something new about his car, and repeat. Overall, the Mustang wasn't a complicated automobile, so he felt satisfied that he wasn't neglecting his surveillance duties.

Once he felt comfortable with everything he could reach from the driver's seat, he opened the glove box and pulled out the owner's manual. He squinted to read a page, only to conclude that the sky had grown too dark for him to see. He was about to return the manual to the glove box when he remembered his smartphone had a flashlight. Turning it on, he began to read.

* * *

A fist pounded on the Mustang's window!

Barry jerked awake.

"Are you okay in there?" a male voice asked.

Barry lowered his window and peered at a husky man partially illuminated by the surrounding city lights. "Um . . . Yeah. Sorry. I . . . I just got tired and parked here to shut my eyes for a moment. I guess I fell asleep. It happens when you're my age."

"Well, okay then," said the man, his scraggly brown beard framing his pale lips. "You'd best be off now. This is a residential neighborhood. There's no place for strangers here."

As the man walked away, Barry reached between his legs to pick up his smartphone, which had fallen to the floor, with its flashlight pointing up. He tapped the icon to turn off the light, brought the Mustang's engine to life, and rumbled down the street.

When he reached the stop sign at the corner, he flicked on his blinker and looked back through his side mirror. The man was climbing the steps to the front door of the house he'd been watching. "Target located," he mumbled to himself.

Rather than return to his apartment, Barry turned onto the cross street and parked far enough down it that the house on the corner would hide his car from anyone who might leave the Andersons' house. He stuffed his smartphone into his back pocket, got out, and hurried down the sidewalk that passed in front of the house. When he slowed to look inside, drape-covered windows blocked his view. On the chance that he'd have a better view looking through a back window, he continued to the next street, walked to the alley, and followed it until he was behind the house.

He opened the back gate, his heart pounding, urging him to run straight for the house before he lost his nerve. Instead, he forced himself to pause and take advantage of the ambient light to scan the backyard for obstacles and escape routes. After noting a swing set, a couple of toy trucks, and open gates on each side of the house, he gave himself a virtual pat on the back for having the foresight to do the proper reconnaissance. Now he could slink to the back porch, like an accomplished cat burglar.

A dog growled and then barked before Barry made it halfway across the yard. Perhaps the whole cat imagery thing was the wrong way to go. He froze until he realized the dog was on the opposite side of the fence. Even so, he had to stop it from barking. If he truly were an accomplished cat burglar, he would have thought out all the possibilities ahead of time and brought along some dog treats. Having failed to do that, he searched his pockets for anything a dog might enjoy. Finding only a roll of Tums, he saved two for himself, shrugged, and tossed the rest over the fence.

That seemed to pacify the dog.

He tiptoed onto the porch and leaned sideways to allow one eye to peer through the bottom corner of a window. There, sitting at the kitchen table, was the man he'd met earlier, a woman, and two young children. Fortunately, no one was looking in his direction.

Although nothing violent was happening at the moment, the scene was depressing nonetheless. The woman appeared to be holding back tears as she stared into the distance, and a dark bruise under her eye and another on her neck convinced Barry that she was, indeed, Megan. The man, obviously her husband, wore a simmering scowl, and their children looked blankly at their plates.

As much as Barry wished he could do something to help Megan and her children, now wasn't the time to intervene. Instead, he needed to shoot some photos, so Beth could positively confirm

Megan's identity and recognize the husband when they conducted their actual caper.

He pulled out his smartphone, eased it into position, and pressed the shutter button icon multiple times. "Shit!" he hissed to himself when his hand shook, causing the phone to rap against the window.

The man swiveled toward the sound!

Barry leaped off the porch, his legs protesting as he landed. His instincts told him to make a break for the alley, but he knew Megan's husband would either expect him to run that way or around the near side of the house. With no chance of outrunning the man, he took the most illogical route, racing around the far side and disappearing through the yawning gate as the back door flung open and the man burst onto the porch.

When Barry reached the front of the house, he realized that beelining for the Mustang would leave him in the open for too long. Instead, he hurried around the neighboring house on the opposite side of the dog, where he spotted a dark alcove. He backed into the corner, sat, and tried to calm his rapid breathing.

"I know you're here!" the man shouted from the front corner of the neighbor's house.

Barry covered his mouth with both hands.

Footsteps approached.

"It'll be easier for you if you give yourself up," the man's voice echoed between the houses.

Barry held his breath.

The footsteps paused, moved away, and faded into the distance.

To ensure that he wouldn't reveal his location if the man returned, Barry stayed motionless for a significant amount of time. Okay, he fell asleep.

When the chill of the night awoke him, he shivered in his corner, conjuring up the will to stand. Eventually, he pushed to his feet, brushed off his pants, and braved a few tentative steps. His aching shins and stiff knees were a not-so-subtle reminder that jumping and running were activities his legs should have retired from long ago. Fortunately, the pain lessened with each successive step.

That allowed Barry to resist cutting in front of Megan's house. Instead, he took the cautious route, walking the opposite way around the block, reaching his car, eager to feel the warmth of the heater cranked up to high.

He didn't stop shivering until he was halfway across town.

CHAPTER 6

The Silver Squad

Upon returning to his apartment, Barry collapsed on his bed and fell asleep in his clothes. He slept through breakfast and was just drying off after a shower when his doorbell rang. He wrapped the towel around his waist, cut across the living room, and flung open the door.

Beth stood there for a moment, with her mouth agape. She composed herself and said, "I've seen all that before. Obviously, everything was a lot firmer back then. But what if it wasn't me at the door?"

"Then, I suppose, whoever was there would think I've always looked like this."

She grinned. "Are you gonna let me in?"

He backed away from the doorway and waved her inside. "I'm going to put on some clothes."

"I think that's a good idea."

When Barry returned from his bedroom, Beth had her face inches from the front glass of Gertrude's terrarium.

"If you can't see her, she's probably inside her hidey-hole," he said.

"Yeah. I kinda figured that out." She turned to face Barry.

"When you didn't show for breakfast this morning, I started to worry. Did everything go okay last night?"

"Well . . . Not exactly." He launched into a recap of his overnight adventure, interrupted numerous times by Beth's giggles.

When he finished, and Beth stopped giggling, she reviewed the photos on his smartphone and announced, "I have a plan."

* * *

For Beth's plan to have the best chance of success, they couldn't delay. That her plan involved the stun gun and using him as bait were features Barry didn't appreciate nearly as much as she did.

Nevertheless, as Barry sat in his Mustang outside Megan's house that evening, he couldn't help but admire Beth's ingenuity. He'd followed her instructions by parking in the same spot as before, turning on the dome light, resting his head against the side window, and pretending to be asleep. Now all he needed to do was wait. And if he actually fell asleep while doing so, he'd only add realism to her plan.

For Barry, however, having permission to fall asleep meant that he was wide-awake when Megan's husband pounded on his window. The man had arrived at just about the same time as he had the previous evening, only this time he had a tire iron in his hand.

"Get out of the car!" he demanded when Barry lowered his window.

"You don't own this street," Barry protested.

"I said get out! If I have to tell you again, I'm gonna break every window in your pretty little car and then move on to you."

Barry waved his hands in surrender and opened the door. As soon as he stepped onto the pavement, the younger man brought his face to within inches of the older man and growled, "Why were you looking in my window last night? Did my wife hire you to spy on me?"

"Step back!" Beth ordered, her voice carrying from a few feet behind the man. "And do it slowly. I've got a gun on you."

The man froze for a moment, as if to process what he'd just heard. Then he peeked over his shoulder, chuckled, and turned defiantly to face Beth. "What is this, the Silver Squad? How stupid do you think I am?" He pointed to the bulge made by Beth's hand inside her coat pocket. "You don't have a gun, and even if you had one, you'd never have the guts to shoot me out here in the street."

Barry pressed the stun gun against the man's neck!

The man screamed and dropped the tire iron! That he didn't fall and convulse, like in the movies, surprised Barry. Instead, he spun around and ripped the stun gun from Barry's hand.

Beth whacked the man in the back of the head with the tire iron!

That worked.

As Barry gazed down at their quarry, his lips trembled. "Oh shit. Did you kill him?"

"How strong do you think I am?"

"Obviously, stronger than you look."

She kneeled down and felt for a pulse. "He's fine. I don't think I hit him squarely."

Barry leaned over to pick up the stun gun and slid it into his jacket pocket. "What do we do now?"

"Let's get him into the back seat and zip-tie his hands behind his back." She pushed on the unconscious man's shoulder. "No, that would be awkward. Let's zip-tie him first, and then drag him into the car."

Barry reached down to pull Beth to her feet. "What if someone sees us?"

"Everything seems quiet," she said, looking up and down the street. "But that could change at any moment. We'd better hurry."

Zip-tying the man was easy, because he'd landed face-first on the pavement. That position also made it easy for Barry to confiscate his wallet.

Positioning of any kind was no help in getting the man into the Mustang, however, as he weighed over two hundred pounds and was noodle-limp in his current state.

"Ugh, he's heavy," Barry squeaked as he lugged the man just far enough into the car to bounce his head on the bottom edge of the doorframe.

"Watch his head!" Beth warned.

"You hit him with a tire iron, and suddenly you're worried about giving him a headache?"

"Well . . . When you put it that way. . . ."

They continued shoving and tugging.

Beth let go of the man's midsection and stood gasping with her hands on her hips. "Why did you have to buy a two-door car? This would be so much easier if we had some room to maneuver the body."

After releasing the man's shoulders, Barry bumped his head on the roof and replied from the back seat, "Sorry, but all the car lots were fresh out of getaway cargo vans."

"Well, if we ever do something like this again, I'm buying a winch." She took a deep breath and said, "Okay, let's get this over with."

Barry counted out, "One, two, three!"

A chorus of grunts accompanied Barry and Beth as they pushed, pulled, and twisted their captive until he was all the way into the back seat. Then a second chorus of grunts accompanied the two as they extracted themselves from the car and returned to the pavement.

Beth held up a finger, taking a moment to catch her breath and decide what to do next. When the solution came to her, she circled around to open the passenger side door, reached into her purse, and dug around inside it until she found a safety pin and a flimsy old cloth grocery bag. She slid her seat forward, slipped the bag over the man's head, pulled it tight around his neck, and secured the overlapping fabric with the safety pin.

Barry shook his head and said, "That's some purse you have. Do you have a wet bar in there too?"

"Hey, a girl must be prepared."

Once they checked the street and settled into their respective seats, Barry tossed the stun gun and pilfered wallet into the center console, started the car, and asked, "Where to?"

"I don't know," Beth said, setting the tire iron on the floor between her feet. "I suppose the Silver Squad lair."

"The Silver Squad? Is that what we're going to call ourselves from now on?"

She smiled. "It's kind of catchy, don't you think?"

He rubbed his forehead and said, "I don't know. . . . Maybe. But more importantly, our so-called lair is my apartment. Even if we borrowed a wheelchair, we couldn't just drag Mister Wife-Beater out of the Mustang, wheel him through the lobby, up the elevator, and down the hall to my apartment. I thought you had this all planned out!"

"I assumed if we got this far, the situation would inspire us to improvise."

"Then improvise!"

"I'm working on it!" she snapped. "Just go."

Barry shifted the Mustang into drive and started down the street. "Oh . . . shit."

"What?"

"Mister Wife-Beater back there has seen me and my car twice, and you once."

"So? You didn't expect him to knock on your window already blindfolded, did you?"

"No, but we were just gonna scare him with your pretend gun and stun him if necessary; not knock him out and kidnap him. Although I doubt he bothered to memorize my license plate number, if we let him go now, there's a decent chance he can work with the police to identify us." He slapped the steering wheel with an open palm. "We aren't very good at this, and I shouldn't have bought such a distinctive car!"

Beth looked at him with doe eyes and said, "Are you saying we should kill him?"

"No! I'm just saying we're fucked."

"I don't think so. He saw me for only a second, and even though he saw you for longer, I doubt Mister Wife-Beater will admit to anyone that he lost a fight with two senior citizens. And if I'm wrong, and he swallows his pride and calls the cops and they somehow find us, we can still punch a hole in his story with a frail old lady and frail old man act. I also wouldn't worry too much about your car. There are probably more similar-looking Mustangs in the Twin Cities than you realize. If we clean it up thoroughly after humbling him, we should be fine."

"Humbling him?"

She grinned. "Yeah. The clouds just opened up, and inspiration hit me like a lightning bolt. I'm ready to improvise. Drive us to the nearest liquor store, and then to a sporting goods store after that. We're gonna need some booze and a *real* sharp knife."

The man in the back seat moaned groggily for a moment before focusing on Beth's last word. "A knife? Don't kill me! I have a family."

"Oh, hello," Beth said over her shoulder, before reaching down between her feet. "I didn't expect you to wake up so fast. You can't see it, but I'm holding your tire iron. Since you didn't believe me, the last time I told you I had a weapon, here, I'll prove it to you." She rapped him on the forehead with a light blow.

"Ow!" he cried.

"Don't be such a baby. I didn't swing *that* hard. I also have a stun gun. . . . Oh, I suppose you can't see that either." She set down the tire iron and pulled the stun gun out of the center console. When she pushed the button and waved it beside the man's head, it made a frightening series of pops.

He recoiled and screamed.

"Relax!" she said. "I'm not gonna use it on you. At least not yet. For now, I need you to lie back and be quiet while I go on a little shopping trip. If you're a good boy, tonight won't be much worse for you than what you typically put your wife through. But if you're a bad boy, you're gonna end up in the trunk with this stun gun pressed against your neck 'til it runs out of power."

Barry cupped a hand to Beth's ear and whispered, "You're one badass lady. Where'd you learn to talk like that?"

"Old Clint Eastwood movies," she whispered back.

CHAPTER 7

Monkey Bars

Beth found the items she needed at a liquor store and sporting goods store that were less than a mile apart. For each stop, Barry dropped Beth off at the front door and parked in a secluded space near the edge of the lot. Then he'd turn off the car, look over his shoulder to remind his captive that he'd meet any quick movements with a whack from the tire iron, and pass the time by riffling through the man's wallet and glancing at the storefront to see if Beth had come outside.

After picking up Beth for the second time, he said to her, "I checked his wallet. His name is Aaron."

She fastened her seatbelt and asked, "Does he have the same address and last name as Megan? I'd hate to think we went through all this and grabbed the wrong guy."

"Yes, on the last name. But since he's the same guy I encountered yesterday, I saw no reason to compare addresses." He reached into the center console and pulled out the wallet. "Here, look for yourself. You can learn all about him while I drive."

"Or you can just ask me," Aaron said.

"Shut up!" Barry and Beth shouted in unison.

"Where to?" asked Barry.

"We need a place that will be dark and quiet tonight, but bright and busy tomorrow morning."

"Like a school?"

"That's perfect. Find one that's at least a few miles away from Aaron's house."

Barry searched for schools on his GPS as he steered out of the parking lot. When they arrived at the school he selected, they found the building buzzing for an evening event. He selected another school from the GPS list and continued on. The second one was exactly what Beth had requested, with no one around, and its shadowy grounds ineffectively lit by widely spaced security lights.

Beth pointed and said, "Park next to all that playground equipment."

He drove over the sidewalk and cut across a small parking area before turning off the engine. "Now what?" he asked.

"We need to get Aaron out of the car."

Barry stepped onto the pavement and tilted his seat forward. "Get out. If you make any fast moves, I'll hit you so hard with the tire iron that you'll lose all your teeth."

Aaron, of course, couldn't see that Barry wasn't even holding the tire iron.

Beth waited until Aaron was beside the car before motioning for Barry to lead him over to the monkey bars. Once there, she backed Aaron up to the ladder and secured his ankles with a set of extra-long zip ties. She also ran a zip tie around the existing one that bound his wrists together and fastened it to a waist-high bar.

"There," she said. "Now all I need is my knife. But I'll be damned if I can remember where I put it."

Aaron relaxed, ever so slightly.

"Oh! Senior moment. It's right here in my front pocket." She unfolded the knife and pressed the point against her captive's chest. "Aaron, we know that you've been terrorizing your wife and children, and if we agree to let you go, we know that you'll promise to never terrorize them again."

"Yes, of course!" he said.

"I'm not finished. We know all about men like you, and that your promises seldom last for more than a week. Therefore, we're gonna make sure you don't forget tonight. And after we're done with you, we're gonna enforce your promise by watching you like a teenage boy watches porn. In fact, observation was how we learned about you. Megan didn't contact us, and she doesn't even know we exist. We have numerous agents in our organization, and it was one of those agents that learned about you and offered your case to us. You'll never know which agent is watching you. One slip-up and you'll yearn for a night that's only twice as hard as what you're about to go through tonight. Do you understand, Aaron?"

"Yes," he whispered.

"Now, hold still. I don't wanna cut you more than necessary."

As Barry watched with his mouth open, Beth removed Aaron's shoes, unbuckled his jeans, and pulled them down.

"Hmm. . . ." she murmured. "I should've thought this out a little better." She took the knife and began sawing the waistband. When she realized cutting through the jeans would take longer than expected, she looked up at Barry and said, "Ba—Bart. Bring me two more extra-long zip ties."

He hurried to the car and found the open package of zip ties, lying next to Beth's purse.

As soon as Barry handed the items to Beth, she said, "Bart, be ready with the tire iron. I'm gonna cut the zip tie around his left ankle, pull off that pants leg, put on a fresh zip tie, and do the same with the other leg."

"I'm on it, Bertha. One move and he loses his teeth."

Beth looked up at Barry and flipped him the bird as she mouthed, "Bertha!"

Aaron didn't resist, and once Beth removed his jeans, she

grabbed the front of his flannel shirt and yanked—buttons flying in all directions. When she tried to pull his shirt all the way off, she encountered the same forethought problem she had with his jeans. She looked at Barry and raised her forefinger before he could make a snarky remark.

Still holding the knife, she contemplated whether to risk cutting the zip tie around his wrists or wrestle with cutting the flannel fabric. Ultimately deciding on the fabric, she made a small incision at the bottom of each side of the shirt, enabling her to rip it upwards to the armpit and downwards along the sleeve. Upon reaching the cuffs, she completed the task by cutting through each one and discarding the torn shirt onto the ground.

"Are you cold, Aaron?" she asked.

"It's October. What do you think?"

"I've got just the thing to warm you up." She pointed at the Mustang and said, "Bart, I need the bottle of whiskey. It's in the paper bag, next to the zip ties."

"Sure thing, Bertha," Barry said sarcastically.

When he returned with the bottle, Beth held up a palm, so he knew to hold on to it, and swirled a finger, so he knew to stand behind Aaron.

She cut an arm off the shirt Aaron had been wearing and said to him, "I'm gonna take the bag off your head and replace it with a blindfold. I think you'll be more comfortable that way. As I do that, I want your eyes closed as tight as you can make them. If I see as much as a sliver of an eye, Bart is gonna use the tire iron to give you a hockey player's smile, and I'm gonna put the bag back over your head. Do you understand?"

"Yes," he whispered.

She unfastened the safety pin that was keeping the bag snug around his neck. "Okay, close your eyes now, and don't open them until I say you can do so." She removed the bag and replaced it with the shirtsleeve blindfold, fastening it behind his head with the same safety pin. "There. You can open your eyes now."

Beth dropped the knife into her pocket and took the bottle from Barry. "I bought you a fifth of whiskey. I can't vouch for the taste, because I don't recognize the brand. I'm sure it'll be fine. You look like the kinda guy who drinks a lot before he beats his wife, so I'm gonna ask you to down most, but not all, of the bottle. Are you ready?"

He nodded.

She raised the bottle to his lips. He choked multiple times, causing some of the whiskey to trickle down his chin and disappear into his chest hair. "That's okay," she said. "I don't mind if you can't swallow it all. Smelling of alcohol is important, too."

Once Beth felt Aaron had consumed enough to be unsteady, she splashed the remaining whiskey onto his chest, gathered his shoes and clothes, and dropped them, along with the empty bottle, into the bag that had been over his head.

"We're gonna leave you now," she said before turning to Barry, handing him the bag, and whispering into his ear, "Start the car, keep the lights off, and pull ahead into that big shadow. Aaron is probably too drunk to remember any numbers, but I don't want to risk him seeing your license plate."

She turned back to her captive. "Here's the deal, Aaron. My preference is to leave you here all night. Unfortunately, I'm afraid you could die of hypothermia before someone discovers you in the morning. My goal is to protect your wife and children, not kill you."

She retrieved the knife from her pocket and cut off Aaron's briefs, leaving him naked except for his socks.

He gasped.

"I'm gonna cut the zip tie from your wrists now, but leave your legs secured. When I do so, I will be directly behind you, so you can't grab me. If you're a good boy, and don't move, I will come around to the front and toss the knife between your feet. You can cut yourself the rest of the way free after I leave. Do you understand?"

"Yes."

She cut the tie and stepped around to face him. "Don't remove your blindfold until Bart honks the horn. I'll be watching you. If you comply, I'll leave your wallet, shoes, the remains of your underwear, and some safety pins on the sidewalk, directly ahead of you. If you fail to comply, you'll have to find your way home without those items. Do you understand?"

"Yes."

"Good. And now I need to hear you make a promise that'll last a lifetime."

He lowered his head and said with a voice full of defeat, "I promise not to hurt my wife ever again."

"I need more than that. Repeat after me: I promise to treat my wife and children with gentle, nonviolent respect for the rest of their lives, and if I can't control myself, I will remove myself from their lives altogether."

"I promise to treat everyone in my family nonviolently . . . and respectfully . . . forever. If I can't do that, I will get out of their lives."

"Close enough. Honor your promise, and you'll never hear from our organization again." She untucked the front of her shirt and wiped off the knife before tossing it between his feet. "The knife is directly below you. Now wait for the horn."

She shuffled sideways to the car, keeping an eye on Aaron the entire time. As soon as she shut her door, Barry accelerated to the edge of the sidewalk, where he stopped and watched in his rearview mirror.

Once Beth had the bag with the wallet, shoes, and other items ready to go, she tossed it out her window.

Barry honked the horn, and they zoomed off with a cheer and a high-five—missing each other's hand badly.

CHAPTER 8

As Good as Sex

Barry and Beth rode silently for a while, both lost in thoughts about their adventure.

When Beth broke the silence, she blurted, "That was as good as sex! I can't wait to do it again."

"Are you talking sex now or sex when we were teenagers? There's a big difference."

"Young sex, of course. Back when we were never sure what was gonna happen next."

"And had much more stamina," Barry added with a smile.

"How was it for you?" she asked.

He merged the car onto the freeway exit ramp and said, "Terrifying. Like the first time I had sex."

"Was I that scary?"

"You weren't the first. Renee was."

"Renee from the danceline team?"

He nodded.

"Didn't she have incredibly long legs?"

"Uh-huh."

"Poor boy." She patted his hand. "No wonder you were terrified. But I bet you were ready to climb right back on that filly and give her another ride. Weren't you?"

He shook his head. "Do you know how lucky we were this time? A million things could've gone wrong that would have resulted in Aaron beating us unconscious in the street or beating us to a pulp at the playground. And who knows what a jolt from your stun gun would have done to either of our hearts?"

"Are you saying you'd rather sit in your recliner with your gecko, waiting to die?"

"No."

"Then let's live a little while we still can."

"I suppose."

"Speaking of living a little, do you wanna see how close we can come to re-creating young sex?"

He choked. "Here? In the car?"

"Oh, God no! I'm not that limber anymore."

* * *

As soon as they returned to Barry's apartment, Beth grabbed her old lover's hand and led him straight into the bedroom.

"Are you sure sex is a good idea?" he asked, his voice wavering a bit.

She chuckled. "I assure you, there's no possible way you can get me pregnant!"

"I know. It's just that . . . I need to go to the bathroom first."

"To pee or take a pill?"

"If I have any pills, they're long past their expiration date," he revealed with a hesitant smile. "Marilyn has been dead for more than a year, and before then we weren't exactly going at it like rabbits."

"I bet you won't even need a pill with me. No disrespect to Marilyn, but it's only human nature that years and years of sex with the same partner loses its excitement."

He nodded. "I still have to pee."

"Hurry up." She winked. "It's been a long time since I've even thought about sex. My post-crime euphoria won't last forever."

"Is that what this is?"

"Do you care?"

He hurried into the bathroom.

Despite Beth's prediction that a pill would be unnecessary, in some ways, their sex was even more awkward than it had been during their first time together as teenagers. Aside from Barry having to deal with feelings that he was somehow cheating on his late wife, he also learned the hard way that what Marilyn liked wasn't necessarily what Beth liked.

"What are you doing?" Beth asked a bit too abruptly.

"Marilyn always—"

"I'm not her." She took his hand. "Here, do it like this."

He went limp.

"Too much coaching?"

He closed his eyes. "One would think that at my age, coaching would no longer be necessary."

"Then I suppose asking you to tell me I've been naughty is a step too far."

He laughed. "Oh, there's no doubt you've been a very, very bad um . . . girl. But if you ask me to spank you, I don't think I can go there."

Eventually, they figured it out.

* * *

For the next few days, Barry worried that at any moment the police would come knocking on his door to take him away. Beth, on the other hand, had no such worries and was already brainstorming for their next caper. One thing they both agreed upon was to be more social with the other Blue Loon Village residents, as they hoped to find some additional candidates for the Silver Squad. Yes, despite Aaron calling them the *Silver Squad* as an insult, neither could deny it was a fitting name—especially if they expanded beyond a two-person organization.

As they savored after-dinner decaf coffees at their corner table in the dining room later that week, Barry pointed with his nose and asked, "What about Walter over there? I think he'd like to go out in a blaze of glory."

Beth set down her cup and said, "He's even closer to death than we are! We can't invite anyone who will slow us down with a heart attack in mid-escape."

"Who says you or I won't be the one having a heart attack in mid-escape?"

"As founding members of the Silver Squad, we get a pass."

They sat in silence for several minutes, watching people come and go.

"There's always Patricia and Bruce," Beth said.

Barry shook his head. "They may be the youngest residents here, but they're way too goody-two-shoes for us—especially Bruce. I heard him mention something about retiring from the military. He'd rat us out in a second."

"This is gonna be harder than I thought."

"There's a reason why *Law and Order: Geriatric Criminal Unit* never became a TV series."

She laughed. "I guess we'll need to keep looking. We still don't know everybody here, and even if we did, turnover in places like this is guaranteed."

"If we're gonna hold off on adding new members for now, what do you wanna do in the meantime?"

"Let's go back to your place and bounce ideas off each other for our next caper. The last one made me feel younger than I've felt in years, and now that you're reacquainted with my tastes in bed, I bet the sex will be better the next time too."

Barry tilted his head. "Are you saying we aren't having sex again until we complete another caper?"

"We'll see. You have to admit, it's a wonderful way to celebrate our accomplishments. And I'd hate to ruin such a great new tradition."

"Oh, yeah," he said sarcastically. "Let's not ruin a *new* tradition."

* * *

"We should rob a church," Barry proclaimed, as he looked up from the newspaper he and Beth were sharing on his couch.

"A church! That may be too extreme, even for me."

"We wouldn't keep the money." He pointed at a headline. "This story about the plight of homeless people in America got me thinking. We could give the money to them."

"Are you aware that most people place checks, not cash, into offering plates?"

He frowned. "Okay, it might not be a big moneymaker—even if we rob multiple churches. But think about it. Are we really cut out to confront men who are much younger and much stronger than we are? That luck won't last for long. But churches don't expect robberies, and the ushers are usually youths or people close to our age. We can grab the money as the ushers are transferring it to the counting room. As long as we don't attempt our robberies too often or follow any pattern, we should be successful."

"Don't churches already help the homeless?"

"Some do. But most could do way more, and their help often comes with strings attached. We'd be eliminating the middleman."

Beth rubbed her forehead. "I don't know. Even though I haven't gone to church in years, it just feels wrong."

"Are you any good with computers and the internet?"

"Sure. I used computers all the time at the university. I also have a desktop computer and printer set up in my apartment—which you'd know if you ever spent any time there."

Barry walked down the hallway to his bedroom and returned with a laptop computer. "I haven't done much with this since moving in. If it doesn't connect automatically to the internet, the password is Gertrude@Gecko1, with the first letter of both words capitalized. I bet you can find a list of Minnesota-based preachers accused of sexually molesting children. If we limit our robberies to the churches where those preachers work, would you feel better about my idea?"

"Yes, I believe I would," she replied, perking up her posture.

He handed her the computer and reclaimed his place on the couch.

Beth quickly got online and found what she was looking for with a single search. She pointed to the screen and said, "Holy shit! Look at this long list of Catholic priests accused of sexual assault within a few hours' drive from us. And that's just the first website I clicked on. I saw others in the search results that listed child-molester clergy for Protestant denominations, too."

Barry leaned sideways for a better view of the page Beth was looking at. "I knew child-molesting preachers were a problem in America, but I never expected you'd find so many that close to us."

Beth tapped a few keys. "I've narrowed my search to just the Archdiocese of St. Paul-Minneapolis, which currently has 222 parishes and 495 priests. In that archdiocese alone, more than 100 priests have been accused of child sexual abuse. Obviously, not every accused priest is guilty; some have been fired, and others are long dead. Even so, the archdiocese settled a lawsuit that required them to pay $210 million to 450 sexual abuse victims."

"I'm surprised that wasn't bigger news," Barry said.

Beth worked silently for a few minutes as she clicked on other websites. Then she said, "Oh, good. The Minnesota legislature passed a bill that temporarily eliminated the legal deadline to file civil lawsuits for child sexual abuse. Oh, wait. The Archdiocese of

St. Paul-Minneapolis had previously filed for bankruptcy. That $210 million was actually a bankruptcy settlement, with the archdiocese paying $40 million and insurance paying the rest."

"How can a church file for bankruptcy?"

"They're a business."

"Then shouldn't they be paying taxes like other businesses?"

Beth shrugged and continued. "This article also states that the Archdiocese of St. Paul-Minneapolis isn't alone in the bankruptcy game. The dioceses of Duluth, New Ulm, St. Cloud, and Winona-Rochester have also filed for bankruptcy. Collectively, their bankruptcy settlements have amounted to over $300 million. Knowing that, we obviously won't have a problem finding deserving targets. Still, I wonder what good we'd be doing. The two of us stealing cash from collection plates would be practically unnoticeable."

"Yes, but we've drifted from the primary goal of my proposal. It's not about punishing churches with child-molester clergy. It's about stealing money from a source that wouldn't make us feel horrible about ourselves and then giving that money to the homeless."

"Sure, but maybe we can do more while we're at it."

"Do more?" He frowned. "We're not gonna kidnap a priest!"

"There are many things we can do that don't involve kidnapping priests," she said.

"Like what?"

"I don't know yet. Let's try your collection plate theft idea first. It'll give me time to think about it."

CHAPTER 9

Watch Your Language!

Early the following Sunday, Barry and Beth passed up breakfast in the Blue Loon Village dining room and instead sat next to each other at the counter between the kitchen and living room in the Silver Squad lair.

Beth took a sip of her tea before saying, "The service starts at nine, which means we must leave here in a half-hour to make it on time. Will you be ready to go by then?"

Barry sliced a piece off his caramel roll and set it on his plate. "I'm ready now, but I still think it's unfair that you get to drive the getaway car."

"How many times do I have to say to you that it's better to be unfair than unsuccessful? Not only will the ushers be much less likely to challenge a man, but if someone does challenge you, you can simply say you work for the archdiocese's accounting firm and need to verify whether they've updated their money handling to the new federal regulations."

"Logically, I know you're right. I'm just a little apprehensive about this."

"Did you test the wireless earbuds I bought you?"

"Yes."

"Do you have any questions about how to use the burner phone?"

"No."

"Then as long as you remember to put in your earbuds, you'll be fine. The connection between our phones will be open the entire time. If you get into trouble, you can't talk your way out of, run for the exit on the parking lot side, and I'll be there with the car."

"My legs retired from running after our last caper."

"Then speed-toddle."

"What if they catch me?"

"The stun gun is still in the Mustang. Slip it into your jacket pocket."

Barry pulled apart the center section of his roll with a knife and fork, seemingly more interested in dissecting the pastry than eating it. "I know this was my idea, so I shouldn't be the reluctant one, but it feels like we're jumping into this too fast. Maybe we should wait another week and use the time to thoroughly check out our target church."

"And waste that sexy suit you're wearing?" She winked and purred, "If we pull this off, I promise you'll have much more fun getting out of that suit than you did getting into it."

"Correct me if I'm wrong, but isn't it abnormal for criminal activities to have an aphrodisiac effect on old ladies?"

"Different strokes, dear. Different strokes."

* * *

Barry timed his entry into the nave to coincide with the priest's opening greeting. He settled into the middle of a pew near the back and whispered to Beth, "I'm in place. . . . I read somewhere that church attendance is down, but this is shocking. I have an entire pew to myself. You could double the number of people in here and still have room for more."

From two pews ahead, a modestly dressed middle-aged woman

looked back at Barry and put a finger to her lips.

Barry nodded to the woman and whispered to Beth, "Sound really carries in here."

The woman swiveled as far around as she could and expelled an audible "Shhh!"

"Going silent," he whispered as softly as he could.

Beth replied with a breathy, "Good luck," before stepping out of the car to stroll around the church and stretch her legs. As she walked, she noted any alternative exits Barry could use if he was unable to reach the one on the parking lot side. Upon returning to the car, she muted the microphone on her burner phone, confirmed that her smartphone was set to airplane-mode-Wi-Fi-only, opened an e-book on it, and tried to concentrate on the story while she waited.

An hour or so later, Beth noticed the first worshippers strolling to their cars. She unmuted her burner phone and asked, "Barry, what's happening?"

Silence.

She raised her voice. "Barry, what's going on?"

"Wha . . . ought?" he mumbled.

"Barry!"

"Oh, shit!" he growled. "I fucking fell asleep."

"Watch your language! You're in a church."

"That would explain the stink-eye the usher is giving me now."

"Grab the money and go!"

He looked around. "I . . . I don't know where it is."

She sighed. "You are so not getting laid today. Come out the front door. I'll drive around to pick you up."

He did as he was told.

As soon as Barry dropped into the passenger seat, Beth snapped, "How could you fall asleep in the middle of a crime?"

"People my age do that. And besides, by definition, I wasn't in the middle of a crime. I was in the middle of a nap." He clicked his seatbelt.

She squealed out of the parking lot.

"Hey!" Barry shrieked. "Be careful with my car."

"Sorry! I wasn't trying to do that. I've never driven a car with this much pickup."

"Are we heading back to the apartment?"

"No. It's only ten-thirty. There has to be a church around here with an eleven o'clock service."

Barry put a hand on the dashboard to brace himself.

Beth tapped the GPS and started searching.

He put his other hand on the dashboard. "Watch out!"

She swerved to avoid a squirrel and slammed on the brakes.

"Are you nuts?" he screamed.

She backed up through the quiet intersection she had just crossed and turned right. "No, not at all," she deadpanned. She raced down the street, turned onto another street, raced some more, and swerved into a church parking lot. "Here we go."

Barry frowned. "But we didn't research this church. How do we know the preacher molests children?"

"Is it Catholic?"

"Yes."

"We should be fine."

Barry facepalmed. "I'm not gonna rob a church I know nothing about. The priests here could be the most ethical priests in the history of priesthood."

Beth turned off the car and squeezed the steering wheel. "You're right. Judging a church because of its religious denomination isn't any better than a church judging a person because of their sexual orientation. But we're here already, and it's not as if we're going to keep the money for ourselves. I guarantee there's not a church in the Twin Cities that doesn't at least claim to give a portion of their offering money to a worthy cause. We're just gonna give that money a personalized escort to such a cause."

"Fine," he huffed. "But how 'bout we switch roles, and this

time I drive the getaway car?"

"We could do that," she said, looking up at the ceiling. "But I can't guarantee it will be much of an aphrodisiac for me."

"Fine," he repeated with a bigger huff. "I'll see you after the service. I've got my phone." He opened the door and ambled toward the church.

As Barry entered the nave, he whispered to Beth, "I'm inside. But I'm not sure how profitable this is gonna be. There are even fewer people here than there were at the previous church."

"I kinda guessed that from the lack of cars in the parking lot. Don't worry about the numbers, dear. It's the thought that counts."

"I'm going to sit now and be quiet. I'll update you as necessary."

Beth muted the mic on her burner phone, reclined her seat a bit, and went back to reading the book on her smartphone. When she finished the chapter, she unmuted and called out, "Barry, are you still awake?"

"Yes," he whispered. "There's absolutely no way I'm falling asleep again."

She read another chapter and repeated, "Barry, are you still awake?"

"Yes. I told you, there's absolutely no way I'm falling asleep again."

Beth was partway through another chapter when a thump and distorted yelling startled her back to reality. The first words she could make out came from Barry's frantic voice: "Pick me up at the main entrance. Now!"

She accelerated from her parking space and hit the brakes directly in front of the church. Barry jumped into the car the moment she stopped.

"Go! Go! Go!" he yelled.

She squealed away from the curb, stealing a glance in the rearview mirror to make sure no one was jotting down the license plate number. She continued checking her mirror as she raced along one street and turned onto another. When she was finally confident no one was following them, she slowed and asked, "What happened?"

Barry held up a finger and squeaked, "Keep driving. I need another minute to catch my breath."

They traveled silently for a few blocks before Barry angled his shoulders toward Beth and said, "Okay, I can talk now. The ushers weren't kids or seniors. They were fit men in their thirties and forties. Physically, there was no way I could just grab the money. My only advantages were my age and the stun gun in my pocket. So I stepped out into the lobby or narthex or whatever you call it until the ushers had collected everything and were waiting for their cue to carry the offering plates to the altar. Then I fell between them, clutching my chest."

Beth's eyebrows rose a notch. "Is that when you stunned them?"

"I didn't have to. One of the ushers was packing. When he leaned down to check on me, his pistol fell onto my chest. I grabbed it, ordered the ushers to set the plates on the floor, stuffed all the cash into my pockets, and backed out as fast as I could."

"Backing out of the church took away your breath? We're gonna have to put you on an exercise program."

"No. I'm not *that* out of shape. I just wasn't expecting such a massive amount of adrenaline to hit me like that."

She slowed for an intersection and shot Barry an expectant look. "Well, count the loot. How much did we get?"

He riffled through his pants pockets, extracted a wad of cash, and set the bills one by one between his legs. "Thirty-two dollars."

"Thirty-two dollars!" she squealed.

"There might've been more in the envelopes. I only grabbed the loose bills."

She shook her head. "I know I said it's the thought that counts, but that's pathetic!"

He reached into his breast pocket. "I got this pistol, too."

"Oh! I had assumed you abandoned it on your way out. Is it loaded?"

"It must be. Otherwise, the guy who dropped it wouldn't have backed off when I pointed it at him." He inspected the gun. "I'm not sure where the bullets go."

"We'll figure that out later. I'm not a fan of guns, but now that we have one, we'll add it to our vigilante tool kit." She smiled. "That makes our take a lot less pathetic."

"Does that mean I'm getting laid?"

"Oh, yeah. Make sure the safety is on, and put it back into your pocket. When we get to your apartment, I'll be the jailer, and you can be my prisoner. Who knows what will happen when I search you and discover what you've smuggled inside?"

He snorted and said, "Let's swing through downtown on the way home. We'll give all the money to the first homeless person we see."

CHAPTER 10

Road Trip

"I've lost my enthusiasm for church vigilantism," Beth said over lunch in the dining room the following day.

Barry lowered his spoon into his soup and said, "I thought you were gonna come up with a bunch of creative ideas for things we could do to punish abusive clergy."

"I know I did. But the courts are already going after them and . . . and I'm a woman and I'm old. I'm entitled to change my mind."

"Maybe we should go on a road trip."

Her face brightened. "That's an excellent idea! But I'm gonna need a really good pillow if I'm going to ride in your Mustang for more than a few hours at a time."

Barry raised a playful finger. "And I'm gonna need to stop at numerous rest areas along the way."

"I'm with you there. And when we're not going to the bathroom or complaining about our aching joints, we'll be an elite team of Silver Squad vigilantes! All we need to do is find some emotionally fulfilling crimes to commit."

"That goes without saying. If a crime can't be emotionally fulfilling, it's hardly worth committing at all."

* * *

Barry and Beth dedicated the next two days to getting ready for their road trip. As part of their preparations, they notified Samantha at the Blue Loon Village that they were going to be gone for a while, paid bills, bought supplies, and packed.

Since they didn't know how long they'd be gone, Barry insisted on bringing Gertrude along. Fortunately, geckos don't take up much space. To ensure Gertrude's comfort, Barry purchased a travel-sized clear plastic reptile container at a pet store and an insulated lunch box and a bunch of heat packs at an outdoors store. That way, she could bask in the sunshine during comfortable temperatures, and he could transfer her to the lunch box if it ever got too cold.

Early on the third morning, Barry loaded the car and started the engine. He waited for Beth to get comfortable before asking, "Are you sure you don't want to head north to Canada?"

"Yes! Canadians are too nice for our purposes."

He chuckled. "No robbing anyone of their loonies and toonies then, eh?"

"I like the adventure of having no pre-set destination, but let's begin by heading south on I-35, not north."

Barry maneuvered the Mustang out of the parking lot and down a collection of quiet streets before merging onto the freeway.

Once they passed beyond the metro area traffic, conversation between the two slowed, and they allowed their minds to wander onto possibilities for the coming days. When Barry finally broke the silence, he tapped the steering wheel with his fingers and said, "Here's an idea. The headquarters for Hormel Foods is less than two hours away, in Austin. We could steal a trunk-load of SPAM."

Beth laughed.

He continued. "It would be safe. No sane person would ever

consider such a theft a crime. Hell, someone might even award us a medal."

She laughed again.

That encouraged Barry to add, "I can see the headlines now: 'Senior citizens rescue hundreds from the plight of SPAM. Parade to be held in their honor.'"

"Oh, you're funny. The Barry I know isn't funny. Who are you, and what did you do with my boyfriend?"

He frowned. "I've been funny before."

"Really? When?"

"I don't know. . . . This certainly isn't the first time I've heard you laugh since our reunion. So either I'm the one making you laugh or you have voices in your head that you haven't introduced me to."

She cackled. "All right, whatever you say, dear." She stared out her window and considered Barry's proposal. "Actually . . . your SPAM suggestion is the best idea we've had all day. It could fit our take from the rich and give to the poor theme too. We could hold up a Hormel Foods truck, fill whatever space we have left in the trunk with cans of SPAM, and distribute them to the homeless."

"Okay, we'll head for Austin and check into a hotel. We probably shouldn't rob a truck at the Hormel plant, but it's certainly the easiest place to find a truck to follow."

"If we stop at an auto supply store, we can pick up a GPS tracker. That'll make it easier for us to follow our target."

"But won't that make it easier for the cops to track us, too? I've never used a tracker before, but I assume we'd have to sign up for a service of some sort."

Beth looked down at her smartphone and searched for an answer. "Yeah, all the ones here require registration. Even so, as long as we remove the tracker at the same time as we remove the SPAM, I think we'll be okay. It would take a determined cop to deduce that we used a tracker and request a subpoena for the GPS records of who knows how many tracker brands. In fact, I doubt our stealing of a few cases of SPAM is going to attract much attention at all."

* * *

Barry and Beth continued on to Austin, checked into a hotel, did some shopping to add to their vigilante tool kit, and eventually ended up sitting in the Mustang outside the Hormel processing plant.

Barry pointed as he said, "The semitrucks are all fenced in, and there's a security station at the entrance. How are we supposed to get access?"

"I guess we just show up tomorrow morning, pick a semi, and follow it."

"Then what good is the GPS tracking device I just bought?"

"Probably no good at all. We're new at this; we're not very organized; and we're gonna make some mistakes. We can return the tracker later if you want. For now, I suggest we carry it with us. If an opportunity arises that allows us to attach it to a semitruck—great. If not, maybe one of us can use it to track the other if we become separated."

"Can't we just call each other on our cell phones if that happens?"

"Sure," she said with a sly grin. "If you wanna do things the easy way."

Barry tapped his knee. "Wait! We're going about this all wrong. If we aren't careful, we could end up following a Hormel truck halfway across the country just to steal a couple cases of SPAM. Instead, we're better off using our burner phones for calling supermarkets to find out when they receive their deliveries. Then all we'd have to do is wait for the truck to arrive, grab the SPAM, and make our getaway."

"That almost sounds organized," Beth said.

* * *

The two seniors retired to their hotel room, where they began calling grocery stores, hoping to find one with a delivery scheduled for the following morning.

After his fourth call, Barry set down his phone and proclaimed, "Being a criminal is hard work! I always thought people entered this field because they were lazy."

"Lazy? Certainly you've been called by telemarketers for scam products and services. It can't be easy for those people to get sworn at and hung up on all the time. Hold on!"

Beth engaged in a rather lengthy phone conversation before looking across the room at Barry and saying, "Finally! Someone who was helpful. It turns out that Hormel trucks seldom deliver directly to grocery stores. Instead, they deliver to wholesalers and distribution centers, which then deliver a wide range of products to the grocery stores, often on a weekly basis."

Barry leaned back in his chair. "That makes sense. If every food manufacturer made direct deliveries, grocery stores would have trucks lined up at their loading docks day and night."

"The good news is that there's a distribution warehouse in Albert Lea, and the woman I was just speaking with was able to confirm that a Hormel truck will be making a delivery there first thing tomorrow morning."

"Perfect. That's only twenty miles away. We'll get there plenty early and try to be organized enough to formulate a plan."

CHAPTER 11

Gunning for SPAM

The Silver Squad arrived at the Albert Lea grocery distribution warehouse well before it opened. Barry drove around the building twice before stopping in the rear, a short distance from a line of loading docks. He cut the engine and lowered his window, allowing the cool fall air to nip his cheek. "I have a plan," he said after a few minutes of careful observation. "But I get to drive the getaway car this time."

Beth zipped up her coat. "I can't wait to hear it."

He raised his window. "We need to borrow a shopping cart from the hardware store next door and get the car out of sight. I'll tell you what I'm thinking while we do that."

* * *

Within minutes of taking their positions, Barry announced into Beth's earbuds, "The Hormel truck will be coming around the corner soon. Get ready."

He watched as the semi entered the front parking lot and lost sight of it when it circled around to the back. Beth's eyes took over, following the truck from her position between two big green dumpsters. Soon the semi angled away from the building, stopped, and began backing toward one of the loading docks. That's when Beth ducked out from her hiding spot, banged on the rear corner of the trailer, and dropped face-first onto the pavement with a shrill scream.

The trucker hit the brakes and leaped out of the cab. "I didn't see you!" he cried. "Are you okay?"

Beth waited until he put a hand on her back before rolling over and pointing her pistol at his shoulder. "Gimme all your SPAM!"

The trucker straightened and raised his hands. "All this for SPAM? Seriously?" He broke into laughter.

Beth resisted the urge to laugh along with the trucker and maintained a serious expression. "You heard me. All of your SPAM. Now!"

He looked her up and down. "Okay. But what are you going to carry it in? I don't think you'll be able to fit more than a few cans into your pockets."

Following Barry's plan to look older than she was, Beth hunched her back as she stood and called out, "Bart. We're ready for you now."

As she and the truck driver stepped to the rear of the trailer, an equally hunchbacked Barry pushed the hardware store shopping cart around the corner of the warehouse. The trucker was already unlocking the doors when he arrived.

"You can put the SPAM in here," Barry said. "And no sudden moves. Bertha is better with a gun than she looks."

The trucker pulled open the doors and chuckled. "Seriously. You don't need to hold a gun on me. I'm not gonna do anything stupid to protect a few cases of SPAM. If insurance doesn't cover the loss, Hormel can just write it off as misplaced stock." He stepped inside and returned with two cases, each containing twelve cans of SPAM. "This is SPAM Classic. Would you also like some low sodium or bacon flavor?"

"Low sodium would be good," Beth said. "And I'm sure Bart would enjoy the bacon flavor."

The trucker pulled a case of each from the trailer and set them in the cart. "You're looking pretty full there. If you'd like to sample some additional flavors, I could give you some cans from our variety pack, or better yet, how about some franks or chili? Hormel makes a wide variety of delicious foods."

"We like our SPAM," said Barry. "Let's stick with that." He turned to Beth and winked.

"All right then. The variety pack it is." He pulled out a case, opened it, and slid in loose cans around what was already in the cart. "Oh, look at that. I managed to fit in the entire case. Will there be anything else?"

"No," Beth said. "You've been a most excellent victim."

He looked down and shook his head. "I'm no victim. I'm always happy to help the poor and the elderly. I will, of course, have to call the police after you leave." He pulled a phone out of his pocket. "Do you mind if I take your picture? You're lucky I'm early today, or someone would have already opened the loading dock door, snapped your picture, and called the police. I just need it for proof that you robbed me. Feel free to lift an elbow to cover your face and point your gun vaguely in my direction."

Beth looked at Barry, and he shrugged.

"Don't worry," the trucker said. "I promise only one picture. You can check my phone afterward to make sure you aren't identifiable. Then I'll give you a ten-minute head start."

"That seems fair," Beth said.

They struck a pose.

"Don't forget your gun," said the trucker.

Beth aimed just to the right of his head.

The trucker chuckled nervously. "I hope you have the safety on."

"Oh, it's not even loaded," she said, clicking the safety back and forth a few times.

The trucker narrowed his eyes and shouted, “It’s not loaded? That changes everything!” He lunged for the gun.

Beth jerked away.

The gun fired!

The trucker jumped back.

Chili oozed from a box near the ceiling, splattering the trailer floor in an unappetizing stream.

Beth covered her mouth for a second before shrugging and declaring, “Oops!”

“Now you have proof of being robbed,” Barry said. “And I’m gonna need your cell phone.”

The trucker returned to his cordial persona. “Of course.” He handed over the phone. “See. I didn’t take any pictures.”

Barry looked at the screen. “Okay. I’m gonna drop this in the first mailbox I come across.”

“Thank you,” he said.

“Now don’t move until we’re out of sight,” Beth said.

Barry pushed the cart, with Beth walking backward, her hand grasping the side to steady herself. He stopped after several steps and turned around. “One more thing. You’ve been robbed by the sometimes tired, always inspired, Silver Squad!”

They continued to the corner of the building, where Beth let go of the cart and stopped to stare at the trucker. That allowed Barry to hurry out of sight, transfer the SPAM, and start the engine. When Barry whistled, Beth blew the trucker a kiss and speed-walked to the open door of the getaway car.

Neither senior said a thing, as Barry weaved them out of the parking lot as fast as he dared. Only when the Mustang blended into traffic did he relax his grip on the steering wheel.

Beth, feeling the tension dissipate, exclaimed, “I thought you removed all the bullets!”

“No. You’ve been in charge of the gun ever since you pretended I was your prisoner and took it away from me. I assumed you either knew it was loaded or removed the bullets yourself."

She pulled a tissue out of her purse and wiped off the gun. "Obviously, that wasn't the case. I didn't even intend to fire it. My finger tensed when the Hormel man lunged."

Barry cringed. "I guess we can chalk that up as another newbie mistake."

Beth slid the gun under her seat. "I think we're okay now."

"Yeah, but we should dump the Hormel man's cell phone before the cops can track us." He pulled the phone from his pocket. "Here. Turn it off and wipe it down."

As she took the phone, her face lit up with a mischievous smile. "We should leave him with a photo to remember us by."

"What do you have in mind?"

"I'm not sure." She stared out her window for a moment. "I've got it! Some guys—not you, obviously—think sending a firm dick pic is funny. If that's the case . . ." She undid her bra and lifted her sweater just high enough to snap a picture. "A sagging boob pic must be hilarious!"

"I have no comment," Barry said wisely.

She dropped the phone into the mailbox on the next corner.

CHAPTER 12

The Fork

Barry and Beth continued south on I-35, stopping in small towns along the way to pass out cans of SPAM. Since the trunk of the Mustang didn't have enough room for all the SPAM, some cans lined the back seat. To rectify their overloaded situation, the two seniors initially expanded their giveaway from solely homeless individuals to anyone who would take the cans. Also, not every homeless person looked homeless and vice versa. As they soon learned, asking the wrong person, "How long have you been homeless?" could induce the rapid-fire return of their gift of SPAM.

Other than learning the proper way to give away SPAM, Barry and Beth considered that they might be leaving a trail of *SPAM-crumbs* for the police to follow. Further thought on that issue led them to discard that worry. After all, would any sane person actually call the police to report an elderly couple giving away cans of processed meat?

Once they'd opened enough space in the Mustang to be selective with their giveaways, Barry shut the trunk and pointed to the fast-food restaurant across the street. "We forgot all about lunch for ourselves. Are you hungry?"

Beth followed his point and said, "I don't know if I'm hungry enough for *that.*" She looked up and down the street. "Is there any other choice in this town?"

"Not out here. But we could probably find a diner or something if we backtracked through downtown." He stroked his chin. "Or we could stay where we are and sample the fruits of our theft."

She grinned. "I haven't eaten SPAM since I was a kid."

"Same here." He reopened the trunk. "What flavor?"

"Classic, of course."

He handed her a can. "That sounds good, but I'd better stick with the low sodium version."

They settled back into their seats and pulled open their cans.

Barry stared down at the meat and said, "How am I supposed to eat this?"

Beth considered her can for a moment before saying, "I might have something we can use inside my purse." She reached down between her feet, unzipped the main compartment, and started searching.

"Don't get lost in there."

"Oh, shut up. I've had bigger purses than this before. . . . Ah! There it is!" She held up a metal fork, decorated with a pinch of red lint and a few gray hairs.

Barry goggled at the fork, as if she were showing him a trampled Pronto Pup she'd peeled off the pavement at a county fair. "I . . . I"

She gave it a blow. "All clean!"

"Ya know, I'm not as hungry as I thought I was. You go ahead."

She smirked. "I forgot all about your germophobia!"

"It's not a phobia. It's a science-based precaution." He stared off into space.

Her expression changed to one of compassion. "My easygoing attitude toward cleanliness has been bothering you all along, hasn't it?"

He nodded.

"And you've been hiding it to impress me."

He nodded again.

"I'm so sorry." Beth rummaged through her purse until she found a packet of sanitizing towelettes. She removed one and wiped off the fork. "There. Are you okay sharing the fork with me? After all, we've already shared spit."

"That's fine. But if you don't rinse off the fork before we use it, the SPAM will taste like alcohol."

She inserted the fork into her mouth and sensually sucked off the residue. "How's that?"

"Are you sure you're really seventy, not seventeen?"

"Oh, I'm much less inhibited now than I was back then. There's no reason to hold back anymore." She dislodged a hunk of SPAM with her fork, popped it into her mouth, and swirled it around as if it were fine wine. "Mmm! I don't know if it's only because it's the fruits of our theft, but this tastes much better than I remember it tasting."

She handed the fork to Barry. He took a bite and chewed with an exaggerated head bob. Once he swallowed, he said, "This isn't bad, but it would be much better if it was fried up in butter, like my mother used to do, and served with eggs and hash browns." He looked up. "Wow, I just got hit with a wave of memories!"

Beth giggled. "Here I am, trying to be sexy, and you're thinking about your mother!"

* * *

They were passing through Des Moines a bit later when Barry switched on his blinker to leave the freeway for a gas stop.

Beth put her hand on the dashboard as they decelerated and said, "We should find a hotel soon."

"Let's get out of the city first."

"We should also decide whether to head west toward Omaha or south toward Kansas City."

"I don't need to think about that at all. I vote for Kansas City. I have a craving for some goo-ood barbeque."

"That's fine with me. Watch out!"

He slammed on the brakes!

It was too late.

CHAPTER 13

Jenny

Barry had been following a box truck up an exit ramp when an elderly woman seemed to come out of nowhere. For a moment, he thought he'd stopped in time, but a horrific bang and the woman falling backward told him otherwise.

He jammed the shifter into reverse, backed the car off to the side, and cut the engine.

Beth jumped out even faster than he did. "Are you okay?" she asked.

"I didn't see you!" Barry declared. "The truck blocked my view."

The woman pressed her side and winced. Then she touched the back of her head and did the same. As she sat up, Beth noticed that the woman's jeans and leather jacket were almost too fashionable for someone so old. Also, the lines on her face looked more deliberate than genuine. Apparently, the Silver Squad was on the opposite side of a scheme similar to the one they had carried out that very morning. Beth doubted that Barry had caught on as quickly as she did, but her curiosity enticed her to play along—at least for a little while.

"I . . . I think I have a cracked rib and maybe a concussion," the woman said, wincing again. "That's a nice car you have there. Have you been drinking?"

"No!" Barry exclaimed.

"I think I smell alcohol. I'm calling the cops." She reached into the bag she was carrying and pulled out a smartphone. "If you give me two hundred dollars right now, I'll forget all about your reckless driving, and we can call it even."

"Seriously? Do you think I just carry two hundred dollars on me?" Barry reached into his pocket, pulled out his wallet, and counted the bills. "The best I can do is sixty-one dollars."

"That's all?" She poked at her screen.

"And a partial case of SPAM," Beth added.

"What flavor?"

"Assorted."

"Deal!"

The woman returned her phone to her bag, and when Beth reached out to help her to her feet, she groaned as she stood.

Beth pointed. "The cans are in the trunk. Stay here while I get them for you."

As she walked toward the Mustang, Barry pushed the key fob button to open the trunk lid.

Beth leaned into the back seat first, to grab one of the low-sided, open-top cardboard boxes that used to contain a full case. Then she ducked into the trunk to pull out stray cans from here and there. When she finished, she held up the box, somewhat unsteadily, and proclaimed, "Oh! This is more cumbersome than I thought it would be."

"Do you want some help?" Barry asked.

"No. I've got it." Engaging in a rapid series of motions, she shuffled toward the woman, tripped, and fumbled the hand-off.

The woman caught the box with surprising dexterity.

"Rib feeling better already?" Beth asked.

The woman winced.

"Too late!" Beth blurted. "And your makeup is hardly convincing."

"What makeup?" she asked.

"Whatever that is on your face that you think makes you look old."

"I am old."

Beth tilted her head. "Yeah, if forty-five is old."

"Okay, maybe I'm not old. But that doesn't change the fact that you ran into me."

Beth hooted. "We didn't run into you. It was all an act. You stepped out from behind that truck on purpose."

Barry returned his wallet to his pocket and crossed his arms. "Maybe I should be the one calling the police!"

Fear creased the woman's face as she pushed out a hand. "Please don't! You're right about everything. I'm sorry. But my husband is a cop—and not the good kind. If you call, he'll . . . I can't let him find me."

"Are you homeless?" Beth asked.

"I guess you could call me that. I mean, I have a home. I just can't go there because . . ."

"Of your husband?"

She nodded.

"How long have you been on the run?" Barry asked.

"Two days. I live in Des Moines, so I haven't run very far. My husband's temper has gotten worse over the years. Leaving an abusive spouse, no matter how violent they are, isn't as easy as people think it is. Each time I threatened to leave, he'd either talk me into staying or I'd rationalize some excuse to stay. This is the first time I've had the courage to follow through. Unfortunately, my husband anticipated my every move. He stole all the checks and money from my purse and even installed a device in my car to disable it remotely. I was at a stoplight, less than ten blocks from my house, when the engine just died. That's when I knew the credit card he didn't steal was only there to taunt me and would be worthless too. So I left the car and everything in it and began walking."

"Oh, dear," Beth said. "Can we drive you to a shelter?"

She cringed. "God, no! My husband has connections all over the city. He'd find me right away. I need to get far away from here."

Barry waved a hand toward the Mustang. "Come on. We'll give you a ride. Is there a friend or relative we can take you to?"

"My husband and I moved to Des Moines when he got his job here, so my friends are his friends. And they all think he's the bee's knees. My closest relatives are in California."

"Well, that's quite a coincidence," said Barry. "We just happen to be heading to California."

Her eyes lit up. "Really?"

He offered a friendly smile. "Actually, we're on our way to Kansas City for some barbeque. But hey, once we get there, we're practically to California. It'll be no problem to drive you the rest of the way." He opened the driver's side door and stood, waiting for the women to join him.

Beth reached out to take back the box of SPAM and asked, "Is the makeup you're wearing to keep people from recognizing you, or is it to help with your car accident con?"

"Both, I guess. Yesterday I pawned my wedding ring. That cheap ring didn't even get me enough money for bus fare to California. I was walking away from the bus station, feeling trapped and discouraged, when I noticed a Halloween display in the window of a closeout store. I went inside, bought the makeup and gray wig, and used the rest of the pawn shop money for a meal at an all-night restaurant. My goal for today was to acquire enough money to buy that bus ticket and a little food. I thought pretending to be an old lady would be the safest way to solicit donations from cars that stopped at the top of the ramp. When that didn't work, I got the idea for the accident con. You two were my first attempt at that. Short of selling my body, one way or another, I was gonna find a way to get out of here."

Beth set the box on the roof, opened her door, and pulled the seat forward. "You're gonna have to squeeze into the back seat. Sorry about the cramped conditions. My . . . um boyfriend, Barry," she pointed, "that's him. Wasn't thinking practically when he bought this car. I'm Beth, by the way."

"I'm Jenny—Jenny Callahan. And I don't care if I have to ride in the trunk, as long as you get me out of Iowa." She slid into the back and yelped!

Beth ducked her head inside. "Jenny, meet Gertrude. Don't worry. She's harmless. Normally we keep her secured inside a box, but she was riding on Barry's shoulder when we ran into you. He only had time to pull her off his shirt before he jumped out of the car." Beth retreated outside, then leaned in again. "Here. Would you like a can of SPAM? I bet you're hungry."

Jenny patted her belly. "I haven't eaten since the all-night restaurant." She took the can, opened it, and stared at its contents.

"Oh! Sorry," Beth said. She reached into the front for her purse, pulled out the fork, and handed it to her.

"Thank you. . . . Hey, can I ask you something?"

"Of course."

"Why do you have so much SPAM? Do you work for the SPAM Corporation or something?"

"No, dear. We're thieves. We held up a Hormel truck."

"You couldn't come up with something better to steal than SPAM?"

"Sure, I guess," Barry said as he dropped into his seat and retrieved Gertrude. "But we're just two old folks looking for adventure. We don't need anything we steal. In fact, we turned right around and started giving the SPAM to people less fortunate than we are—like you."

Beth returned the rest of the SPAM to the trunk and eased into the passenger seat. "If you're still hungry after finishing that can, let me know. You can have all the SPAM you want."

Jenny put a hand on the back of Beth's seat and said, "Just so both of you know, I wouldn't have called the cops. In fact, I turned off my cell phone right after my husband disabled my car and haven't dared to turn it back on. Once we're well out of Des Moines, I'll turn it on just long enough to call my stepsister to let her know I'm on my way."

Beth twisted around to face Jenny and said, "We wouldn't have called the cops on you either."

Barry started the car and drove to the top of the exit ramp. He paused there for a moment before turning to Beth and saying, "I don't have the slightest idea why we left the freeway."

"I think we needed some gas."

He glanced at the gauge. "Oh, yeah. That's right."

Beth grinned at Jenny and said, "If you're gonna ride with us, ya better be prepared for some senior moments." She pointed with her thumb. "Especially from him."

The trio proceeded a short distance down the road to a convenience store with gas pumps. There, they took care of the three basic traveler's needs of fuel, snacks, and bladder relief. Jenny also removed her wig and washed off her face.

As they merged back onto the freeway, Barry made eye contact with the suddenly attractive woman in his rearview mirror. "You cleaned up pretty good. I like the wavy blond hair, and I'm glad your wrinkles weren't permanent."

"Thanks," she said, holding a forkful of SPAM at chin-level. "I thought about leaving everything on until we were far away from Des Moines, but you two seem trustworthy. I'm gonna keep the wig and makeup in my bag for a while, however."

"That's a good idea," Barry said. "You'll probably wanna put it back on when Beth and I rob our next target."

"You're gonna rob someone else?"

He nodded. "I hope that doesn't make you uncomfortable. Since you're making good headway on that stolen can of SPAM, technically, you're already an accomplice."

She swallowed and said, "I was committing a crime when we

met, so I'm not exactly an innocent angel. As long as you're only doing a modern-day Robin Hood thing and not physically hurting anyone, I'm perfectly comfortable, and you can trust me not to tell the cops. In fact, I'm all in."

Beth reached back to shake Jenny's hand. "Welcome to the Silver Squad! You're a little young, but—"

"A *lot* young," she interrupted.

"Okay, a lot young. How 'bout if we make your Silver Squad membership an honorary one?"

"I like that. Who or what is our next target?"

Barry looked into the rearview mirror again. "We haven't thought that far ahead. Before we met you, our most distant plans were to check into a hotel somewhere near Des Moines and enjoy a barbeque dinner in Kansas City the following evening. For your safety, I think we should go a bit farther today. Perhaps Osceola."

"Thank you. But I don't have any money to pay for a room. If you can set me up with another can of SPAM, I'll be happy to sleep here in the back seat."

"You'll do no such thing!" Beth declared. "One of the few advantages of Barry and me growing old is that we've had a lifetime to save our money. While you're traveling with us, your room and board are courtesy of the Silver Squad."

Jenny burst into tears. "You two are so kind. Less than an hour ago, I was trying to con you out of two hundred dollars."

Beth patted Jenny's knee. "You were only trying to survive, dear. That's different."

As the three continued south on I-35, Barry and Beth used the hour-long drive to give Jenny an overview of their dating in high school and meeting up again at the Blue Loon Village. They also spoke in a vague manner about their crimes so far. Jenny, in turn, shared with them a summary of her marriage to a chauvinistic, hard-drinking cop who had regressed from verbal to physical abuse.

In all, the ride proved to be a valuable bonding experience—especially for Beth and Jenny. Barry wasn't yet ready to trust the fresh addition to the Silver Squad unconditionally, and while he felt for the woman and her predicament, he could also feel the interpersonal dynamics in the car changing. By the time they reached Osceola, the two women were engaged in such rapid-fire conversation that he couldn't slip in a word and even felt like an outsider.

He sulked, just a little.

Rather than driving around town to find the ideal place to stay, Barry simply pulled up to the first motel he saw and parked the car.

"Really?" Beth asked. "This motel looks a bit sleazy. Let's see if we can find something nicer. If it's the money, I can—"

"It'll be fine for tonight," he interrupted with a gruff voice. "We can live it up tomorrow when we reach Kansas City. For now, I just want a room, a quick meal, and some sleep."

A perplexed expression crossed Beth's face. "Are you upset about something?"

"No. It's just been a long day. Let's check in, grab some hamburgers across the street, and call it a night."

"You're gonna make us eat fast food?"

"No. That's what I'm going to eat. If you two want to take the car and drive around looking for something better, go for it."

"I'm fine with hamburgers," said Jenny.

"See? Jenny is fine with fast food too."

Beth scowled.

Barry wanted to smile at his minor victory, but he knew it would get him into trouble. Instead, he maintained a neutral expression and said to Beth, "Let's ask the person at the front desk if we can have two adjoining rooms. That'll give Jenny some privacy. Unless, of course, you'd like a room for yourself too."

"Two rooms will be fine," she huffed.

After checking into side-by-side second-floor rooms, Barry stepped into the bathroom and immediately realized the trouble his stubbornness had gotten him into. There was a pubic hair on the counter next to the sink! And more in the shower! At least he thought they were pubic hairs.

He hurried into the bedroom, where Beth was unpacking. "Honey, do you have any more of those sanitizing wipes?"

She shot him a frosty frown. "You're the one who wanted to stay here!"

"Please. There are drifts of pubic hair in the bathroom."

"Drifts? Oh, I doubt that. Let me see." She walked into the bathroom and inspected a hair on the shower wall. "Hmm. . . . It could be a pubic hair. It might also be an armpit hair."

He cringed.

She turned on her heel and strutted back into the bedroom.

Barry followed. "Well? Honey?"

"Well, honey what?"

He sucked in a deep breath, letting it out so it vibrated his lips—just a little. "I'm sorry for being such a jerk. It won't happen again. Now, *please,* can I have some of your sanitizing wipes?"

"And?"

"And what?"

She mimed spooning food into her mouth.

"And I will take you and Jenny wherever you want to go for dinner tonight."

She pulled the packet out of her purse and held it in the air. "Was that so difficult?"

"Thank you." He snatched the packet and began to clean.

CHAPTER 14

A Road Trip Story Plus a Mustang Equals . . .

A frantic early morning knock startled Barry and Beth awake. Barry pushed out of bed and was just about to open the door leading to the outside landing when he heard the knock again. The sound was coming from the door between theirs and Jenny's room. He adjusted his route and opened the door.

"My husband, Joe, is standing outside my room," Jenny whispered.

"How'd he find you?" Barry asked.

"I suppose it's a cop thing. I turned on my cell phone last night to call my stepsister in California. My phone was on for only a few minutes, but obviously that was long enough for Joe to track me here. Then, just now, as I was crossing the landing on my way to the lobby for a coffee, the faded green chamois shirt he wears all the time caught my eye. What a way to wake up—seeing that fucker staring up from the parking lot. If I'd missed him and descended the stairs, he would've grabbed me already."

"Did he get a good look at you?"

"I turned right away, but a husband knows his wife from any angle."

Barry held out a hand. "Give me your shirt."

"What!"

"Rather, give it to Beth."

When Barry looked away, Jenny took off her shirt and tossed it to Beth, who then grabbed a shirt from her suitcase and tossed it back.

As Beth pulled on Jenny's shirt, she crinkled her nose and let out a long, "Ewww!"

"Sorry," Jenny said. "When Joe disabled my car, I expected him to show up at any minute and got the hell out of there. Even carrying the suitcase I'd packed was too risky, because it might've slowed me down too much. I've been wearing the same clothes ever since."

"We'll take care of that problem after we ditch Joe." Beth reached into her suitcase, pulled out a scarf, and used it to cover her hair the best she could. Then she put a hand on Barry's shoulder and said, "Now, to make sure we're thinking the same thing, I'm gonna go into Jenny's room, step out her door, and try to convince Joe that he mistook me for Jenny and has been watching the wrong room."

He turned around and shrugged. "It's not a perfect plan, but it's all I've got."

Beth tilted her head toward Jenny. "Before I go out there, do you have a better idea?"

"If you had a gun, I could shoot him," she said.

"Actually, we do have a gun," Beth said. "But let's file that away as Plan D."

"Then at least take your phone," said Jenny. "If Joe gets belligerent, make sure he sees you filming him."

"Will do," Beth said, grabbing her phone from the bedside table. "Wish me luck."

She slipped into Jenny's room and locked the door between the rooms. Jenny stayed where she was, and after locking the door on her side, joined Barry by the main door so she could listen.

Beth stepped from Jenny's room onto the landing and pretended to be shocked by the sight of the muscular, buzz-cut man who was leaning against the railing, smoking a cigarette. "Can you smoke somewhere else? You're right outside my room!"

Joe lifted his aviator-style sunglasses and asked, "Who are you?"

"Why is that any of your business?"

"I saw my wife go into that room."

Beth tilted her head, as if trying to get a better look at the object in his hand. "Are you smoking a joint?"

He glared. "I'm a police officer!"

"Oh, like that changes anything." She backed up a step and opened the door wide. "Do you see your wife in here?"

He pushed past her and strode into the room.

"Hey!" Beth pulled the smartphone from her back pocket and tapped the record icon. "What are you doing? I gave you permission to look in from the landing, not to step inside. You're trespassing!"

Joe took a quick look into the closet, under the bed, and in the bathroom. "Sorry, I thought I saw her go in here." He meandered back outside.

"Go away. Now!"

He walked to the stairway and stopped. "I'll wait here."

Beth continued filming. "No. You're not wearing a uniform and you didn't show me your badge. That tells me that you're either impersonating a police officer or that you aren't on official business. If I don't see you drive away in thirty seconds, I'm gonna call the cops and show them this video."

Joe stared at Beth for a moment as he took a long, final drag off his cigarette. He snuffed it out on the railing, flicked it in her direction, and descended the stairs.

Beth stayed on the landing, with her camera following Joe, as he started his car and departed the parking lot. Only when he was out of sight did she put away her phone and announce, "He's gone. Let me in."

Jenny opened the door. "I know I'm only your guest, but we

should get out of here. Joe isn't the type to give up so easily. He's likely searching for someplace where he can observe the motel without anyone spotting him."

"Was he driving a police car?" Barry asked.

"No. He had a white SUV of some sort," said Beth.

"It's a Jeep," Jenny confirmed.

Barry took a step back and stroked his chin. "I don't know how fast a Jeep can go, but I'd be willing to bet that my Mustang is faster."

"I'm sure it is," Beth said. "But Joe's reflexes are much younger than yours are, plus he has the high-speed driving experience of a cop."

"While it's true that my reflexes aren't what they once were, SUVs aren't known for being nimble around corners. Superior speed plus superior handling minus inferior reflexes equals, well . . . there aren't any numbers involved. But our odds don't suck."

Jenny shut the door and said, "Maybe you should drive us directly to the freeway and floor it."

"Between Des Moines and here, I saw at least three highway patrol cars. If there's one thing I know about cops, it's that they stick together. Cop-loyalty plus a plethora of highway patrol cars equals, well . . . once again there aren't any numbers involved. But I like our odds better if we stick to the back roads."

Beth walked the rest of the way into the room before looking over her shoulder at Jenny and fanning the air with an open hand. "You can keep my shirt. But I've got to get out of yours!"

* * *

As soon as everyone was packed and ready to go, Barry handed Jenny the box containing Gertrude and said, "I'm gonna pull the car around to the bottom of the stairs. Stay inside until I toot the horn."

The two seniors carried their suitcases down the stairs and

loaded them into the trunk. At the sound of the horn, Jenny descended with Gertrude, sliding into the back seat the moment Beth opened the door.

Since no one knew for sure if Joe was watching, Barry proceeded out of the parking lot in an unhurried fashion. Three blocks later, he spotted a white Jeep in his rearview mirror and said, "Jenny, look behind you. Is that your husband?"

She turned as far as the cramped back seat would allow. "Yep. That's him."

Barry tapped his GPS until it gave him a wide view of the back roads leaving Osceola. "Tighten your seatbelts, everyone, and Jenny, hold on to Gertrude's box. The chase is on!"

Until that moment, Barry hadn't driven his Mustang faster than a few miles per hour over the speed limit. Even so, he distinctly remembered the saleswoman at the car lot telling him it could do 146 miles per hour. Though he doubted he'd have the guts to drive that fast, the mismatch of vehicles meant that Joe could only catch them if he was too timid to let the Mustang do its thing, got into an accident, or turned onto a dead-end road. That was his theory, anyway.

Barry continued driving at the speed limit until he found a quiet two-lane highway that his GPS promised would go nice and straight for a considerable distance. Then he floored it!

Joe obviously wasn't expecting such a maneuver. His delayed reaction, plus the Mustang's superior power, seemingly ended the chase in an instant. Barry's eyes flitted toward Beth, just long enough to see her fingernails digging into the dashboard, then his eyes returned to the road, only to drop to the speedometer, which was clocking his speed at 127 miles per hour. He eased up on the gas and held the speed steady, just long enough to appreciate the roar of the engine and the reserve of power awaiting his foot's command. It was during that moment that Barry felt as if he and the Mustang had become one—their ages irrelevant. The next moment, which featured two bright orange signs, ruined it all: Road Work Ahead, Be Prepared to Stop.

"Shiiit!" he screamed, pumping the brakes.

Only a dry road prevented disaster.

Barry looked into his rearview mirror to confirm that no vehicles were behind him, squealed into a U-turn, and raced in the opposite direction. When the white Jeep rose out of a depression, he squeezed the steering wheel.

But it was too late for Joe. The Mustang blurred by before he could react, and his more cautious U-turn left him hopelessly behind.

Barry let up on the accelerator, swerved onto the first major road to his left, tapped his brakes, veered onto the next major road to his right, further reduced his speed, and ultimately zigzagged through a residential area at close to the posted speed limit.

"All right already!" Beth blurted. "You've lost him."

"At least five minutes ago," Jenny added.

"Can't either of you just say you were impressed by my driving skills?"

Beth reached over and patted his knee. "In all my life, I've never been more impressed with a getaway driver. In fact, if we didn't have a guest riding with us, I'd take you right now."

"Don't hold back on my account," Jenny said playfully. "If two people *your age* can do it in a Mustang, I'd be happy to go for a walk to give you some privacy. Just be sure to document your feat, so you can report it to *The New England Journal of Medicine* or at least the *Guinness Book of World Records.*"

"Hey!" Barry retorted. "This old man just kicked your much-younger husband's ass in a high-speed chase."

Jenny bowed her head. "I'm sorry. I shouldn't have said that. We don't know each other well enough yet for me to give you shit."

Barry broke into a smile as he looked at Jenny in the mirror. "I should say the same thing. I'm giving you shit too."

They both laughed.

Once the residential streets gave way to a major road, Beth pointed at a fast-food restaurant and said, "I'm hungry! We didn't get a chance to eat breakfast before bolting from the motel."

"*Now* you wanna eat fast food?" Barry asked. "I didn't think we were doing that."

"I'd suggest something more relaxing, but I think we should keep moving until we reach Kansas City."

"I agree." He turned into the parking lot and entered the drive-thru lane.

They ordered and pulled ahead.

Noticing a few cars in front of them, Jenny took the opportunity to rearrange the various items that shared the back seat with her. When she finished, she said, "There! Now I can sit a little sideways without worrying about my knees pressing into the back of either of your seats." She swiveled her head to stretch her neck. "Oh, shit! Look who's behind us!"

Barry glanced in his mirror. "How'd he find us?"

"I didn't turn on my phone, I swear!"

"Then he must be using something else to track us," Beth said.

Jenny combed through the contents of her handbag. "Everything I brought from home is in here—and there's not much." She went silent for a moment as she continued looking. "Unless Joe used some sort of miniaturized tracking device, it's not with me."

"Then he must've attached something to the Mustang," Beth said.

"How could he have done that?" Barry asked. "There were at least a dozen cars in the motel parking lot. He couldn't have attached tracking devices to all of them."

Jenny leaned forward and said, "Remember, we were all together by the front desk when you registered and provided your vehicle make, model, and license plate number."

"So?"

"Any time after I called my stepsister, Joe could've flashed a badge at the front desk clerk and asked a bunch of intimidating questions. He's quite good at getting information out of people. And while my phone was on, he might have even been able to narrow my location to just a few rooms. After that, he could've simply walked by your car and attached a tracker. I'm guessing that's also why he wasn't directly outside my door when I went for coffee. He knew he could follow me at will and had the flexibility to wander around if he needed to grab a donut in the lobby or stretch his legs."

"What do we do now?" Beth asked.

"Nothing," said Barry. "If Joe dared to grab Jenny by force in public, he would've already done so. As long as we're here, we have a truce. Let's enjoy our breakfast in the parking lot. When we finish, we'll commence part two of our chase."

Beth unbuckled her seat belt. "While we're stuck here in line, I'm gonna get out and find the tracker. It's probably attached to someplace obvious, like a bumper or a wheel well."

"No, don't do that here," Barry said. "I'm willing to bet that Joe already knows we've spotted him and has puffed up his ego by thinking we must be in awe of his brilliant detective work. Hell, if he believes he can track us at his leisure, he's probably not even concerned about the possibility of losing us again and might even be curious about where we're going. I'd like to use that to our advantage. All we need to do is lose him long enough to find the tracker and attach it to another vehicle."

"Like a train heading straight for hell," Jenny suggested.

Barry pulled up to the delivery window. After paying for the food, he selected a parking space he could escape from by driving forward, thereby preventing Joe from boxing them in, should he grow bold.

The trio enjoyed their fast-food breakfast as much as anyone pursued by a wife-beater cop could enjoy such a thing. Joe, who they all hoped would choke to death on whatever he was eating, sat parked two spots away. More realistically, they hoped their imminent getaway attempt would coincide with Joe taking a big sip of hot coffee.

As soon as everyone finished their meals, Barry began watching the traffic while Jenny kept her eyes on the cars departing the parking lot. Their plan was to accelerate forward, avoid the departing cars, and merge just in front of a long line of traffic. If they timed everything correctly, they would achieve a significant head start that Barry could build on with additional maneuvers.

"It's all clear behind and to the side," said Jenny.

"I see an opening coming up," Barry added. "Here we go!" He started the car, slammed the shifter into drive, and spun into traffic.

Beth fanned her face with an open hand. "Not bad for an old man!"

"I think *someone's* getting laid tonight!" Jenny said in a sing-songy voice.

Barry ignored the women and concentrated on weaving between cars whenever he spotted an opening. Rather than engaging in a series of deceptive turns onto side streets, which he knew Joe could track, he stayed on the main road, racing toward the freeway as fast as the traffic would allow. Once there, he accelerated down the entrance ramp and risked 110 miles per hour until he saw a rest area sign. "Everyone out as soon as we stop," he ordered.

What happened next resembled a teenagers' prank, frequently called by a racist name, in which the occupants of a car stopped at a red light jump out, race around the vehicle, and jump back in. Only this time, the rapid, synchronized exit featured the occupants feeling underneath the car instead of racing around it.

"Found it!" Jenny declared.

"That was quick," Barry said.

"I've been finding things hidden by Joe for years, usually mementos from whoever he was fucking at the time. Since he's an ass-man, the first place I thought to look for the tracker was near the tailpipe."

"Is he really that predictable?" Beth asked.

"Mostly. I also remembered a tan van parked beside the Mustang in the motel parking lot. That van would've prevented us from spotting Joe from the landing if he were attaching the tracker to the rear of the car, but not the front of it."

Barry scanned the line of semitrucks in the opposite parking lot and said, "Oh, I can't believe it. There's a Hormel truck!"

"You're not suggesting we rob it to replenish our supply of SPAM, are you?" Beth asked.

"No. We can get SPAM anytime we want. This is an opportunity to—"

"Oh!" Beth's eyes lit up. "Now I'm following you." She turned to Jenny. "Run over and attach the tracker to that Hormel truck."

Barry pointed. "Hurry! I think that's the driver, walking toward the truck right now. I'll swing the car around to pick you up."

Jenny raced across the parking lot, angling her approach to make sure the Hormel truck remained between her and the driver. She attached the tracker and strolled nonchalantly ahead. When the Mustang pulled alongside and stopped, Beth stepped out, Jenny jumped in, Beth did the same, and Barry accelerated onto the freeway.

Soon realizing that speed was no longer necessary, Barry slowed the car and began monitoring his rearview mirror. "Here comes the Hormel truck!" he declared. "We timed that perfectly."

Beth squirmed in her seat. "I need to pee."

"Me too," Jenny added.

CHAPTER 15

A Night on the Town

Barry veered the Mustang off at the next exit, to give everyone a proper bathroom break, and they arrived in Kansas City, Missouri, less than two hours after that. As they unloaded the car in the hotel parking lot, the last remnants of apprehension or tension anyone felt melted away. Barry was no longer feeling overwhelmed by girl talk, Beth was delighted they'd be staying in an upscale hotel, and Jenny was relieved to be in a state unoccupied by her husband.

After checking in and arranging for adjoining rooms, Barry headed straight for the bed, where he collapsed for a nap. Beth hesitated in the middle of their room and contemplated whether to join him. Concluding that it was too early in the afternoon for a nap, she wrote Barry a note, grabbed the car keys from the bedside table, stepped into the hallway, and knocked on Jenny's door.

"Come on!" she announced when Jenny answered. "We're going shopping. You need some new clothes and a travel bag to carry them in."

"You know I don't have any money."

"Don't worry about that. It's my treat."

Jenny's face twitched with a range of emotions, ultimately

favoring breaking into a smile over bursting into tears. "I'm so fortunate that you were in the car I bumped into! Still, a girl has her pride. You can treat me now, but only if you'll accept an IOU from me to pay you back after—one way or another—I make Joe hand over at least half of everything we own."

"You have a deal."

* * *

Several hours later, a bright light accompanied by the sounds of giggling women and crinkling bags startled Barry awake. He slammed his eyes shut, then slowly opened them to the sight of two hovering faces, their lips painted black cherry; their eyes accentuated with dark makeup. "Jesus Christ," he groaned. "It's the Goth Sisters."

"Sit up," Beth ordered. "We've been shopping!"

He swung his legs over the side of the bed. "How many bags. . . ? My God, did you leave anything for the other shoppers?"

"Nothing cool, that's for sure." Beth reached into a bag and pulled out a skimpy black dress for Barry to see. She held it against her body and wiggled her hips. "What do ya think?"

"It depends on who's wearing it."

She feigned anger and stuck out her tongue at him. "Come on, Jenny. We'll change in your room and present a fashion show for Mister Grouchy here. If he doesn't properly appreciate us, I bet we can perk up some of the businessmen downstairs in the lounge. Is the between-rooms door on your side locked?"

"I unlocked it as soon as we checked in."

"Good." Beth grabbed what she bought for herself, opened the door between the rooms on her side, pushed open the door on Jenny's side, and dramatically departed.

Jenny followed with her bags, whispering over her shoulder, "We'll be back."

Barry listened to the giggles coming from the other room and couldn't help smiling. He wondered if Beth was starting to think of Jenny as the daughter she never had. They certainly shared a similar amount of spunkiness. He also wondered what he'd be doing now if he hadn't reconnected with Beth and embarked on this exciting yet exhausting adventure. The answer to that question was easy. He'd be sitting in his recliner with Gertrude, passing the time until he died. So why was he feeling grouchy again? The answer to that question took more thought. Perhaps grouchiness was his natural state at this stage in life, or perhaps he was still crashing from their latest adventure high. Whatever the case, he vowed to loosen up and allow himself to have some fun.

He hurried into the bathroom, ran a brush through his hair, changed into a fresh shirt, and dropped into the armchair beside the bed.

Beth popped her head through the doorway and said, "The show is about to begin!"

"Bring it on!" he said.

One at a time, Beth and Jenny entered the room, strutting past Barry and striking exaggerated runway model poses. Even though some of their outfits were just casual pants and shirts, Barry oohed and aahed as each woman passed by. When they finished, he said, "I assume you're going to put on your gothiest outfits and expect me to take you out for dinner tonight."

"And dancing," Beth added with a smile.

"Do you have a place in mind?" he asked.

"You wanted barbeque, and we saw multiple options between here and the mall. Pick one out. Later, Jenny will select the dance venue."

"I'm thinking country-western line dancing," Jenny said.

Barry widened his eyes. "But you're all made up for goth or dark wave music. Isn't that a bit incongruous?"

"That's the whole point. The cowboys won't know what to make of us, and they'll leave us alone. I've had enough of macho men for one lifetime."

Barry shifted in his chair. "It's already dark out. We should head to the restaurant as soon as you two are ready."

"But you're not ready," said Beth.

"Sure I am."

"Oh, no. You're not getting off that easily. I bought some clothes for you too!" She reached into a bag, grabbed a pair of pants and a shirt—both in black—and tossed them to Barry. "After you put them on, we'll do your makeup."

"Men my age don't wear makeup!"

"I bet you were a fan of The Cure in the 1980s."

"Well, sure. I think most of our contemporaries were back then."

"The band's lead vocalist, Robert Smith, is close to our age, and he's worn goth makeup for his entire career."

Jenny sat on the edge of the bed, facing Barry. "Way too many people spend their lives being way too serious. Then, when they realize their best years are behind them, they lament the time they wasted not having fun. I'm pretty sure that's why you started on this road trip in the first place. Don't forget that."

Barry knew Jenny was correct. In fact, he was reasonably sure he had said something similar to someone older than him many years ago. He pushed up from his chair. "You're right. Bring on the makeup." Carrying his new outfit toward the bathroom, he added over his shoulder, "But I don't think either of you has the skill to give me Robert Smith's hair."

"We'll see about that," Jenny said.

Barry quickly changed, eliciting devilish smiles from the women as he exited the bathroom and struck a runway model pose of his own. Preparing Barry took only a tad longer than the lengthy stares the Goth Trio earned as they strolled through the hotel lobby, laughing a bit too loudly on their way to a totally incongruous night on the town.

* * *

Despite feeling self-conscious from the near-continuous gawking of other diners, Barry enjoyed a barbequed pulled pork sandwich that was as close to perfection as any he could remember eating. The women enjoyed their meals too, making exaggerated sounds of pleasure that forced the conservatively dressed family next to them to seek a distant table.

While they waited for their desserts to arrive, Barry handed Jenny his smartphone so she could research places to go dancing. She selected Benny's Country Dancehall, a few miles down the road, and began humming a Shania Twain song.

Following their eager consumption of every last morsel, Barry paid the bill and chauffeured the women to the nightclub Jenny had selected. They crossed the parking lot to the main entrance, where a sign on the door announced that the KC Roundups—obviously the house band—would be playing "today's hottest country hits."

Barry led the women inside, paid the cover charge for everyone, and said, "Tonight, drinks are on me."

They grabbed one of the last open tables and ordered the first round.

The band took the stage shortly after their order arrived, breaking into a song that sent a rush of patrons to the dance floor. Jenny took a long sip of her drink and tapped Barry on the arm. "Do you know how to line dance?"

"All I know about line dancing is what I've seen in the movies. You and Beth go first. I'll join in later."

She shook her head. "Oh, no. This isn't the kind of dancing that requires pairs. We can all dance at the same time."

As Jenny and Beth stood, Barry remained seated. "Everyone's going to stare at me," he said. "I need a cowboy hat."

Jenny grabbed his hand and tugged. "Even in a cowboy hat, you'd be . . ." she gasped and tugged harder, "one of a kind."

When Beth grabbed Barry's other hand, he put up just enough resistance to feel as if he'd gained some sort of point he could cash in later, before letting the women pull him onto the dance floor.

To Barry's surprise, a few awkward minutes were all it took for him to get the hang of line dancing. With each passing song, he grew more confident. Soon the rhythm of the music was flowing through him, and he was gliding gracefully across the dance floor, syncing his steps with the other dancers.

When the band took a break, he and the women returned to their table, much sweatier than they were when they started, and ordered another round of drinks.

Beth looked at Barry and tilted her head. "So was that as bad as you thought it would be?"

He grinned. "Tomorrow, I expect several body parts will vigorously remind me how old I am, but yeah, I'm having a blast."

"Don't dis those old body parts too much. We really are a spectacle. If we were younger, I suspect some of the people here wouldn't be as tolerant of three goths invading their country dance floor. It's that respect your elders thing."

"Either that, or they think we're totally nuts and scare the shit out of them."

Jenny raised her glass to salute Barry and Beth. "Don't either of you worry about anyone else. You guys are doin' great. Taking me out dancing like this only adds to the deep appreciation I already have for both of you."

"It's our pleasure," Beth said. "And we appreciate you too. You've turned our road trip into much more of an adventure than it would've been otherwise."

Jenny looked down and swirled her drink with a straw. When she looked back up, she asked, "Do you guys wanna stay for another set?"

The two seniors exchanged glances before Barry smiled and said, "Sure, Jenny. One more set."

They hit the dance floor as soon as the band started playing again. The extra drinks loosened them up—especially Barry. They line danced and partner danced. Each time they switched to another dance, Jenny shouted the name to Barry, and each time he promptly forgot what she said. After all, now wasn't the time to get caught up in remembering such things. Now was the time to live in the moment.

Finally, exhausted, they returned to their table to order another round of drinks and watch a group of advanced dancers who had taken over the dance floor.

Bang! Bang! Bang!

Bang! Bang! Bang! Bang!

Barry was unfamiliar with the song the band was playing and hadn't been paying attention to the lyrics. It didn't occur to him that the noise wasn't coming from their instruments.

Bang! Bang! Bang! Bang! Bang!

"Everyone, get down!" screamed the vocalist.

"Shooter!" someone else screamed.

Barry grabbed Beth to his right and Jenny to his left as he yelled, "We're too exposed here!" but neither could hear him above the screaming. His visual communication was unmistakable, however, when he hunched down and pulled them to the half-wall that separated the tables from the bathrooms. They dropped to the floor. It wasn't much, but with a little luck, the shadow provided by the wall would make them less obvious targets.

It was from there that Barry's gaze landed upon the stout, bald man with a bushy, light brown beard. The man was cradling an assault rifle, carrying a handgun holstered at his side, and wearing a protective vest. He had positioned himself to block the main exit, while still being able to pick off almost anyone remaining in the building at will.

For the time being, at least, the barrage of bullets had stopped. Instead, the shooter was scanning the room as if trying to decide whom to murder next. His change in tactics caused the screams to give way to silence as people huddled in corners and under tables, trying not to attract attention to themselves.

At the same time, the jumble of panicky and protective instincts in Barry's brain cleared enough for rational thought. He whispered to Beth, "Do you have the gun in your purse?"

"No," she whispered back. "I haven't touched it since I slid it under my seat in the car."

"I was afraid of that. At least we're in a country music bar. Certainly, someone here is armed. We just have to survive until that person has a clear shot."

Bang! Bang! Bang! Bang! Bang! Bang!

A man dressed in full cowboy regalia had dashed for the door, only to skid across the floor on his own blood after the bullets pierced his back.

Screams filled the room again.

Barry put a hand to Beth's ear. "I take that back! We can't wait for some mythical good guy with a gun. Do you have anything in your purse I can use as a weapon? The stun gun, hairspray, a nail file, anything?"

She cupped a hand around her mouth and replied, "You're too old to be a hero."

"My age is exactly why I need to be the hero. I'm expendable. Half the people in here are barely old enough to drink."

Beth did her best to lean lifelessly against the wall as she plunged her hand into her purse, feeling for something that could become a weapon. She turned her head and hissed into Jenny's ear, "Check your purse. Do you have anything we can use as a weapon?"

"I've already checked. I've got nothing."

Beth tilted back to Barry, her hand still working its way to the bottom of her purse. "Sorry, neither of us has . . . wait. Oh, never mind, it's just a can of SPAM."

"I'll take it!"

"Don't be stupid."

"Give it to me!" he roared, not realizing how much the screams had died down.

As Beth handed him the can, the shooter turned toward the sound of Barry's voice. He swept his gun right and left.

No one dared breathe.

The only sound anyone could hear was the shooter's boots, plodding toward Barry and his companions—each step like a slow, ominous drumbeat. He stopped two tables away and said in a gravelly voice, "You. Freaky guy with the gray hair. Get up!"

CHAPTER 16

SPAM vs. Rifle

Barry stood.

The shooter chuckled. "What the hell are you wearing? Is that makeup or are you already dead?"

"Something like that."

He squinted. "Who's with you?" He motioned with his gun. "Get up!"

Beth and Jenny stood.

The shooter chuckled again. "What the fuck? Y'all are in the wrong bar!"

"We'd be happy to leave," Barry said.

"Oh, it's way too late for that."

While they were talking, a woman behind the shooter was slinking her way toward the main door. She might have made it, if she hadn't panicked and tried to run the last twenty feet.

The shooter wheeled and fired!

Barry pitched the SPAM!

If the can had been a baseball, the spin might have indicated a four-seam fastball. And if that baseball was hurtling toward the batter's head, the batter might have had the reflexes to duck, or, if unable to do that, at least the protection of a helmet. In this instance, the shooter possessed neither the reflexes nor the helmet. Therefore, it didn't matter that the object flying through the air was a can, not a baseball, and that it was only traveling at the best speed a seventy-year-old arm could generate. All that mattered was the dent the corner of the can left in the shooter's temple—an instant before he crumpled to the floor!

Barry screamed, "Fuck!"

Jenny launched herself into the air, landing atop the shooter, with her knee jammed against his neck!

Beth piled on top—slamming her knee into the small of the shooter's back while grabbing his sidearm in one quick motion. She pressed the gun against his temple and said, "Don't move, dear, or I'll blow your fucking brains out!"

Barry continued screaming, "Fuck! Fuck, that hurts!"

Beth's eyes darted to her partner, his arm dangling by his side. "Oh, my God! Have you been shot?"

"No! There's a reason men my age don't pitch in the Major Leagues. Something popped in my elbow, and it hurts like hell."

"We'll get you some Johnny Thom surgery later. But right now . . ." she craned her neck toward the bar and shouted, "Has anyone called nine-one-one?"

"I did!" a woman yelled.

"It's Tommy John," Barry said between whimpers.

Beth's expression grew confused. "The shooter? How do you know his name?"

"No! The baseball pitcher the surgery is named after."

"Well, you'll live." Beth allowed her knees to slide onto the floor as she made eye contact with Jenny. "I think you can get off this asshole now. Just don't touch his manhood compensator."

Jenny put her foot on the barrel of the assault rifle as she stood and shouted, "Hey! Can someone with gloves, or at least a handkerchief, come and help us? We need to move this rifle away from micro-dick here, before he gets any ideas for round two."

A bartender hurried over with a towel. He maneuvered the strap off the man's shoulder and carefully carried the rifle to the bar.

That allowed Beth to push up from the floor and sit on the closest chair while still holding the handgun on the shooter. It also allowed Jenny to tend to Barry, even if she couldn't do much other than help him onto the next closest chair.

Only then did the three allow their eyes to focus on the surrounding horror. Blood and body tissues were splattered on the walls, on the floor, on the tables, and on the people. The shooter's victims lay like fleshy islands in a sea of red. Some were only injured; others were obviously dead. Among the physically unharmed, some were silent, some wept, some prayed, some left, and some helped.

Beth and Jenny were among the helpers. Both had expected the police and Emergency Medical Technicians to rush through the door at any moment, but when they didn't hear any sirens, Beth handed the gun to Barry and said, "Keep an eye on this fucker. Jenny and I are gonna do what we can to keep some of these people alive until the EMTs get here."

The women hurried to the nearest people not already receiving assistance—a man bleeding from his abdomen and a woman with a wound just under her collarbone. Although both victims were alert, blood was pooling on the floor between them. Jenny and Beth fought off waves of nausea and the urge to curl up and weep as they comforted the man and woman and applied pressure to their wounds.

The Tactical Response Team, EMTs, and media arrived outside virtually all at once. A platinum blonde reporter and her cameraman slipped inside first, forcing a contingent of heavily armed cops to rush in after them. As one cop escorted the TV crew back outside, the other cops raised their guns at Barry and ordered, "Drop your weapon!"

Barry set the gun on a table as he stood and pointed. "I'm not the shooter. He—"

Two cops tackled him before he could finish.

"No!" Barry cried out. "My elbow! Don't bend—"

Beth, now sticky with blood, shouted at the cops, "What the fuck is wrong with you? He's the hero!"

"He's the hero!" someone else echoed.

"He stopped the gunman!" yelled another.

The cops didn't let up until they had Barry secured in handcuffs.

The shooter scrambled to his feet and dashed for the door! As people screamed and pointed, a huge cop lunged with surprising speed, tackling the man and pinning him to the floor.

A cacophony of raised voices reverberated through the dancehall until a sinewy cop with salt-and-pepper hair shouted above the others, "Quiet, everyone!" He motioned for the cop guarding the main door to let in the EMTs and stepped over to where the two cops had Barry face down on the floor.

"Pull him to his feet," he ordered.

Barry winced as the men used his arms as handles.

The sinewy cop looked Barry in the eyes and said, "I'm Detective Rodriguez. What's your name, sir?"

"Barry Swanson."

"Tell me what happened."

Barry swallowed before saying, "I was having drinks and listening to the band with my friends Beth and Jenny." He pointed with his nose. "Her and her. I don't think any of us processed that the gunshots weren't part of the music until the band abruptly stopped and the singer screamed for everyone to get down. During the initial chaos, we hid over there." He pointed again. "The shooter spotted us after the room grew quiet. I thought we were goners, for sure. The only thing that saved us was a woman behind him making a break for the door. When the shooter spun around to fire at her, I hurled a can of SPAM at his head. Somehow, I hit him, and when he collapsed onto the floor, my friends jumped on him and took his guns."

Rodriguez crinkled his nose in disbelief. "Two *women* disarmed the gunman?"

"Yeah, why not? I stunned him pretty good, and my friends were pissed that he ruined their night of dancing."

Rodriguez looked around the room and threw out a question to all who were listening and able to answer, "Is that what happened?" After multiple people expressed their agreement, the detective shushed the rest with a flick of his hand and turned back to Barry. "Are you injured?"

"Not seriously, but something popped in my elbow when I threw the can of SPAM. It hurts like hell, and the officers who tackled me didn't make it any better."

Rodriguez nodded to his associates, and one of them uncuffed him. "Where's the SPAM now?"

"I'm sure it's around here somewhere. I haven't been too concerned about getting it back." He squinted and pointed. "Oh, there it is, under that table."

Rodriguez waved to a gloved officer, who picked up the can and dropped it into an evidence bag. Then he turned back to Barry and said, "You took quite a chance confronting an armed man with a can of SPAM."

Barry smiled sheepishly. "Well, you know what they say, 'Cold or hot . . . SPAM hits the spot!'"

"Where'd you get the SPAM?"

"I stole it."

Rodriguez frowned. "Sir, this isn't a time for jokes. I need a straight answer."

Barry pointed at Beth, who had turned over the victim she was helping to an EMT and was now standing a few feet away with Jenny. "My lady friend, Beth, found it in the bottom of her purse. It was the only thing handy I could use as a weapon."

Rodriguez did a double take between Barry and the women. "What's with the makeup? Aren't you and Beth a bit old for that sort of thing?"

"That's what I said to her! She insisted that Robert Smith of The Cure still wears goth makeup, and that made it cool. I'm not sure if anyone near our age—even Robert Smith—can still be cool. But then, I just bought a Mustang as my second teenage-hood car. So it's possible that Beth is just going through her second goth-hood and dragging Jenny and me along."

The detective vigorously shook his head, as if trying to make sure he wasn't hallucinating. "I need y'all to stick around, in case I have more questions. For now, take a seat and don't move."

Rodriguez walked over to the shooter, who was handcuffed and about to be transferred to the police station, asked the accompanying officers a few questions, and did the same with the shooter. From there, he began a tour of the room, checking with officers and questioning witnesses.

Beth watched for a few minutes before growing impatient. She raised a hand as she yelled, "Detective!" When he didn't respond, she turned to Barry and asked, "What's his last name?"

"Rodriguez."

She tried again, yelling louder, "Detective Rodriguez!"

He turned. "Can I help you?"

"Yes! All this sticky blood on me is grossing me out. I also have to pee."

"Same here," Jenny added.

"You need to let us go to the bathroom and clean up."

The detective's jaw tightened for a moment before he said, "Wait for the police photographer. Then you two can do what you need to do. But don't touch anything and return directly to your seats."

"Yes, sir!" Beth said with a tinge of sarcasm.

Rodriguez talked to an officer, who talked to another officer, who talked to the police photographer, who weaved through the bodies to introduce himself as Dustin. He appeared to be right out of college, and he was so nervous that his face was as pale as the dead around him. Dustin's nervousness, and his dash to the men's room to vomit, slowed his work. By the time he finished capturing all the images he needed, the desperate women raced to the restroom, prepared to shove aside anyone standing—or sitting—in their way.

Time passed slowly for Barry, Beth, and Jenny as they sat together at a table, occasionally answering questions from Detective Rodriguez and others working the crime scene. Whichever of the three answered the question immediately followed up with a question of their own: "Can we leave now?"

Eventually, the detective grew weary of their requests. After verifying that he had everyone's correct contact information, he handed each of them his card, and released them, saying, "Call me if you think of anything, and don't leave town."

During their detention in the bar, Barry, Beth, and Jenny had watched people of various specialties work the scene, as well as people who could never again specialize in anything depart the scene—in body bags. If there was a positive side to their time sitting there, it was that it gave everyone the opportunity to begin processing their feelings. When they finally trudged to the main door, their emotions were a mishmash of anger, sadness, and yes, relief.

A media mob was waiting for them outside.

"There they are!" a slick-haired reporter exclaimed into his microphone. "The three brave heroes who saved the lives of countless people tonight! Tell me, sir. What's your name, and how did you find the courage to take on a killer armed with an assault rifle?" He thrust the microphone into Barry's face.

"I'm just a good guy with some SPAM. Now, please. We're all tired and just want to get cleaned up and go to bed."

"How about you, ma'am? Witnesses say you and the gray-haired woman held down and disarmed the shooter." The reporter swung his microphone toward Jenny.

"I used to live with a man who relied on guns to compensate for his insecurities. This guy was no different. Once we separated him from his weapons, he was just another fucking wimp!"

The reporter turned back to the camera and said, "I apologize for the language! We're live at Benny's Country Dancehall, interviewing the heroes who brought down an armed man. Seven people are confirmed dead, and at least a dozen others have been hospitalized. As bad as this tragedy is, it could've been much worse without these three heroes." He stepped toward Beth. "Let's get a word from the third hero. Ma'am, I can't help noticing that you're all wearing makeup that seems to be in the goth style. What's that all about?"

Beth flinched when the microphone swung toward her face. "Please. We're all exhausted and just want to be left alone tonight."

"I understand. But by tomorrow morning, you're all going to be famous. Can you please, at least, tell the world who you are?"

"Fine," she said in an exasperated voice. "He's Barry, she's Jenny, and I'm Beth. We're the sometimes tired, always inspired, Silver Squad!"

She turned on her heal and marched for the Mustang, with Barry and Jenny directly behind her.

The passage of time, and an ice pack a bartender brought to Barry while he was waiting to be released, had eased much of his elbow pain. Nevertheless, Beth overruled Barry's contention that he was in fine condition to drive. She held out her hand and cemented her eyes on him until he relinquished the keys.

No one said a word during the short drive back to their hotel.

And no one noticed the car following them, either.

CHAPTER 17

Going Underground

Exhausted, Barry, Beth, and Jenny dropped into their beds, only to be haunted by horrifying mass shooting images looping through their brains. Then, early that morning, the telephones in both rooms rang, inducing Barry and Jenny to unplug the phone lines from the wall. That might have given them some peace, if it weren't for the media and others congregating outside on the sidewalk and in the parking lot—and not being quiet about it. Any sleep anyone got for the remainder of the morning was fitful at best.

When the trio finally resigned themselves to being up for the day, Beth leaned against the doorframe between the adjoining rooms and said, "Obviously, one or more cars followed us here from the nightclub, and after that, word got around. I'm sorry, as the driver, I should have been more observant."

From the third-floor room window, Barry counted all the satellite dishes atop the news vans before saying, "Don't beat yourself up over it. We were all too stressed last night to be concerned about anyone following us. Instead, what pisses me off is that somehow those people figured out what rooms we are in."

Jenny and Beth padded across the carpet to join Barry at the window.

As Beth gazed down at the crowd, she said, "The hotel probably pays its night staff close to minimum wage. That doesn't buy much loyalty. All it would take was one enterprising employee accepting bribes from unscrupulous reporters, and not only would our room numbers be out there, but so would the personal information Barry supplied when he arranged for our rooms."

Jenny clenched her fists. "I always thought it would be cool to be famous, but now I long for anonymity. That circus down there leaves no doubt that Joe will come after me again. And this time he'll be better prepared."

"He'd come all the way here?" Barry asked.

"Des Moines is less than three hours away. He might be here already."

Beth turned sideways to perch on the narrow windowsill. "Two women and a man armed with a can of SPAM overpowering a mass-shooter is a story that stands out like none other. It also means that the Hormel Foods truck driver Barry and I robbed back in Albert Lea will probably recognize us and alert the police."

"We need to get outta here," Barry said.

"What about Detective Rodriguez?" Beth asked. "He ordered us not to leave town."

"Did he offer to pay for our hotel rooms while we waited? Besides, it wasn't a court order, and we did nothing wrong at the nightclub. We'll send him a text, telling him that the stress of the media hounding us was too great, and we had to blow town. That way, he can text us back if he has an urgent question, and if we aren't in too much trouble for other things, we can return later to testify at the shooter's trial."

"I'm so sorry for getting both of you into this," Jenny said. "First I put my husband on your tail, then I selected the nightclub where you were almost killed. Why don't you just put me on a bus to California? I'll pay you back for the ticket as soon as I get there."

Beth grabbed Jenny's hand and directed her to sit beside her on the bed. "Don't you understand? For Barry and me, living out the rest of our lives with quiet acceptance in a retirement home is almost as frightening as a crooked cop or a mass shooter. Turning seventy was a big deal for us. Many of our contemporaries have already died or are experiencing age-related health problems. We're still in relatively good shape, and the best way for us to stay that way is to remain useful. And last night we were all pretty damn useful. If you didn't pick Benny's Country Dancehall, if I didn't have a can of SPAM in my purse, and if Barry didn't have one final Jimmy John's-worthy pitch in his arm, many more people would have died last night."

"Tommy John," Barry corrected. "Jimmy John's is a sandwich shop."

"Either way, it was an amazing pitch, dear. I'm sure Elton John would have been proud of you."

Barry stepped away from the window as he said to Jenny, "Now she's doing it on purpose."

"Ya think?" she replied.

He leaned down to plug in the room phone. "Okay, since someone from the hotel obviously gave out our information, breakfast downstairs in the restaurant is out of the question. I'm gonna speak to the manager, raise holy hell, and demand complimentary room service. While we wait for the food to arrive, let's do whatever we need to do to be ready to depart after we eat."

* * *

Ninety minutes later, everyone was fed, caffeinated, and packed.

Barry stuffed the box containing Gertrude under his arm and opened the door. "Let's all push through the gauntlet and go directly to the car. Don't answer any questions."

With a coffee in one hand and a suitcase handle in the other, Beth replied, "That'll only make things worse. Let's answer their questions. Otherwise, they're just gonna follow us."

"I agree with Beth," Jenny said. "It's too late for anonymity now. Let's just limit ourselves to a few questions apiece. That'll also give me a chance to scan the crowd for Joe."

Everyone nodded.

When the elevator opened on the main floor, no one was waiting for them, thanks to the temporary security guards the hotel had to hire for the occasion. The new celebrities followed the hallway to the lobby, where they paused to indulge in a few calming breaths. Their collective tension returned the moment someone spotted them through the glass doors and screamed a first-sighting announcement. The crowd writhed like a garter snake mating ball on a warm spring day.

Barry handed the keycards to the woman at the front desk and led Beth and Jenny out the door.

Those in the crowd who weren't in the media broke into applause. Everyone else shouted questions and thrust microphones in front of the nearest Silver Squad hero.

Overwhelmed by the tangle of voices, which made it impossible to distinguish one reporter from another, Barry shouted, "Please! One at a time."

A voice separated itself from the others. "Mr. Swanson! Did you really hit the shooter with a can of StarKist tuna?"

The question caught Barry off-guard, then he shook his head and snarked, "No. I don't always hit mass shooters with cans of food, but when I do, I prefer SPAM."

"Were you scared?"

"Of course," he replied.

"Ms. Potter! Ms. Potter!" called another reporter.

Beth looked in his direction. "How do you know our last names?"

The reporter appeared taken aback for a moment before replying, "That's the job of our outstanding research staff! But research alone can't tell the entire story. Witnesses say you jumped on top of the shooter after Mr. Swanson knocked him to the ground. Can you take us through what happened?"

"Actually, Ms. Callahan gets the credit for that. Not that I'm too old to be jumping atop men, but in this situation, I simply followed her lead and added my weight to the pile. Somehow, amidst the chaos, I was able to seize the shooter's strap-on manhood-compensator and press it against his temple."

"You disarmed him?"

"That's what I just said."

"Ms. Callahan!"

Jenny gave the reporter a little nod.

"What made you think you could take on a man so much bigger than you are?"

"This isn't the first time I've had to deal with a tiny man in a large body. My survival instincts kicked in, and I did what I had to do."

"I taught her everything she knows about self-defense!" a voice shouted from behind the media line.

The reporters turned to see a uniformed police officer weaving his way through the spectators.

Jenny didn't even look. Instead, she mouthed to Barry and Beth, "It's time to go."

As they pushed through the throng, Joe caught up and grabbed Jenny's elbow.

"Let go of me!" she screamed.

He let go and looked back at the shocked reporters. "It's okay," he said with a friendly smile. "It's only natural for Ms. Callahan to be jumpy after such a traumatic experience. I'm Officer Joe Callahan, her husband. I taught her the move that saved so many lives last night. But this morning I'm just a public servant, here to give my wife and her elderly friends a police escort back home to Des Moines."

Even though Jenny, Barry, and Beth had moved too far away to hear everything Joe said to the reporters, seeing his police car squeezed onto the sidewalk near the Mustang told them all they needed to know.

After swiftly wedging their luggage into the trunk, Barry opened the passenger-side door, flung the seat forward, and said to Jenny, "Hurry! Take Gertrude and get into the back." Once she jumped in, Beth stepped forward and hesitated. "Get in!" he demanded. "My arm feels much better today." He pushed the door shut as soon as Beth was inside, and dashed around to the driver's side, where he dropped into his seat and locked the door as he yanked it shut.

A heavy metal ring rapped on the window.

Barry looked at Joe through the glass and shook his head.

Joe rapped again, and stooped so Barry could read his lips. "Roll it down or I will break it."

Barry lowered the window a few inches.

Joe spoke quietly, so the trailing reporters couldn't hear him, yet firmly, so no one in the car would doubt him. "I'm gonna escort you outta here nice and easy. Don't try to run. My squad car can keep up with your Mustang. I've also attached another tracking device, and this one will be much harder to find. If you try anything, I'll nail you for the bag of cocaine you have in your trunk."

"Lead the way, Asshole." Barry raised the window and looked over at Beth. "Please tell me you recorded that with your smartphone."

"I hit the record icon the moment he knocked on the window."

"Good. Send a security copy to my phone. He's probably bluffing about the cocaine, but I have little doubt he'd plant some on us later, if it suits him."

Barry followed the squad car—its lights flashing—out of the parking lot, as reporters and their camera crews scrambled for their vehicles, trying not to get left behind.

"You're not really gonna follow Joe all the way back to Des Moines, are you?" Jenny asked.

"Oh, hell no! One advantage we have now that we didn't have in Osceola is that Kansas City undoubtedly has multiple tunnels and parking ramps where we can hide the car underground. If we can lose both Asshole and the media long enough to get to one of those, the ground should block the tracking device signal, allowing us to find the tracker and check the trunk for drugs."

Beth opened a browser on her phone and started thumbing.

"Got it!" she said a few minutes later. "I-29 and I-35 are going to split in a few miles. Make Joe believe you're gonna follow him north on I-35, then veer off on I-29 at the last possible moment. We're gonna backtrack a little to the Parkville Commercial Underground, which is located underneath Park University."

Jenny shook her head in disbelief. "Joe has never been the brightest bulb in the pack, but instructing us to follow his car instead of the other way around is stupid, even for him."

Barry glanced at Jenny's reflection in the rearview mirror and said, "Escorts lead, and he's confident that his threat and tracking device will make us behave. Besides, bad cops do stupid things all the time. Think of how often cops get caught beating black men because they recorded the entire assault with their own body camera."

"Yeah, Joe would be one of those. It's not like he had to go through years of training to get his job."

Beth looked up from her phone. "We're approaching the split."

"I see it." Barry accelerated almost to the point of tailgating Joe's car before swerving abruptly onto I-29.

Jenny leaned forward and extended a middle-fingered wave. "Buh-bye, asshole!"

Beth checked the traffic in her side mirror. "Speed up if you can. I think your move surprised the media as much as it surprised Joe, but that won't last for long. They'll both be able to take the next exit and catch up with us quickly."

"Maybe not quite as quickly as you think," Jenny said. "If the media is still following Joe, he'll probably rethink his plan, cut his flashing lights, and ditch them before coming after us."

Barry pressed his foot partway to the floor and asked, "How far?"

Beth looked back down at her phone. "Maybe four and a half miles. Take the Highway 45 exit; go west for two miles to Highway 9; then go south for another two miles; look for the Park University sign, but don't turn there; instead go to the next road; take a left; and follow Hoslett Street to the President Mackenzie Underground Entrance."

"I'm fucking seventy years old! Do you really expect me to remember all that?"

"Just drive. I'll tell you when to turn."

Following Beth's turn-by-turn instructions, Barry rushed them to the university, where they descended underground before Joe or anyone else could catch up.

"Holy shit!" said Barry, as the road leveled off. "This place looks like it goes on forever."

They had entered the white limestone tunnels of an abandoned mine that traversed below the college. Lights lined the tunnel surrounding the main road, but darker tunnels branched off here and there, going to who knows where.

"It also looks like a great place to get lost," Jenny said.

"Yeah. No worries about any tracker giving away our location," Barry said.

"Joe will still be able to track us to the entrance," Jenny added. "It won't take him more than a second to figure out what we're doing."

Barry tilted his head toward Beth. "Is there another way out of here, or do we have to come out the way we came in?"

"I don't know." She looked at her smartphone and tried to tap back to the tunnel map she had up earlier. "I can't find that map again! And there's no signal down here."

"We can't return the way we came without risking a run-in with Asshole." He paused to think. "There *has* to be a second entrance. Otherwise, a cave-in, a fire, a mass-shooter, you name it, could trap people down here."

Beth set her phone into the drink holder. "I agree. Let's go in a good distance and pull off into one of the side tunnels."

"What's a good distance?" Barry asked, his shoulders tensing. "We have no idea how big this place is."

Beth closed her eyes and tried to recall the map she had looked at. "I remember a field aboveground and off to the side—probably a football field. If everything on the map is to scale, you could fit about ten of those fields down here. Does that help?"

"Okay, I'll try to drive in the equivalent of five football fields."

"I didn't say they were end-to-end. This place is shaped like a fat, deformed mushroom."

Barry tapped his brakes and said sarcastically, "Oh, that *really* helps. I'm gonna drive what feels like two more football fields and take the first side tunnel I see after that."

They continued deeper inside, occasionally passing white vans with Park University logos on their doors.

"Pull in there!" Jenny said.

Barry veered into a tunnel that dead-ended at a parking area. He switched off the car, opened his door, and said, "Let's work fast. If Asshole guesses this same tunnel, we'll be trapped."

Using smartphone flashlights, Barry and Jenny dropped to the ground to look under the car while Beth searched the trunk for cocaine or anything else Joe could have planted there.

As Barry felt for the tracker, he voiced a running commentary of aches and pains brought on by each arm stretch and shoulder twist.

Jenny cut short his commentary with a shout, "I found it!" She extracted herself from under the car before continuing, "This time, Joe didn't use a magnet to stick it to a metal surface. Instead, he tried to be sneaky and glued it to the plastic beneath the front bumper." She reached back underneath and grunted. "He used some really strong glue. I can't pry it off. Is there a flathead screwdriver in the car?"

"I don't think so," Barry said. "But there should be a tire iron with the spare in the trunk. Beth, can you check?"

She moved some items around. "I don't see a spare."

"Look under the carpet."

She removed some suitcases and pulled on the tab. "This car doesn't come with a spare!" She paused for a moment. "Instead, it has an air compressor that injects some tire sealant."

Barry joined Beth and peered into the trunk. "A car without a spare?"

"Apparently so," she said.

A distant siren blast echoed through the tunnel.

Jenny glanced over the hood. "He's almost here! Are we out of SPAM?"

Beth reached into a corner. "We have a few cans left."

"Throw one to me."

She tossed the can.

Jenny caught it and peeked at the label. "Jalapeño? I didn't know they made that flavor. I hope it has some kick to it." She ducked back under the car and grunted as she repeatedly rammed the can against the tracking device. "Got it!"

She removed the battery pack and waved it in the air. "I deactivated the tracker, but I'm gonna hold on to it for now. Later, if we find someplace to stick it, I'll fire it back up."

Barry stuffed the luggage back into the trunk and slammed the lid.

Joe's voice crackled through the squad car's PA, "Hey Jenny-Jenny-Jenny! I know you're down here. If you give yourself up, I won't arrest your friends."

Beth hurried to her door and held it open for Jenny. "We should go. Your husband will be here any second."

"Oh, please! He hasn't acted like my husband in years. Call him *Joe* or use Barry's name of *Asshole.* Better yet, combine the two and make it *Joe Asshole.*"

"Okay. Joe Asshole will be here any second," she said.

As soon as everyone took their places, Barry spun the Mustang in a tight circle, squealing the tires. The car shot out of the parking lot, down the short tunnel, and back into the main tunnel.

Headlights from Joe's squad car glared in the rearview mirror.

"That was bad timing," Barry said.

"I guess the chase is back on," Beth declared.

Barry pressed the accelerator partway to the floor. He wanted to go faster, but there were too many blind curves, university vans, cars, and—he slammed on the brakes!—pedestrians.

A startled student pounded on the hood, yelled, "Slow the fuck down!" and finished his warning with a pair of one-fingered-salutes.

Barry lowered his window and shouted, "Sorry!" Leaving the window down, he sped back up, glanced in his rearview mirror, and said, "Jenny, do you have that can of SPAM handy?"

"I tossed it on the floor."

"Pick it up."

"Got it."

"How good are you at throwing things?"

"Not as good as you are, obviously, but I played shortstop on my high school softball team."

"That'll have to do."

"Are you right-handed or left-handed?"

"Right-handed."

"That means you're gonna have to lean out on my side. Pop open the can. I'm going to move my seat forward and position the car to give you enough room to maneuver. When I give the signal, try to toss the can so the open end hits the driver's side windshield.

With any luck, it'll create enough of a mess that Asshole will have to stop and wipe it off."

Jenny opened the can.

Barry looked ahead. A sharp curve was coming up. Since he was driving in the middle of the narrow road, Joe couldn't pass him or force him to the side here. He slowed way down and said, "When the road cuts right, Asshole won't be able to see you lean out the window. Make your throw as soon as he straightens out behind us."

They curved right.

Jenny leaned out.

The SPAM sprang from her hand and thwacked against the windshield!

She pulled back in and said, "Damn! The can landed on its side, and the meat stayed put. I can't see any mess or damage to the windshield."

Beth watched in the passenger side mirror as Joe turned on his windshield wipers, sliding the can harmlessly onto the road. "I guess there's only so much heroing processed meat can do," she said.

Jenny opened the gecko's box and said, "I bet Gertrude would like to be the new hero."

"No!" Barry cried. "What kind of sick suggestion is that? You're not throwing my gecko at the squad car!"

Jenny's face flushed. "No! No! No! I wasn't suggesting that. All this getaway driving has made a mess of Gertrude's little home. Her water has soaked the sand, or whatever it is you put in the bottom as a substrate, and it looks like she pooped and threw up too. I think I can compress some of it in my hands and throw it like a dirty snowball."

"Do it fast," said Barry. "I see another curve coming up. Same side."

Jenny reached in and cringed as she made the ball. "Oh, God. This is disgusting stuff!"

"Hurry!" Barry slowed way down and turned on the flashers.

"Ready!"

He sped up to give the impression he was going to make a run for it, swung the Mustang around the curve, and slowed down again.

Jenny let it fly!

Joe tried to swerve out of the way, but he was already too close to the wall.

"Got 'im!" she cheered.

Joe turned on his windshield wipers again.

Bad idea!

Now, hopelessly unable to see through the mess smeared across his windshield, Joe lowered his window and leaned out, looking for a place to pull off to the side.

The Mustang shot into daylight two turns later.

CHAPTER 18

The Supermarket

Jenny cleaned her hands with the wet wipe Beth had given her. Then she asked, "Where to now?"

Barry's eyes flitted to the rearview mirror. "Are you in a hurry to get to California?"

"Not at all. I'm numb from what happened last night, and I'm sure we'll all experience nightmares or worse, once everything sinks in. Knowing that, I'd like to hang out with you two for as long as you'll have me. And can afford me! Since I can't help financially at the moment, you can count on me to help with driving, laundromat runs, cleaning Gertrude's box, and anything else that comes up."

Beth looked over her shoulder. "Don't worry about money, dear. Barry and I have enough for all of us. And I have a hunch that somewhere down the road your youthful athleticism is going to come in handy."

A crossing gate descended as they approached a railroad track. Barry slowed to a stop and turned off the car. Looking to his left, he could see that the train was going to be a long one. "Jenny, I think Beth's hunch is gonna come true sooner than she thought it would."

Jenny's expression grew confused for a moment before she realized what Barry wanted her to do. She grinned, waved the tracker in the mirror, and said, "I'm reinserting the battery pack now. Let me out, and we'll see if Joe Asshole can catch a train!"

Barry opened his door and slid his seat forward. Jenny hopped out and stood beside the Mustang. She watched the train until she saw a flatbed car, loaded with two huge spools. She started running alongside the tracks as the flatbed approached, and once it caught up to her, she tossed the tracker into the center of the second spool.

For just a moment, Jenny stood there frozen, as if the stench of everything Joe was sliding off her and clickety-clacking on down the track. When the moment passed, she spun around to perform a little victory dance for Barry and Beth before jogging back to the car and squeezing into her seat.

When the crossing gate ascended, Barry started the car and said, "We aren't far from the geographical center of the contiguous forty-eight states. Any suggestions on which way to head: north, south, east, or west?"

"It's fall," Beth said. "Let's go someplace warm."

Jenny leaned forward. "Since none of us appear eager to travel directly to California, it seems to me that the obvious direction is southeast. Perhaps we could loop through Nashville and Atlanta on our way to Miami, and then hit New Orleans, Dallas, and Phoenix before parting ways in San Diego."

"That's way too many big cities for me," Barry said. "But I don't object to the general direction of travel."

"I'm with Barry," Beth added. "A few big cities are fine, but I think small towns and rural areas better fit our purposes."

Barry tapped his GPS to set a route. They'd head east on I-70 before cutting southeast on a series of county roads, heading vaguely toward Nashville.

No one spoke more than a sentence or two for the next hour, as so much had happened that everyone needed a little quiet time to live with their thoughts. Only when Barry announced, "We need to stop for gas," did conversations of any substance resume.

"We're getting a bit low on SPAM too," Beth said.

"Is that a problem?" Barry asked. "After the events of last night and this morning, I'm too exhausted to even think about another giveaway. And if you desire it for our personal consumption, I don't care how many flavors it comes in, I'm no longer SPAM-curious. The can I ate earlier in our trip satisfied that question for the rest of my life."

"Really?" Jenny said. "I kinda like it."

"Oh, to have young and inexperienced taste buds," he replied.

"We don't have to rush to give it away, and you don't have to eat it," Beth said. "But it's been our lucky charm. We might all be dead without it, and who knows how many homeless people considered the can we gave them the only thing even close to luck they had all day."

Barry sighed and glanced at his GPS. "It looks like there's a midsize town coming up. We can fill the tank there and find a supermarket where we can buy some SPAM."

"Buy?" Beth asked. "I'm not sure the SPAM gods would approve. I think we have to steal it."

"SPAM has gods?"

"Uh-huh. What were the chances of you ever throwing a can of SPAM as hard and as accurately as you did last night?"

"I'd like to think it was because I dug down deep to summon my inner hero."

She reached across the center console and patted his thigh. "You believe what you want to, dear, and I'll believe what I want to."

"So I don't get any hero credit?"

"Of course you do. The SPAM gods merely blessed your old arm with a moment of youthful strength and accuracy. The creative thinking and bravery were all yours."

"Well . . . okay." He flicked on his blinker. "Here's our exit."

Gas was first on the list. After all, nothing ruins a quick getaway like an empty gas tank. From there, Barry's GPS directed them two miles down the road to a large supermarket.

"What's the plan?" he asked, turning off the car in the parking lot.

"Give me a second." Beth raised a finger while she thought. "Okay. How does this sound? You and I will fill a cart with SPAM, and Jenny will serve as our lookout. When she signals that no one is watching, we'll walk the cart out to the car."

"That sounds overly simple," Barry said.

"Does our plan have to be complicated?" she replied.

Jenny leaned forward and said, "To do that, you're gonna need some grocery bags, preferably the reusable cloth kind. That way, you two can fill the bags directly from the shelf, and your theft won't look so obvious when you walk out."

"How do we get those?" Barry asked.

"If one of you will lend me a credit card, I'll go in first to buy some drinks, sandwiches, and snacks for our trip, and add a couple of cloth bags to my purchase."

Beth handed over her card. "A Diet Coke and chicken salad sandwich for me, please."

"I'll have the same," said Barry. "Only make it an iced tea and a turkey sandwich."

* * *

When Jenny returned from the supermarket, she handed Barry and Beth their orders and said, "You'll find the SPAM in aisle eight. They have a decent selection of flavors and enough stock to make use of the two cloth bags I picked up. I recommend collecting the SPAM and pushing the cart over to the bathrooms, which are at the front of the store, on your right. Step inside those bathrooms and wait. I'll use one of the burner phones to send each of you a text when all the cashiers are busy. Once you get that, you should be able to push the cart right out the main door. If our plan goes awry, and someone notices that you're leaving without paying, just pretend you're forgetful senior citizens."

"That last part won't require much acting," Barry said dryly.

Beth added, "I like how you've taken my simple plan and enhanced it to decrease the likelihood of us getting into trouble."

"I've learned a few things as a cop's wife. Mostly from Joe telling me stories about stupid thieves who got caught."

After finishing their sandwiches, Barry and Beth entered the supermarket. Jenny followed a few minutes later. The store was servicing a moderate number of shoppers at the time.

Barry pushed the cart down aisle seven as Beth walked alongside. Upon reaching the far end, they looked down aisle eight and waited until the one shopper there moved on to the next aisle. Then the two executed their plan to perfection: loading up the bags, toddling to the bathrooms, and leaving the cart outside the doors. Neither was sure if they were supposed to make use of the bathroom they were in, but they both reasoned that a potential car chase with full bladders was just as bad as a potential car chase with an empty gas tank.

When the texts arrived, Barry and Beth exited the bathrooms and spotted Jenny partway across the store, pretending to sort through a rack of greeting cards. She nodded subtly.

Beth nodded back and took hold of the side of the cart, hoping to shield its contents as Barry pushed it toward the door.

"Hey!" the nearest cashier yelled before she hurried over to stand in front of the cart. "My manager just rang from the back room. He spotted you on one of the security screens and told me not to let you leave until he gets here."

Barry and Beth looked at each other, unsure if they should make a run for it or pretend to be forgetful senior citizens.

Barry was just about to shout, "Run!" when a stocky man came barreling toward them with surprising speed. He stopped three feet away, looked them up and down, and wiped the sweat off his forehead with his apron.

"I couldn't let you get away," he panted.

"Who said we were going anywhere?" Barry asked.

"Oh, I saw you slyly pushing that cart straight for the door, hoping no one would recognize you." He reached into an apron pocket and pulled out a notepad and pen. "Can I have your autograph?"

Barry winced. "Autograph?"

"You don't need to play coy with me. I watched both of you on TV and read about you on the internet. You're the heroes who stopped the Benny's Country Dancehall Shooter! The Silver Squad, right?" He rocked back on his heels. "Wasn't there a younger woman with you, too? A pretty blonde?" He swiveled on his hips and rotated his neck, spotting Jenny as if he were an owl on a perch. "There she is!" he cheered, summoning her with a vigorous wave.

Jenny cautiously approached.

He thrust the pad and pen toward Barry's stomach. "I'm Anthony."

Barry quickly signed and handed back the pad and pen.

He looked down and frowned. "Can you please personalize it *To Anthony?"*

Barry took the items back and added the correction.

Anthony checked the autograph and smiled. He turned to Beth. "Can you please sign too, and personalize it To Anthony?"

"Of course, dear."

As soon as he retrieved the pad and pen and inspected Beth's autograph, he slid over a step to present the items to Jenny. "Can you please sign too, and—"

Jenny pointed to his chest as she finished his sentence in a friendly lilt, "Personalize it To Anthony."

He beamed.

All the excitement caught the attention of nearly every employee and shopper in the store. Barry, Beth, and Jenny played along with what was building into a celebrity frenzy, patiently signing autographs and posing for selfies with everyone who asked for them.

After another wave of shoppers arrived, including a woman who insisted that Barry hold her toddler while she posed with him for a selfie, Barry grumbled into Beth's ear, "I'd rather face a man with an assault rifle than hold someone else's kid. Children that age are breeding grounds for the flu, colds, rabies, and whatever else is going around. Let's get outta here before I have to hold another one."

Beth held up a hand and announced, "I'm sorry. We're on a tight schedule and must be moving on."

When voices rose in protest, Jenny waved the waiting people closer. "All the rest of you, hand your phones to one of the nice cashiers and gather 'round. We'll do one final group photo."

With that, the trio posed with their new fans, leaving everyone happy, and enabling them to depart through the main door, serenaded by a vigorous round of applause.

"Wait!" Anthony shouted, as he pushed a cart through the still-open door. "You forgot your groceries." He tapped a palm to his forehead. "How rude of me. Lead the way and allow me to personally load these bags into your car."

They proceeded into the parking lot, where Barry used the key fob to pop open the trunk lid. He peered inside at the cluttered mess, made worse by Beth's search for the cocaine Joe claimed to have planted, and rearranged some luggage and other items to carve out enough space for the two grocery bags.

Anthony didn't mind the wait, as every extra moment he spent with the biggest celebrities he'd ever met was another moment he could add to the story he'd be telling others for months.

When Barry pointed to the spot he'd opened up, Anthony gently set in the bags of SPAM and backed away with a deep bow. "Thank you all for gracing my store today. And safe travels!"

The trio climbed into the Mustang and bid farewell with exaggerated waves.

Silence filled the car until they reached the highway, where a soft chuckle bubbled up from Barry's chest. As the women joined in, their chuckles crescendoed into howls of laughter.

The absurdity of Anthony personally delivering their stolen SPAM was just what they needed to take their minds off of everything they'd gone through since the bullets began flying at Benny's Country Dancehall.

CHAPTER 19

Three Kittens and a Lady

After a morning of escaping from Joe, and an afternoon of stealing SPAM and signing autographs, Barry, Beth, and Jenny elected to pull off the highway at the next exit that displayed a hotel sign. There, Jenny donned her gray wig, borrowed Beth's credit card, and booked two rooms near the end of a hallway at a chain hotel.

Once settled into their rooms, everyone dozed for the rest of the day and part of the evening, awakening only when the pizza delivery arrived. Subsequently, Barry and Beth returned to slumber, while Jenny retreated to her room, where she indulged in some TV time before drifting off to sleep as well.

* * *

Having achieved their short-term goal of catching up on their sleep and putting the past few days a bit further behind them, the trio began a new day with the new goal of distributing the fresh supply of SPAM that was taking up space in the trunk.

As they continued southeast, they learned that finding homeless people in the small towns they passed through was going to be a challenge. The homeless were there, of course, but they weren't as visible as those they'd previously seen living out in the open in larger towns and cities.

So whenever they saw someone walking along a street, dressed in clothes that appeared to be even remotely tattered, Barry would steer the Mustang alongside and Beth would lower her window, waving a can as she called out, "Hey! Would you like some SPAM?"

"Get away from me, lady!" was a frequent response.

While only a few people recognized them during their car-window SPAM giveaways, their stops for any other reason were quite different. Frequently, those recognitions would start with a double take, followed by a stare and a shout-out. Jenny and Beth enjoyed the attention; Barry felt irritated.

With no hurry to get to anywhere, they traveled slowly, taking multiple days to cross Missouri. Even so, they soon realized the importance of keeping visits with their newfound fans brief. If they stayed too long, even in the tiniest of towns, someone from the media—usually a local newspaper reporter—would show up requesting photos and an interview. Although they accommodated the local reporters, they did so with trepidation, because those interviews could also give Joe or anyone else looking for them assistance in tracking them down. With that in mind, they always ended their interviews by giving the reporter a false destination for their next stop.

"How long is all this gonna last?" Barry grumbled as he started the car in a far eastern Missouri town.

"Oh, I'm sure they'll forget about us soon," Beth said with a wink. "Certainly when the next good guy with some SPAM stops a mass shooter."

Jenny held up Gertrude's box so Barry could see it in his rear-view mirror. "I'm sure Gertrude would be happy to take your place during the next interview. No doubt, she'd be just as informative."

"Are you saying I'm bad at interviews?"

"I'm saying you could be more open. These people admire you. Don't take that away from them."

He humphed. "I never asked to become a hero."

She reached into the box and placed the gecko on her shoulder. "Few people ever do."

* * *

They were traveling along a lonely two-lane highway in northwestern Tennessee when Beth pointed and asked, "What's going on up ahead?"

Barry squinted. "It's just a car on the side of the road."

"I know it's a car, but I thought I saw someone throw something into the ditch."

When Barry slowed the Mustang, the car they were watching accelerated back onto the pavement. "Are you thinking what I'm thinking?" he asked.

"Pull over!" Beth shouted. Waiting just long enough for the wheels to stop, she jumped out, ran to the ditch, and pulled a burlap bag out of the water.

Barry knew exactly what was in the bag the moment she returned. "We can't keep them," he said, as a chorus of soft meows squeaked inside. "Cats and geckos are a terrible combination."

Beth untied the twine at the top of the sack and looked inside. "They're kittens! Three of them, and they aren't old enough to harm anyone." She held up what appeared to be an orange tabby.

Jenny leaned forward and cooed, "Oh, let me hold it."

"Not unless Gertrude is safe," Barry said.

"I put Gertrude away a long time ago." She held out her hands, and Beth set the wet, shivering kitten into her palms. When the frightened little face looked up at her, Jenny burst into tears. "Who could be so cruel as to dump a bag of kittens?"

"Well, obviously whoever was driving that green car," said Barry.

"We must seek justice for these kittens!" Jenny demanded.

"Justice?" Barry asked.

She sniffed. "Isn't that what the Silver Squad does?"

"Once in a while, I suppose. But the car is long gone."

Beth held up the other two shivering kittens for Barry to see. "I'm with Jenny. And we're not in a fucking Mustang for passenger comfort! Either you put this speed-demon into gear and catch up to that car, or switch places with me, and I'll do it."

Barry recoiled, surprised by the forcefulness of Beth's demand, and shifted into drive. "Hold on, then."

The Mustang's tires spun on the gravel shoulder before taking hold on the pavement. The next town was less than ten miles away. If they were going to catch up to the car, they needed to do so before it reached the city limits, where it could disappear down any street.

Barry brought the Mustang to a satisfying purr—well over the speed limit, but less than when he was trying to lose Joe—and soon blurred past a sign warning of a reduced speed limit ahead.

Beth shouted, "There it is!"

Barry pumped the brakes. "What do we do now?"

Jenny rubbed her cheek against the kitten she was holding. "Nothing too nice, I hope."

"We do nothing now," Beth said. "Stay back and follow. No one travels too far from home to dump kittens. Let's figure out where the driver lives and make our plans after that."

As if proving Beth's assumption, the car traveled partway through the small town, turned onto a street, proceeded two blocks, turned again, continued for another block, and pulled into a driveway.

Barry parked the Mustang a few houses away, and they watched a leggy woman in her thirties with long auburn hair and tight blue jeans get out.

"We must've followed the wrong car," Barry said.

Beth shot him an angry look. "Are you saying a beautiful woman can't be ugly on the inside? It's definitely the right car. I remember that red and white bumper sticker."

Barry shook his head. "Hey, it was one thing when we zip-tied and stripped that wife-beater back in the Twin Cities. He deserved it. But I just can't go there with someone who looks like her for the crime of being a kitten dumper."

Jenny leaned forward until she was almost between Barry and Beth. "Holy shit! I knew you guys took on a wife-beater, but this is the first time either of you revealed any of the details."

Beth placed a hand on Jenny's shoulder. "We were just getting to know you the first time we mentioned it, dear."

"So what are you guys, Dexter-lite?"

"Something like that," Beth said.

Jenny leaned back and clapped her free hand on her knee. "I'm loving you two more by the minute! So what are we going to do to this kitten dumper? Tie her up and give her a taste of what it feels like to be sealed inside a wet burlap bag?"

"No!" Barry roared.

"That's not a bad idea!" Beth said. "Only it needs some modifications."

Barry bumped his forehead against the steering wheel as he bellowed, "No! No! No! If you two want to abduct a woman over *kittens,* you're on your own."

"You haven't heard my modifications yet."

CHAPTER 20

Revenge of the Kittens

Once Beth laid out her plan, Barry reluctantly agreed to go along with it. The Silver Squad had a new mission, and that mission would require a multi-night stay. The town they were in was too small for a chain hotel, but it did have a mom-and-pop motel with two clean side-by-side rooms. Well, clean from Beth and Jenny's point of view. Barry still had to wipe down every hard surface using multiple sanitizing towelettes, plucked from the giant economy-sized pack he'd purchased when they were still in Missouri.

After settling in, Jenny joined the seniors in their room, where Beth was busy jotting down everything they would need to do before implementing her plan. Included on her list was divvying up surveillance duties. Until they knew the auburn-haired woman's schedule, and how many other people lived with her, they couldn't do any vigilantism on behalf of the kittens. They would also need to make a supply run and coordinate it with their time spent conducting surveillance.

And what were they going to do with the kittens they rescued? Barry flipped through a tattered old phone book he found in the bedside table drawer and said, "I think I know why the woman dumped the kittens. There's not an animal shelter here." He picked up his smartphone and tapped the screen. "I'll see if I can find one in a nearby town."

"We can't drop the kittens anywhere near here now that we're famous," said Jenny, who was sitting in a side chair, nuzzling a kitten. "Someone might recognize us."

"Oh, yeah," Beth impishly chimed in from her position on the bed, leaning against the headboard with her legs stretched out to corral the other two kittens. "We certainly can't leave any clue near here that could lead the cops to us for the crime we're about to commit."

"In the meantime, these kittens need food and a litter box." Jenny turned her kitten so she was nose-to-nose with it and switched to a singsongy voice, "I hope you're old enough to eat solid food."

Beth stroked her kittens as she mused, "My guess is that they were recently weaned, and the kitten dumper lady was able to give away the rest of the litter. These three are the leftovers."

Barry pushed up from the corner of the bed and said, "Jenny, come with me. We'll find a place to buy some pet supplies. Then I'll drop myself back here, and you can take the car for the first surveillance shift."

She handed her kitten to Beth and followed Barry out the door.

* * *

Saturday arrived two days later. Since that meant the auburn-haired woman's schedule would likely change over the weekend, they abandoned their surveillance and turned their attention to preparing for a strike on Monday.

When the three met up in Barry and Beth's motel room after breakfast, Barry leaned back in the desk chair and raised his objections again. "By the time we leave, we will have been here almost a week."

"Are we in a hurry to get somewhere?" Beth asked, her voice echoing from the bathroom where she was cleaning the litter box.

"Apparently not," he said.

Jenny opened a can of kitten food and looked up. "Try to relax and enjoy your retirement!"

"How am I supposed to relax when we could all be in jail cells by Monday night?"

"Oh, come on!" Beth said as she stepped out of the bathroom. "Are you still having reservations about this because the woman we're going after looks hot?"

"No!" he protested.

Beth shot him a dose of side-eye. "Assuming that after all the illegal things we've already done, you're *suddenly* worried about jail: we know the woman's schedule; we know that no children live in the house; and we know that two men have stopped by when she's at home. Whether they're friends, lovers, or brothers is still a mystery, but that doesn't matter, since we haven't seen anyone show up unless the woman is at home. Overall, our chances of getting caught are minimal. All we need now are supplies, and we're gonna have to drive to an actual city to get them."

"We also need cash," Jenny added. "Take it from a cop's soon-to-be ex-wife. If we use a charge card to pay for anything we leave at the crime scene—even if we purchased it from a store in a different city—the cops will track us down."

"What about this motel?" Barry asked. "I put our rooms on my charge card."

"I suppose we have some exposure, but we aren't the only ones staying here. Cops don't investigate the guests at every local hotel and motel every time there's a crime. The unusual purchases we're gonna make are a different matter, however. In fact, since we're all famous at this moment, I should put on my gray wig, a hat, and sunglasses, and be the one to go through the checkout line."

Beth pulled a kitten out from under the bed and handed it to

Barry. "Why don't you stay here with Gertrude and the kittens? Jenny and I will do the shopping and try to be back in time for dinner."

His face brightened. "That's a job I'm happy to handle."

Beth and Jenny had to travel more than an hour away to find the items they needed. Throughout their shopping trip, both women wore floppy hats and sunglasses, though only Jenny needed a gray wig. No one seemed to recognize them.

* * *

When Monday morning arrived, Barry parked the Mustang several doors down from the auburn-haired woman's house, and the trio of vigilantes watched until she left for work. As soon as she was out of sight, everyone stepped out of the car. Jenny turned on one of the burner phones and moved to the driver's seat. Beth pocketed the other burner phone, and after she and Barry put on gloves, they both hurried around to the back door of the house.

The flaw in their plan was how to get inside. Since they hoped to avoid having to break a window, Beth had purchased some tools to help them pick the door lock, and she and Barry had watched a video on YouTube that made doing so look easy.

Barry tried first and only succeeded in bending one of the tools.

Beth tried next and was soon puffing out her cheeks in frustration.

"Here, try this," Barry said.

She looked over her shoulder and smiled. "Where'd you find that?"

"Under one of the flowerpots."

She took the key from Barry and turned the knob. "Under a flowerpot is just about the worst place to hide a key."

"And yet neither of us thought to look there until now."

Beth texted Jenny: *Door opened. Going inside.*

A cat, presumably the mother of the kittens, met Barry and Beth in the back hallway and followed them into the kitchen. Reasoning that getting on the cat's good side might be important later, Beth pulled a bowl out of the dishwasher, found a carton of milk in the refrigerator, and poured a little of it into the bowl for the cat.

"Remind me to put the bowl back before we leave," she said.

With the cat occupied, Barry and Beth explored both floors of the two-story house, making note of any floorboards or stairs that creaked, closets where they could hide, and electrical outlets they could use. They also checked the basement, where they located an additional hiding spot.

Before leaving, they walked through the house one more time to make sure they didn't miss anything. Then they stepped outside, and after Beth locked the door, she took out her phone and started to text Jenny.

She stopped and hissed, "Shit."

"What's wrong?" Barry asked.

"You forgot to remind me to put back the bowl."

"So it's my fault?"

"I think that goes without saying." She unlocked the door and returned the empty bowl to the dishwasher.

Rejoining Barry outside, Beth locked the door again and finished her text: *Mission accomplished.*

Jenny texted back: *Street is clear.*

They hurried around the house and ducked through the open door of the waiting Mustang, with Beth taking the back seat and Barry taking the front passenger seat.

"We did it!" Beth exclaimed. "Other than Barry's senior moment, when he forgot to remind me to return the bowl I used to give the mother cat some milk, everything went swimmingly."

"You had a senior moment, too," Barry said.

"No, I didn't."

"Are you saying that me forgetting to remind you about the

bowl qualifies as a senior moment, but you forgetting about the bowl in the first place doesn't qualify as the same thing?"

"Uh-huh."

He looked over his shoulder and bit his lip. "Uh-oh. I don't remember you returning the back door key, either. Who gets credit for that senior moment?"

Beth leaned forward. "The back door key? I thought you put it back."

"No. You never returned it to me."

She reached into her pocket and sheepishly held up the key. "Okay, maybe I had one tiny senior moment. Slide your seat forward and let me out."

"Do you know which flowerpot to put it under?"

"No."

Barry held out a hand. "Give it to me. I'll return it."

He stepped onto the pavement, and after scanning his surroundings, walked to the rear of the house and stared. Before him were two flowerpots, one on each side of the flagstone walkway. He remembered that he looked under both pots before finding the key, but not which one he looked under last.

"Come on, old man," he whispered to himself. "Which pot? Which pot?"

He closed his eyes to visualize the moment, opened them, and placed the key under the left pot. He started back toward the Mustang, returned, and switched the key to the one on the right.

"What took you so long?" Beth asked after Barry dropped into his seat and buckled his seatbelt.

"Oh . . . No reason."

She chuckled. "You had another senior moment, didn't you?"

"I did not."

Jenny put the car into drive and said in a voice laced with amusement, "Do I need to chauffeur you two to the drugstore for some Prevagen?"

"Jellyfish protein?" Beth waved a hand dismissively. "Oh, please. We're mammals."

* * *

Upon returning to the motel, Barry and Beth prepared everything they would need for the evening, while Jenny gathered together all the packaging and discarded it in a dumpster on the opposite side of town. With everyone anticipating an adrenaline-filled night, Barry and Beth retired to bed shortly after dinner, and Jenny, who was wide awake, relaxed with a movie on the TV in her room.

Since their plan was to enter the house two hours after the auburn-haired woman went to bed, someone had to watch the house and note when she turned off all the lights. As the person assigned to lookout and getaway-driving duty, that task fell to Jenny.

To avoid the possibility of neighbors later mentioning to the police that they saw a black Mustang that didn't belong, Jenny had planned to park a few blocks away from the house and walk past it every fifteen minutes or so. But since the night was cold, she searched for an alternative and discovered that if she parked in just the right spot, one street behind, she could stay in the car, peer across a back-neighbor's yard, and still see two sides of the target house. As long as she could see light coming through at least one window, she knew the auburn-haired woman was awake. Only when those windows went dark did she walk past the front of the house to confirm that no other lights were on.

She noted the time, sent a text to Beth's phone, and returned to her motel room to watch some more television. She managed to watch for only a few minutes before a wave of exhaustion convinced her to click off the TV and go to sleep.

* * *

The alarm Beth set after receiving Jenny's text buzzed loud enough to wake up not only her and Barry, but also Jenny in the next room. Apparently, there was at least one advantage to staying in an old motel with walls seemingly unencumbered by sound-dampening insulation.

Everyone met at the Mustang fifteen minutes later.

Beth whispered to Barry, "Are you sure you packed everything?"

"Of course," he whispered back. "Check for yourself if you want."

Beth tried to resist, but their recent senior moments convinced her to stride back to their room to make sure they'd left nothing on a desk, bed, or chair. She returned to the parking lot and whispered over the roof of the car, "Okay, now I believe you."

Jenny was already in the back when Barry and Beth slipped into their seats. After quietly clicking their doors shut, Barry eased the Mustang onto the road. Minutes later, he drove slowly past the target house and parked two blocks away. He switched off the engine, handed the car keys to Jenny, and said, "No joy riding while we're gone."

Beth took both burner phones out of the center console, turned them on, and handed one to Jenny. She sent a test text before stepping onto the sidewalk with a bag full of supplies. Barry skulked alongside her, carrying a bag of his own.

Upon reaching the house, Barry and Beth scanned their surroundings. The neighborhood was fast asleep. They hurried to the back door, turned on their headlamps, retrieved the key from under the flowerpot, and stepped inside.

The cat greeted them with a loud meow!

Beth sprinkled a pocketful of cat treats on the floor as she and Barry tiptoed through the kitchen and into the living room.

She texted *We R inside* and returned the phone to her pocket.

Neither Barry nor Beth said a word, since they'd rehearsed what they needed to do. The only sound either made was the tiniest squeak of laughter escaping Beth's mouth before she sealed it shut with her hand.

Setting up everything took only minutes. That was the easy part. The hard part was coordinating turning on the electronic items with waking up the auburn-haired woman at just the right moment. If she came charging down the stairs with a gun while they were still in the house, a can of SPAM wouldn't be able to save them this time.

Among the tasks they completed were plugging in multiple spooky flashing lights, wetting the original burlap bag, and turning on the three battery-powered kittens inside the bag. The mechanical kittens meowed, but probably not loud enough to wake the sleeping woman one floor above. To solve that problem, Barry brought along a cordless sound bar, which he'd loaded with a micro SD card containing an endless loop of cats yowling. The two vigilantes took a few seconds to admire their work before he pressed play, cranked the volume, and slid the sound bar under a table.

They hurried out the back door as fast as their not-so-fast legs could carry them.

Once they'd progressed partway down the block, Barry felt confident their getaway had been successful and allowed his shoulders to relax. That's when Beth stopped suddenly and declared, "I need to go back! I forgot the cat bu—"

"No!" Barry interrupted. "Good things never happen when the hero goes back for the cat. Besides, we already have three kittens."

She chuckled. "Would you let me finish? The cat bumper sticker, not the cat inside the house." She pulled the bright red and yellow sticker out of her inside coat pocket and held it up for Barry to read. *I Dump Kittens,* it said. "I made it at a self-service kiosk at a mall." She handed her burner phone to Barry. "Text Jenny to pick us up."

Beth jogged back to the driveway, where the auburn-haired woman's car sat. She slapped the sticker on the back curve of the trunk and rubbed as hard as she could. She glanced up at the house. Steady burning lights had replaced the flashing lights she and Barry had set up.

The outside light flicked on!

Beth was already huffing and puffing, but that didn't stop her from rushing to the curb when the Mustang pulled up. She tumbled inside and yanked the door shut as they sped off into the night.

CHAPTER 21

Goth Again

The Silver Squad returned to the motel as quietly as they had left. Doing so was difficult, because their successful revenge on behalf of the kittens deserved the proper amount of laughter and celebration. That celebration would have to wait for the next evening in another town.

What town that would be was anyone's guess. All they had planned at the moment was a late morning checkout, so as not to raise any suspicion that they were vacating with urgency. That was Jenny's suggestion, as Barry and Beth continued to rely on her experience as a cop's wife to keep them out of trouble.

And when morning ultimately arrived, a leisurely checkout was about as fast as anyone could move, anyway. Winding down after their kitten caper hadn't been an easy thing to do, and their collective lack of quality sleep stayed with them as they headed southeast on a lonely two-lane highway, traveling for miles with no one saying a word. Those moments allowed Jenny to reflect on her final days with Joe and her new friendship with Barry and Beth. When her mind finally returned to the present, she knew what she had to do.

"We're heading in the opposite direction of California," she said from the back seat. "I know that doesn't matter to either of you, but my tagging along has given me second thoughts about running away. As you've already witnessed, Joe is more than just an abusive husband; he's also a dirty cop. Unfortunately, I'm the only one who knows the full extent of his true nature. If I escape to California and file for divorce, he'll still be able to hide behind the hero worship he receives from so many in the community and his cozy relationship with numerous Des Moines judges. Using that cover, he'll find another woman to seduce and abuse and add to the list of people he's beaten up or arrested under false pretenses. It's an endless cycle that will continue until someone stops him. And I intend to be the person who does that."

"We'll take you wherever you want to go," Barry said as he reclined his seat a notch.

Beth turned to look at Jenny. "And we're happy to help in any way we can. Having already scared the crap out of that wife-beater in the Twin Cities, we've got some experience with this sort of thing."

Jenny leaned forward and said, "No! What I want to do to Joe is much worse than stripping and zip-tying him. Hell, he'd probably get off on that. But I could never ask you two to help me commit the crime I have in mind. Just drop me off at my house while Joe is at work. All I need is a gun, and I can do what I should have done instead of running away."

Beth reached under the seat and pulled out the pistol she'd hidden there. "You're welcome to use this, dear."

Jenny jerked back and pushed out her hands. "I don't want your gun! You've both been so good to me. I won't take any chances on anything that could lead the cops to either of you. Besides, once I get home, Joe has more than a dozen guns I can choose from."

"Well, if you change your mind, there are no worries about anyone tracing this gun back to us." She smiled. "It belonged to an usher who dropped it when Barry was robbing a church."

As Jenny chuckled, she noticed that Barry had flicked on the blinker and was preparing to exit the highway. "Bathroom break, already?"

"No," he said. "I just thought I'd point us in the general direction of Des Moines."

Jenny shook her head. "I wasn't suggesting we go directly to Des Moines. If I'm able to do to Joe what I want to do—and survive—a prison sentence will most likely be in my future. I'd like to have a little more fun before that happens."

Barry completed the exit. "Bathroom break, anyone?"

* * *

Once back on the road after a quick stop at a gas station, Beth twisted open an iced tea and said to Jenny, "If you wanna have fun, I suggest we head south to New Orleans."

Barry's eyes shifted to the rearview mirror. "We could also go north. New York City is fun too."

"Both sound wonderful," said Jenny as she reached forward to flash a thumbs-up. "Either is fine with me."

Beth shook her head. "If you're gonna go to prison after our road trip, our next destination is solely your choice."

She thought for a moment. "We're closer to New Orleans. Let's go there."

Barry tapped the screen on his GPS and entered a random location on Bourbon Street before turning to Beth and saying, "You'd better call Samantha at the Blue Loon Village to let her know we haven't abandoned our apartments. She's probably wondering what happened to us."

Beth reached into her purse. "I'll also make sure she's still holding our mail and that our rents are paid for next month."

"What about the kittens?" Barry asked. "Shouldn't we be thinking about dropping them off at an animal shelter?"

"Shelter!" Jenny squealed. "No!"

He continued. "Who knows how long we're gonna be on the road? We'd have to buy a crate for them, make sure we never leave them in a hot car, and only stay in hotels that allow cats. Then, once we get home, neither Beth nor I will be allowed to keep any of them at the Blue Loon Village, and, apparently, your home could be a penitentiary. None of that is fair to the kittens."

Jenny wiped a tear from her cheek. "I hadn't thought of that. We should probably find an animal shelter in the next major city. I don't wanna get more attached to these kittens than I already am."

"I'm sorry," Barry said. "I may not show it, but I've become attached to the kittens too."

* * *

On the following morning, Barry parked the car in front of an animal shelter in Jackson, Mississippi. When he reached back, Jenny handed him a kitten. His throat burned and his face trembled as he stroked the fuzzy ball of fur. Beth whispered little nothings to the kitten on her chest, and Jenny tried not to let her tears wet her kitten too much.

"They're all so innocent," Jenny said with a sniff.

Barry wiped a tear from his cheek. "Yes, they are. And we've given them a chance. Kittens as cute as these won't remain at the shelter for long before someone adopts them."

Beth unbuckled her seatbelt and twisted to face Jenny. "Why don't you and Barry stay here with the kittens for a while? So far, I'm the only one successfully holding back the tears, making me . . ." She paused to force down the lump in her throat. "I'll go inside and arrange for their care." She kissed her kitten and handed it to Jenny. A vagrant tear streamed down Beth's cheek as she opened her door and willed her feet toward the entrance of the animal shelter.

* * *

As they continued toward New Orleans, Jenny did her best to cuddle Gertrude, though neither human nor gecko felt totally satisfied with the endeavor. Nevertheless, all the humans could feel their moods brighten as they neared their destination. By the time they reached the city, the women were chattering back and forth, and Barry was even able to squeeze in a word or two while driving them to wherever they pointed. They didn't stop until they found a charming hotel in the French Quarter.

When everyone stepped up to the front desk to check in, Barry's demeanor reverted to the default setting, and he was prepared to complain about the room prices. Then he learned the rate wasn't much more expensive than what the hotel in Kansas City had charged them. That, of course, made him wonder what was wrong with the rooms.

"Bedbugs?" he asked.

The front desk clerk looked up from his screen. "Huh?"

Barry enunciated each word: "Do your rooms have bedbugs?"

The clerk looked back down and punched a few keys before raising his head and saying flatly, "I'm sorry, sir. We don't have any bedbug rooms available for tonight. If you'd like, I can check with one of the hotels down the street. They might have one for you." He winked.

"Smartass," Barry mumbled.

They moved into their rooms, this time across the hall from each other. Soon afterward, Jenny knocked on Barry and Beth's door.

Beth greeted Jenny with a finger pressed to her lips. "Shhh! Barry is sleeping."

"Already?" she whispered. "How can anyone fall asleep so quickly?"

Beth pointed. "You're looking at a man who fell asleep in the middle of robbing a church."

Jenny covered her mouth to keep from laughing out loud, then said, "I was hoping you two would wanna go out for dinner and dancing."

Beth aimed a dismissive wave toward Barry. "Oh, let's just leave him here. I'll write him a note. He can call my cell if he wakes up and wants to join us later. Until then, we'll have a girls' night out."

"That sounds delightful."

"Give me fifteen minutes to get ready. I'll meet you downstairs in the lobby."

Jenny raised an eyebrow and asked, "Goth?"

Beth tilted her head. "Hmm. . . . Okay. No one will think anything of it here, but it'll be fun for us, anyway. Give me five minutes to change outfits, and I'll come over to your room with the makeup."

* * *

The Goth Sisters partied their way along Bourbon Street, first stopping at a crowded Cajun restaurant for dinner, then weaving from one live music bar to another. They stayed at each bar just long enough to buy a drink, flirt with the youngest man they could find, and dance like Robert Smith and Siouxsie Sioux. Their goth dance moves didn't always mesh with what the bands were playing, but that only added to the fun.

The two were standing—somewhat unsteadily—in the middle of Bourbon Street, well past midnight, when Jenny asked, "Do you remember where our hotel is?"

Beth pointed. "I think it's four blocks that way and two blocks the other way."

Jenny squinted. "What d'ya mean, 'the other way'? Is it left or right?"

She pointed left and said, "Right."

Jenny chuckled. "I told you not to accept another drink from that extremely handsome young man."

"Why? Do you think he spiked it?"

"I watched your drink all the way to our table. No one but the bartender dropped anything into it. You just drank way more than you should've."

"But he was so cuuute!"

"And way too young. . . . Even for me."

"How 'bout you? You drank as much as I did."

Jenny didn't answer right away and instead looked up to watch a dark figure step out onto a balcony to light a cigarette. As she returned her gaze to Beth, she swayed a bit and said, "I'm doing just fine. Are you okay with walking back to the hotel, or should I call for a ride?"

"I think walking will do me some good."

"Then let's go. We'll work together to remember our corner."

They meandered for a little over two blocks, providing support to one another when necessary. Neither noticed the other's backward glances until Jenny whispered, "Three men are following us."

"Oh, do you mean those *black* men?" Beth said too loudly.

Jenny put a finger to her lips. "Shhh!"

"I noticed them earlier. I think they were in the second bar we were in. Or maybe it was the fourth."

"We should be careful."

"Why? Because they're black?"

"No! . . . Well, maybe a little. Joe always warned—"

"Joe is an asshole!"

"Yeah, I know. It's just that when you hear something all the time from someone in his position, you tend to believe it."

Beth straightened and gave Jenny's wrist a slight tug. "Shall we stop and ask the men if they intend to mug or rape us?"

"Boy, you sure sobered up fast."

"It's a skill that comes with age."

Jenny pointed. "I think we turn right at the next corner."

"Agreed."

The lighting on the street they turned onto wasn't as efficient as the lighting on Bourbon Street. The women quickened their pace, neither looking back until they were halfway down the block.

Beth looked first. "They're still behind us," she said, her voice revealing a subtle quiver that betrayed the bravado she had displayed moments ago.

Jenny squeezed Beth's hand. "Okay. If those men weren't black, would you feel less nervous?"

"I don't know. . . . I might."

"Does that mean we're racist-white-privileged-Karens if we run?"

"Maybe. . . . A little. But I'm willing to take that chance."

They ran!

* * *

A call to Barry's smartphone went directly to voicemail. Since Barry had turned off his phone, the second and third calls went there too. The hotel room phone would've rung next, but after the incident with the media in Kansas City, unplugging the landline phone was the first thing Barry did each time he moved into a new room.

Only a vigorous knock on the door was able to startle him awake.

"Go away!" Barry shouted. "I'm sleeping."

A loud voice followed a second knock. "Mr. Swanson? It's the night manager. I need you to come to the door."

Barry fumbled for the lamp on the bedside table, brushing Beth's note to the floor and knocking over a bottle of water in the process. "Damn it!" he shrieked. He continued fumbling until his fingers found the lamp and climbed to the switch, his eyes wincing when the harsh light filled the room.

He shuffled out of bed and cracked open the door.

"Mr. Swanson?" said the man. "The hotel van is waiting outside the lobby to take you to the hospital."

CHAPTER 22

Selfies

"The hospital! What happened?" Barry asked from his hotel room doorway.

The night manager shrugged. "All I know is that someone in your party suffered a head injury."

"A head injury!" Barry looked over his shoulder. "Beth? Beth! Are you in here? Shit!" He turned back to the night manager. "I'll be down in three minutes."

Barry hurried into the bathroom and growled when his old man urinary tract wouldn't pretend to be young, just this once. After the last dribble, he flushed, and dashed to the door. As he stepped into the hallway, he instinctively checked his pockets for his smartphone, wallet, and keycard.

He kicked out a foot to stop the door from closing. His boxer shorts didn't have pockets.

Back inside he went to put on some pants and find his phone, wallet, and keycard. Necessities confirmed, he rushed to the elevator and reached the van only a few minutes later than promised.

The trip to the hospital didn't take long. Barry popped out of the van the moment it stopped, pushed past the automatic doors, and was marching straight toward the front desk when Jenny waylaid him with a tug on the arm. That it was Jenny, not Beth, who grabbed him, told him who was injured.

"What happened to Beth?" he asked.

"She has a significant gash on the side of her head." Jenny pointed to three college-aged men who were standing nearby. "This is Tyrone, Jamal, and Robert. If it weren't for their quick actions, Beth would've lost a lot more blood."

Jamal arched an eyebrow, making the freckles on his forehead shift. "All we did was bind her wound and drive her to the hospital. And if we're to be perfectly honest, we were the ones who made her nervous and caused her to fall."

Barry shot Jenny a fierce stare.

She shuffled back a step and said, "Beth and I were both tipsy, and when we saw these men following us, we thought the worst and ran. Beth would have been fine if she hadn't taken a second glance over her shoulder. She tripped and hit her head on a fire hydrant."

Barry cringed. "What! Did you two run because they're black?"

"No!" Jenny declared, a bit too forcefully. She tried not to look at the men, but her conscience made her do so anyway. "Maybe. . . . A little. I'm sorry! We didn't know your car was parked just up the street."

"It's okay, ma'am," Tyrone said, his head swaying atop his muscular shoulders. "We're kinda used to it."

Robert, the tallest of the men, leaned down slightly as he said, "You should go check on your friend. What's your name again, ma'am?"

"Jenny."

"And your name, sir?"

"Barry."

Robert stared at the ceiling and repeated the names, "Jenny, Barry, and Beth. Jenny, Barry, and Beth. Wait a minute. I knew y'all looked familiar! You three are the heroes who overpowered the gunman at that dancehall in Kansas City."

"You're thinking of someone else," Barry said.

Robert placed his hands on his hips and asked his friends, "Didn't we see these two on TV?"

"Oh, yeah," Tyrone said, smiling widely. "I never forget a woman who can rock the goth look. I just couldn't place where I'd seen her until you made the connection."

"The Silver Squared," added Jamal.

"Squad, not squared," Barry clarified.

"Aha! I knew if I said it wrong, you'd correct me."

Robert put a reassuring hand on Barry's shoulder. "Don't worry. Your secret is safe with us. Now go check on Beth. We'll be here when you get back."

"And we'll be expecting selfies and autographs from all three of you," Jamal added. "No excuses from Beth."

Barry nodded and followed Jenny into the elevator.

Once the doors closed, Jenny said, "When Beth hit the fire hydrant, I was so scared for her."

"But she's going to be okay. Right?"

"No one has told me one way or the other. But head wounds often bleed a lot, making them look worse than they really are. I think the doctor just wants to be sure she doesn't have any swelling or bleeding inside her brain."

When the elevator doors opened, Jenny led Barry to Beth's room. It was empty. "A nurse said they'd place Beth in here once the doctor is done with her."

They backed out, claimed some chairs down the hall, and waited.

Soon, two hospital attendants wheeled Beth's bed around the far hallway corner, past Barry and Jenny, and into the empty room.

Barry glimpsed Beth and commented to Jenny, "At least her face looks okay."

"Much of what happened tonight is a blur to me, but that's how I pieced together that she was taking a second glance over her shoulder. When she tripped, it was the side of her head, not her face, that collided with the fire hydrant."

Barry shuddered. "That was lucky. . . . I think."

When a heavyset man with a high forehead rounded the far corner, Jenny announced, "Here comes the doctor."

They both stood as he approached.

"I'm Jenny. I spoke with you earlier. And this is Barry, Beth's um . . . significant other."

After the doctor introduced himself and the two men shook hands, Barry asked, "How's Beth?"

"Very lucky," he said, launching into a detailed explanation of what he had found.

Barry interrupted, "Can you repeat that in English?"

"Ms. Potter has a mild concussion, with no skull fracture or internal bleeding. Her wound required eight stitches, but other than suffering from headaches for the next few days, I don't expect her to have any problems. I'm going to hold her here until noon for observation. If nothing unexpected pops up between now and then, she can go home."

"How soon can she have visitors?" Barry asked.

"A nurse will let you know. I'd guess a half-hour from now."

"Thank you," said Barry.

"Thank you," Jenny repeated.

The doctor nodded and continued down the hall.

As Barry returned to his chair to wait, Jenny descended in the elevator to update the men. She located them in the primary waiting area, and they rose as she neared.

"Tyrone, Jamal, Robert—I have good news. Beth got eight stitches and has a mild concussion. Other than that, she's fine."

Robert whistled in relief. "Thank God. All that blood had me worried."

"Well, ya know . . . head wounds," said Jenny. "I'm sure you guys are tired. You're under no obligation to stick around."

"Oh, no," Jamal said with a smile. "I told you we aren't leaving until we get autographs and selfies."

Tyrone shook his head and said in a serious tone, "Mostly we just want to say hi to Beth, so she knows we meant her no harm. If she has a concussion, she probably doesn't remember much of what happened."

"I'm sure she'll appreciate that. I'm gonna go back upstairs and see about getting you guys into her room. If the wait will be longer than an hour, I'll come down to let you know."

Jenny ascended in the elevator and reclaimed her chair next to Barry in the hallway. There they both sat silently until a nurse approached them to say, "You can see your friend now."

As soon as they stepped into the room, Beth said in a groggy voice, "Oh, good. Familiar faces. Can either of you tell me how I got here? All the nurse would say was that I hit my head."

Jenny sidled to the bed and reached for Beth's hand.

Beth pulled away. "The only time you grab someone's hand in a hospital is to tell them bad news. Am I bleeding inside my brain or something?"

"No! You just headbutted a fire hydrant."

"A fire hydrant! How drunk was I?"

"You had quite a few. But it was my fault. I was the one who got us nervous about the men walking behind us."

"I remember something about that. Did my head hit the fire hydrant when they mugged us?"

"No. They were walking to their car, which just happened to be in the same direction we were going. When we got scared and ran, you tripped and your head bounced off the fire hydrant." Jenny paused for a moment. "I take that back. Since we're talking now, and you only have a mild concussion, your head must've glanced, not bounced, off the hydrant. No matter what actually happened, those men carried you to their car and raced both of us to the hospital."

Beth frowned. "Oh, dear. We must find those men so I can thank them."

"Don't worry about that. They're waiting in the lobby. And get this: they figured out we were the people who stopped the Benny's Country Dancehall Shooter, and they're refusing to leave until they know you're okay and get selfies and autographs from all three of us."

"Then let's not keep them waiting. Bring 'em on in!"

"Are you sure you're up to it?"

"Thank science for whatever drugs I'm on! My grogginess is fading away, and I'm feeling pretty good at the moment. We should do this before any of that changes."

"I'll go get them," Barry said.

As Barry walked out the door, Jenny reflexively reached for Beth's hand again. This time, she didn't dodge.

When Barry returned a few minutes later, three suddenly shy men followed him partway into the room.

Beth found the switch for her bed and raised herself into a sitting position. "Come all the way in, boys . . . men. I hear you saved my ass."

"We just did what any decent person would do if they found a lady bleeding on a sidewalk," Robert said.

"But I was running because I was scared of you."

He shrugged. "It was dark. You probably thought we were white."

Beth laughed. "Tell me your name, dear."

"Robert, ma'am."

"Come closer, Robert. I'd like to shake your hand." As he approached, she peered past his shoulder. "You men, too. What are your names?"

"I'm Jamal."

"Tyrone."

"It's a privilege to meet all of you." She shook each man's hand before continuing. "Jenny tells me you'd like some autographs and selfies. While I can't understand why anyone would want those things from us, who are we to say 'no'? But before we do that, I need a promise from all of you."

"Sure. Anything," said Tyrone.

She looked beyond the men to make sure no one was directly outside the door before saying, "Barry, Jenny, and I are on the run."

Jamal choked down a laugh and said, "I've seen you run. You're not very good at it."

"A different kind of run. Jenny is running from an abusive husband, Barry and I might be running from the law—we're really not sure—and all three of us are running from mass media attention. So before posting any photos on social media, you must let us get out of New Orleans first. Give Jenny your cell phone numbers, and she'll let you know when you can post."

"Of course," Tyrone said. "We promise."

"We promise," Robert repeated. He turned to face Jenny. "And if you'd like some help dealing with that abusive husband of yours, let me know."

"Let all of us know," Jamal added.

"My husband is a cop," said Jenny.

"Well then, you're screwed," Jamal said with a slight grin.

Tyrone shook his head. "Don't take Jamal seriously. We're all suckers for pretty ladies in distress. If you need us, we'll be there."

Barry stepped forward and blurted, "Shall we get on with the selfies?"

Jenny reached over and playfully slapped Barry's hand. "Don't be such a curmudgeon. When a lady my age is called pretty by a gentleman his age, you give that lady a moment to enjoy it." She closed her eyes and raised her hands, as if she were at an evangelical tent revival.

"I have to agree with Barry this time," said Beth. "I'm growing tired again, and I'm sure these gentlemen would like to get some sleep too."

With that, the Silver Squad signed autographs and posed for selfies with Tyrone, Jamal, and Robert. Jenny also borrowed Barry's smartphone, so she could enter into it the men's phone numbers and shoot some selfies to document the moment.

When a nurse showed up to shoo everyone out of Beth's room, it provided the perfect excuse for Barry and Jenny to accompany the men downstairs and accept their offer of a ride back to the hotel.

After the short ride and a round of warm goodbyes, Barry and Jenny took the elevator up to their floor, said goodnight to each other, and retired to their respective rooms.

Lack of sleep had left Barry feeling exhausted, and now he intended to reclaim a chunk of what he'd lost. He closed the curtains extra-tight, stripped down to his underwear, flicked off the lights, and collapsed onto the bed. Despite his exhaustion, he fidgeted under the covers, unable to turn off his brain. Finally, just when he was about to give up and get dressed for breakfast, he fell into a deep, wonderful sleep.

A knock on the door jolted him awake.

"Housekeeping!"

CHAPTER 23

Makin' Whoopee

The three friends hung around New Orleans for several more days. Even though Barry wasn't much for the nightlife, he enjoyed the food and people-watching along the riverfront. Jenny and Beth, on the other hand, split their time between enjoying the food and sights with Barry and going off on their own for attractions that appealed more to women than to men.

Whenever Beth felt the side of her head throb, she'd take a couple of ibuprofen. Other than that, she had experienced no complications since leaving the hospital. Well, she did have a bald spot on the side of her head where the stitches were. "That," she declared mischievously, "is merely an excuse to go hat shopping!"

On their final morning in New Orleans, the trio ate breakfast in the hotel restaurant, and Jenny texted Tyrone, Jamal, and Robert to say goodbye. It was then that Barry announced to Beth, "Unless you have a plan for upgrading my Mustang to a motor home, there's only enough room in the car for you to bring along a couple of the hats you bought. You're gonna have to ship the rest."

"Or I can give them away," she said.

"Give them away? Why spend all that time shopping and all that money just to do that?"

"What am I gonna do with my money after I die? Shopping for the hats was almost as much fun as wearing them. And if I blow through all my savings on this trip, I'm okay with that. My pension and Social Security are more than enough to live on."

"So are you planning on giving away your hats to homeless people, like we did with the SPAM?"

"Uh-huh. I already have several people in mind. After all, shouldn't every bag lady wear a fabulous hat?"

Barry laughed.

Beth continued. "If you and Jenny help me, it'll only take us a few hours. I know where some of the women hang out. And since you mentioned SPAM, do we have any left from our last heist?"

"I'm sure we have a few cans. We kinda got distracted with the kittens and everything else. Check the trunk."

"I will. And to make sure we have enough, let's see if that little corner market down the street has any in stock. That place doesn't look like it does much business, so I think the SPAM gods will forgive us if we pay for the cans this time. Then I'll give the ladies a free hat with every free can of SPAM. . . . Or should I give them a free can of SPAM with every free hat? I've never been good at marketing."

"I think *free* is the key term here. You can't go wrong either way."

"Checkout is at noon," Jenny chimed in. "If we're gonna do this before then, we'd better finish up here and get moving."

* * *

Taking a cue from the bag ladies who push around their belongings in shopping carts, Barry borrowed one of the hotel's luggage carts and stacked it with hats and SPAM. Then they paraded down side streets, looking for the women Beth had in mind. She didn't find everyone, but she did find most. And when all the hats were gone, they continued distributing cans of SPAM to any homeless person who would take one.

The last few dusty cans of SPAM Classic, from the corner market, were particularly hard to give away. That's when Beth realized the problem. They needed some Cajun SPAM. Using her smartphone to check the Hormel Foods Corporation website, she learned that the closest flavor to Cajun was Hot & Spicy. She shrugged, clicked over to the contact page, and thumbed in Cajun as a flavor suggestion.

* * *

Later that afternoon, the trio was back in the Mustang, traveling northeast. They weren't yet ready to head to Des Moines, but they weren't sure where to go either. So as Barry drove at a leisurely speed, waiting for someone to suggest a destination, he spoke into his rearview mirror, "Jenny, can you take out Gertrude and put her on my shoulder? She's been spending way too much time in that box. I think she'd enjoy the ride more if she could look around."

Jenny opened the box. "Sure. But do you really think a gecko cares about the view from a car?"

"Do you know for sure that she doesn't?"

"I guess not." She placed Gertrude on his right shoulder.

Barry reached up and gently scratched the gecko's neck, which she may or may not have enjoyed.

"Do geckos live in the Everglades?" Jenny asked.

"Of course," Barry said.

"Perhaps we should head there. I've always wanted to see the Everglades, and maybe we can find a mate for Gertrude."

"We can go to the Everglades, but finding a mate for Gertrude is out of the question. She's a leopard gecko, native to countries like Afghanistan and Pakistan. In fact, we'll have to be extra careful to make sure she doesn't escape. Invasive species are a major problem in the Everglades, and I'd feel almost as bad about contributing to that problem as I would about losing Gertrude."

"Wow! I didn't expect that much knowledge coming from you!"

Barry glared into the rearview mirror.

Jenny covered her mouth. "I'm sorry! I didn't mean it that way. I was trying to compliment you on your knowledge of geckos and invasive species."

"I know my reptiles," he said before glancing over at Beth. "Are you up for the Everglades too?"

"Sure. As long as you promise to protect me from cobras."

"Cobras? There aren't any cobras in the Everglades."

"Not even as an invasive species?"

"Well, I . . . I guess it's possible."

"Then you'll have to protect me."

"Me too," Jenny added.

"Okay, ladies." He tapped a random Everglades City business into his GPS. "We know where we're going next."

If they were in a hurry, their journey from eastern Louisiana to Everglades City would take less than twelve hours, but since none of the three had anyplace to be, they aimed to complete their journey in two days, maybe three.

* * *

Ultimately, they achieved their destination in two days, staying in a hotel near Tampa along the way. Even though they hadn't previously made reservations for lodging during their road trip, this time Beth called ahead to secure a two-bedroom condominium on Lake Placid. Having accommodations waiting for them was a convenience they all appreciated when they arrived stiff and tired late in the afternoon.

Jenny set her travel bag on the coffee table in front of the couch and rolled her shoulders. "I know I have no right to complain, but have either of you ever spent any length of time in the back seat of a Mustang?"

Beth plopped down on the far side of the couch and smiled. "Barry and I once had back-seat-Mustang-sex. Although I can't remember exactly how much time it took."

Jenny cringed as she eased onto the near side cushion. "On the bare seat? Why didn't you say something when I joked about it when we were in Osceola? No offense, but before I ride back there again, I'm gonna have to wipe down the seat with one of Barry's sanitizing towelettes."

Beth laughed. "We didn't have sex in the current Mustang! Barry drove a beat-up old Mustang when we were in high school. I think that's why he bought this newer one."

Barry had been listening to Jenny and Beth's conversation as he gave Gertrude some fresh water. When he finished, he set her box on the counter that separated the kitchen from the living room and headed straight for the recliner. Sinking into the chair, he said to Beth, "Those were good times, weren't they? Remember when we'd go to the drive-in theater and barely even watch the movie? I'd start by kissing your neck, eventually move down to your—"

Jenny covered her ears and interrupted with a chant, "Nah! Nah! Nah! Nah!" She lowered her hands and said, "Both of you are old enough to be my parents. And since my parents are no longer around, you've kind of replaced them. Joking about sex is fine. But no daughter, even an adopted one, wants to hear graphic details about her parents makin' whoopee. It's just gross!"

"Makin' Whoopee?" Barry hummed a few bars. "That song is even older than we are!"

"It's a song?" Jenny asked. "I thought it was just a phrase."

"Yeah, you're definitely young enough to be our daughter." He resumed humming, and when Beth joined in, he pushed up from the recliner, reached out for her hand, and pulled her into a dance. They waltzed gracefully around the living room and down the hall before collapsing with giggles on the bed in the master bedroom.

CHAPTER 24

See You Later, Alligator!

Everglades City isn't a city—at least in the true sense of the word. Instead, it's a town of less than five hundred people. In fact, it's so small and so quiet that restaurants, the grocery store, the post office, and anything else Barry, Beth, or Jenny could want were all walkable from the condominium they were renting.

In the morning, Jenny and Beth strolled over to the grocery store to buy supplies for two days of breakfasts and bag lunches. "Barry can spring for our dinners at a restaurant," Beth said over her shoulder as she paid the cashier.

The three friends ate a quick breakfast on their lakeside balcony before setting out for a day of exploring. Unsure of where to go first, they headed south on the causeway, because Barry claimed it was the most logical direction to travel. Soon they reached Chokoloskee Island, a tiny resort community with a mixture of paved and gravel streets and a dock-lined shore. When the road dead-ended on the far side of the island, Barry looked around and humphed. "I was hoping to see alligators."

"Be patient!" Beth said. "We just got here."

Barry turned off the car, said, "I'll be right back," and walked over to a ramp, where a truck with an alligator logo on its door was backing up to launch a boat.

He stood watching until he caught the eye of the driver, a mustached man wearing a camouflage baseball cap. The man stopped the truck and asked from his open window, "Can I help you?"

"Perhaps. I drove down here looking forward to a native wildlife adventure, particularly one with truly wild alligators, but I'm new to Florida and don't really know how to go about it."

"I can help you with that, but not today. I'm fixin' to take some men out hunting." He reached into his shirt pocket and pulled out a wrinkled business card. "Call my office and ask for Sandy. Tell her Darrell sent you. Our hunts are usually booked out weeks in advance, but if you're in a hurry, she can put you on the waiting list. Sometimes we have cancellations."

"You can hunt alligators in Florida?"

"Sure! We guide both public and private land hunts, though for the best experience, I always recommend our own pristine private lands. There, you'll have more freedom to hunt the way you want, won't be restricted by any hunting season, and have access to some of the biggest gators around. Trust me. It'll be truly wild!"

Barry took the card, muttered, "Thank you," and walked back to the car.

"What'd you find out?" Beth asked as soon as he clicked his seatbelt.

"I think we're gonna need some more SPAM."

As Barry drove the Mustang back toward Everglades City, he explained what he'd learned and what he intended to do about it. He finished by saying, "We need to make Gertrude proud. This one's for her—or at least her distant cousins."

Jenny tapped Barry on the shoulder. "Can I borrow your smartphone?"

"Of course." He retrieved his phone from the center console and handed it to her.

She opened a browser and thumbed in a search. "Are we going

to steal or buy the SPAM?"

"Let's buy it this time," Beth said. "If we want to avoid getting caught, I think stealing more SPAM in order to use it to commit another crime is pushing our luck. We really are just amateurs at all of this."

"I was hoping you'd say that." Jenny looked down at the screen. "We shouldn't buy the SPAM at the grocery store in Everglades City. It would be too obvious, and they likely don't have much of a supply there, anyway. Instead, I recommend that we go north to Naples, where we can spread our shopping over multiple stores."

"That sounds reasonably competent to me," Barry said. He reached forward, tapped a random Naples grocery store into his GPS, and pressed enter.

"Wait!" Jenny said.

"What's wrong?"

"Don't go there yet. I'll tell you why after I finish reading this."

He pulled to the side of the road and turned off the car.

When Jenny finished, she looked up and said, "Okay, I suspect the man you just spoke with guides hunts for a variety of animals, not just alligators, because near where we are now, we have Everglades National Park, Big Cypress National Preserve, and Fakahatchee Strand Preserve State Park, and none of them allow alligator hunting. The Everglades that are not part of any park or preserve continue north of those areas, all the way to Lake Okeechobee. It's in that belt, between the public lands and Lake Okeechobee, where some of the most prominent alligator hunting outfitters are located."

Beth gave the dashboard an excited little pat. "So if we want to see alligators or any other animals, we should do that first, while we're here. And if we want to create mischief on behalf of Gertrude's distant cousins, we should do that last, when we're ready to leave the state."

"Exactly," Jenny said.

"Are you okay with that, Barry?" Beth asked.

"Um. . . . Sure. Then where do you gals wanna go today?"

"Let's continue driving north," Jenny said. "Take a right when we reach the Tamiami Trail, which is four miles past Everglades City, then watch for the Loop Road. That'll take us into the Big Cypress National Preserve, where there are supposed to be lots of alligators."

Barry started the car and eased back onto the road.

* * *

The Loop Road didn't disappoint.

Barry beamed as he pointed out his window. "I've never seen an alligator in the wild before. Look at that one! And that one! She's absolutely stunning." He steered off to the side and cut the engine. "Let's go for a walk."

Beth frowned. "Is it safe?"

"I think so. It's not like we're gonna be one of those Yellowstone National Park idiots you see on the internet, trying to pet bison. At least I hope not. We'll give the alligators plenty of space."

He opened his door and stepped onto the gravel road. The women hesitantly followed.

An alligator hissed!

Barry jumped back. "Oops! Sorry, big girl. I didn't see you there."

"We're all gonna die!" Jenny said, her puckish smile giving away that she wasn't totally serious.

"We're gonna be fine!" said Barry. "I didn't realize the roadside bushes could hide alligators so effectively. Now that I know, it won't happen again."

They strolled along the road, stopping frequently to admire alligators, anhingas, little blue herons, great egrets, butterflies, lizards, and snakes. Most of the animals weren't on the road or in the bushes. Instead, they were in the crystalline water swamp or the haunting cypress trees that stretched out to the left and right.

Jenny pointed to ten or so large white birds wading among the trees in the swamp and said, "Oh, look at those!"

"What are they?" Barry asked.

Jenny held out her hand. "Can I borrow your phone again?"

He reached into his back pocket. "Sure, but I doubt there's any service out here."

She took the phone from Barry and glanced at the screen. "One and a half bars!" She squatted to capture an image, searched the internet for a bird identification site, and uploaded the photo. A moment later, she declared, "They're white ibises."

"They sure are beautiful," Beth added.

"Jenny," Barry said with a wide smile. "Thank you for finding this magical place! Here we are, within a few hours of multiple large cities, yet we're all alone with this amazing wildlife."

Beth grinned. "I don't know about you, Barry, but now that I've overcome the nervousness of walking on a road through an alligator swamp, I'm beginning to feel younger."

Barry added a little bounce to his walk and said, "I believe you're right. I feel younger too. Do you think if we jumped into the water, we'd revert to our youth?"

"I doubt that, but I'm sure we'd be fresh meat."

Another alligator hissed!

Everyone scurried to the far side of the road.

This one was only five feet long, but it was unwilling to give up the warm patch of sunlight it had claimed on the strip of grass between the road and the swamp.

Once the people and the alligator felt comfortable about the distance between them, Barry put his hands on his knees and hunched down to admire the sight before him. "I wish we hadn't left Gertrude back at the condo. She would've been impressed with this reptile cousin of hers."

Jenny kneeled for a better view. "Not to take anything away from Gertrude, but do you really think she'd appreciate seeing an alligator?"

Barry furrowed his brow and playfully snapped, "Oh, let an old man anthropomorphize for a bit, will ya?"

Jenny laughed. "Well, when you put it that way. Yes, I'm sure Gertrude would be in absolute awe of such a magnificent sight!"

"Damn right she would!"

They continued along the road, stopping frequently to admire whatever nature had in store for them next.

Eventually, the youthful feelings Barry and Beth were experiencing gave way to the reality of the aged bodies they occupied. Barry arched into a backward stretch and moaned, "Oof! My back is killing me."

"Oh, good!" Beth said. "My knee is grinding like a wheel that's lost its bearings."

Even though Barry knew what Beth was implying, he scowled at her anyway. "You're glad my back is killing me?"

Her mouth gaped open. "No! That's not what I meant. My knee has been bothering me ever since we stopped to watch that anhinga do the hypnotic gyrating thing with its neck. I didn't want to say anything because you and Jenny were having such a good time. Now I assume you're ready to turn around, too."

Barry smiled. "I'm just teasing. We both had similar thoughts. I didn't wanna complain about my back, when you and Jenny were having such a good time." He pulled the car keys from his pocket and dangled them in front of Jenny. "I think it's your turn to drive. Beth and I will wait for you here."

She snatched the keys and marched several steps down the road before looking over her shoulder and saying, "Goodbye, old folks. I've always wanted a Mustang!"

The two seniors eased onto a pillow of unoccupied grass, where they watched in silence until Jenny disappeared around a curve.

"She wasn't serious, was she?" Barry asked.

"If she was, that would make us the ultimate suckers, wouldn't it?" Beth replied.

CHAPTER 25

Blaze of Glory

Jenny returned to find Beth grasping Barry's wrists, desperately trying to stop whatever was dragging him through the bushes and into the swamp.

"Help!" Beth screamed.

Jenny leaped out of the car, wrapped her arms around Beth's waist, and pulled.

The septuagenarians surreptitiously provided just enough counter resistance to make the fight seem real. Then, on Barry's nod, they reversed their resistance and fell into a heap of laughter atop Jenny.

A car approached. Its occupants unsure of what they'd just witnessed. The driver lowered his window and asked, "Is everyone okay?"

Jenny brushed herself off as she stood, swallowed to regain her composure, pointed, and said, "An alligator stole his dentures." She swallowed again. "And . . . and they fit so well, it took all three of us to pry them out of its mouth."

That Barry still had all his own teeth didn't stop him from reinforcing Jenny's words by pushing to his feet and tilting his head to display a broad, somewhat demonic smile.

The driver punched the accelerator, spinning the wheels, as his car vanished into a swirling cloud of dust.

Beth accepted Jenny's offer of a hand to pull her to her feet and said, "Okay. Are we all even now?"

Jenny grinned. "As far as I'm concerned, we are. But I knew from the beginning you two were faking."

"You did not," Barry said.

"I did too," she replied.

* * *

The trio kept their Everglades City condominium for two more nights, spending the next day exploring Fakahatchee Strand Preserve State Park and the day after that enjoying nature wherever they could find it. Throughout their visit, Beth attempted to maintain a mental list of all the bird and butterfly species they observed, but eventually gave up. Barry, on the other hand, knew they had seen precisely twenty-three alligators.

They would have stayed longer, if someone else hadn't previously reserved their condo for a weeklong visit. So rather than try to find another vacancy in Everglades City, they packed up and headed for Naples. At that point, their road trip took on the more serious tone associated with completing the mundane tasks of finding and checking into a hotel and shopping for more SPAM.

After departing the final supermarket, everyone huddled around the trunk, searching for open spaces to wedge in cans of SPAM. That's when Beth threw out a suggestion she hoped would lighten everyone's mood. "Since SPAM seems to be playing an oversized role in our endeavors, instead of the *Silver Squad,* shouldn't we be calling ourselves something like the *SPAM Commandos?"*

"That makes us sound like one of those militias, where out of shape men dress up in military gear to play with their guns," Barry said. "How 'bout the *SPAMinators*?"

Beth laughed. "I know you're referring to a character Arnold Schwarzenegger played in the movies, but it still sounds obscene. How 'bout *The Three SPAMeteers*?"

"Oh, that's awful!" said Jenny as she found a space for the last can of SPAM.

Barry shut the trunk. "I'm with Jenny on that one. I'm also reluctant to tie ourselves to a corporate product. A week from now, we might be bored with SPAM and on to something else. If we're sincere about a name change, we could be *The Geezers and the Gal*."

Beth opened the passenger-side door and said, "I'm pretty sure geezers are exclusively male. But we could reconfigure it into *The Geezer and the Gals*."

Jenny followed Barry over to the driver's side door and exclaimed, "I've got it! *Jenny and the Geriatrics*."

Beth snorted. "That's the best one yet, but no way do you get first billing."

Barry opened his door and slid the seat forward to allow Jenny to step inside. "I agree with Beth. Besides, we're a ragtag band of vigilantes, not a slick band of pop stars."

Beth fastened her seatbelt. "Our sudden burst of creativity aside, I have to admit that I brought up the possibility of a name change more for fun than anything else. If we're being serious, we're already locked into the Silver Squad name. I know it's not terribly creative, or even fitting, now that Jenny has joined us, but the time to come up with something better was before we became famous in Kansas City. If we ever end up on TV again, we'll confuse the media and our fans if we suddenly call ourselves by an unfamiliar name."

Barry started the engine and said, "Jenny, even though we can't change our name to give you equal or accurate billing, this next job depends on you. We're gonna need your internet skills to figure out what alligator hunting organizations to hit and how we can damage them without getting shot."

Jenny leaned forward to put a hand on Barry's shoulder. "I can't guarantee none of us will get shot, but I've already done much of the research."

"You have?"

"Yeah. You two go to bed much earlier than I do, and during the past few nights we were together in the condo, I worried that the TV would disturb your sleep. So instead of channel surfing, I occupied myself by borrowing your smartphone to browse online."

"Without asking?"

"Oh, come on. You were leaving it lying out on the counter, and it's not like you have porn on it or have ever said no when I've asked to use it before."

"You checked my phone for porn?"

"Um . . . ," Jenny's face flushed. "Let's just stay on topic. I've already located some worthy prospects and even looked at satellite images of their headquarters and surrounding grounds. But before we do anything, I want to show both of you some of the alligator hunting videos featured on their websites. The cruelty the hunters display in those videos is sickening, and the celebratory grins they flash would make Satan blush. One outfitter even has a slogan that claims, 'If it flies, swims, or runs—we slay it.'"

"Why would we want to see any of that?" Beth asked.

"Because those videos will help us calibrate the level of vigilantism we administer. This is much worse than a one-time incident of a woman dumping kittens. These macho-micro-dicks run ongoing entities worthy of the Deluxe Silver Squad Package."

* * *

Later that evening, everyone gathered in Barry and Beth's hotel room to watch the horrific alligator hunting videos Jenny had found. The videos, which showed everything from baiting alligators—so glory-seeking hunters could spear the unsuspecting reptiles from platforms above—to men armed with heavy-duty fishing poles, gleefully snagging and reeling in one alligator after another, made Barry and Beth feel ill. Most of the hunting methods they watched would be illegal on public lands, but on private lands in Florida, almost anything goes. Barry brought the viewing to an abrupt halt when he slammed his eyes shut and cried, "Enough!"

Knowing that no outfitter wishing to stay in business would post videos of illegal activities, Barry likened what he saw to billionaires who game the system to pay less taxes than schoolteachers do. In other words, just because something is legal doesn't make it ethical. He opened his eyes and said, "If ever there was a situation that screamed for us to be vigilantes, this is it."

But private land alligator hunting is a lucrative industry, with some outfitters charging ten thousand dollars or more for a trophy-sized kill. Therefore, the longer the three friends discussed potential targets and retributions, the more hopeless they felt. More outfitters existed than they could realistically visit, and most, if not all, of those outfitters would be armed. Also, as they could see from satellite images, none of their potential targets left their equipment out in the open, presenting opportunities for vigilantes to vandalize them. Clearly, the Silver Squad was out of their league.

Beth stared at the ceiling and said with dejection in her voice, "Feeding the alligators all the SPAM we just purchased might do them more good than anything we can do to the outfitters on their behalf."

Barry looked at the floor and shook his head. "SPAM isn't good enough. Say we force some of the meat into a bunch of gas tanks. Maybe we screw up a few boat engines, but any established outfitter is gonna have backup boats, and even if by some miracle we get to them all, whatever damage we do will be covered by insurance, anyway."

"We have the gun," Beth said. "If we shoot up the headquarters of a couple of outfitters, I bet they'll get the message."

"What!" Jenny shouted. "Are you crazy?"

"Hey, that's not a bad idea," Barry said. "But the little pistol we have won't be enough. We're gonna need some AR-15s and lots of ammunition."

"Any idea where we can get all that?" Beth asked.

"We're in Florida. They probably have AR-15s and ammunition in vending machines, right next to the candy bars."

Jenny pounded her fist on the bedside table. "You two are insane! This isn't what I meant when I suggested the Deluxe Silver Squad Package! You know these people are hunters, don't you? All of them will be much better shots than either of you are."

Beth bobbed her head in satisfaction. "Well, Barry, deep down isn't this what we really wanted when we began this trip—to go out in a blaze of glory, like senior citizen Bonnie and Clydes? We'll be even more famous than we were after Kansas City!"

Barry posed his hands as if they were holding an invisible assault rifle. He walked over to the floor-to-ceiling mirror and pretended to shoot. "All my life, I've wondered if anything could piss me off enough to grab a gun and go ballistic. Seeing all those slaughtered alligators strung up on poles gave me that answer. Yeah, a blaze of glory is the way to go."

Jenny stood, arms tensed at her side, hands balled into fists. "This is where we part ways! It's one thing for me to use a gun to go after my abusive husband. It's quite another to use one to go after people who, despite their vile behavior, are technically following the law. I won't die—or even go to jail—for that!"

She stormed out of the room.

CHAPTER 26

Upgrades

Barry stared at Beth for a moment before saying, "Do you wanna go after her, or should I?"

"I think you'd better let a woman do it." She pushed off the bed, stepped out the door, and crossed the hall to Jenny's room.

She knocked.

"Go away!"

"Jenny. We weren't serious."

"You sure sounded serious to me."

Beth stood as close to the door as possible and explained, "Barry and I grew up together in a small town and were friends long before we started dating. Back in school, the two of us and some of our classmates used to play a game to help us whenever a teenage problem required a creative solution. That game involved proposing the most outrageous solution possible and chewing on it for a while. Often just the visualization of the extreme would open our minds to something workable that was more realistic."

"If that's true, why didn't you tell me before you played it?"

"I don't think either of us was aware we were resurrecting the game until it happened, and telling you during the process would've destroyed our momentum."

The women stood silently on opposite sides of the door for a moment. When Jenny finally responded, she said, "I still need you to go away."

"What? I just told you what happened. At least let me give you enough money to cover bus fare to wherever you wanna go."

She opened the door. "Bus fare? No, I think we're gonna need much more money than that."

Beth frowned. "Okay, now you're pissing me off."

Jenny broke into a wide smile. "The money isn't for me. I'm trying out your game in my head, and it's already working. Go back to your room and let me, as you say, 'Chew on it for a while.' In fact, since it's getting late, let me sleep on it too. I'll knock on your door in the morning. I just might have an awesome solution to our problem!"

* * *

When Beth answered the morning knock, the junior member of the Silver Squad strutted straight into the room and plopped down on the corner of the bed. "How much are you two willing to pay to do some serious damage to the private land alligator hunting industry?"

Beth sat next to her and said, "Remember the conversation we had about money back in New Orleans? Nothing has changed. I'm already set for my day-to-day expenses. I also don't have any children waiting for an inheritance. So, really, the best way for me to enjoy what I've saved over the years is to witness it doing some good. I don't know exactly how much money I have, but for now, we can use whatever I have stashed in my money market account. Later, if necessary, we can even explore dipping into some of my other investments."

Barry leaned back and twirled in the desk chair. "I can contribute some money too. Probably not as much as Beth can, but enough to be helpful."

Beth patted Jenny's knee. "I can't wait any longer. What do you propose?"

Jenny's gaze alternated between Beth and Barry as she said, "We all know that what happened in Kansas City made us famous. Even though our fame won't last forever, we still have time to take advantage of it. To do that, I'll need a laptop computer, some video editing software, and my own smartphone—a good one. With the proper equipment, I can create some effective videos. We won't be able to end private land alligator hunting, but I think we'll be able to give the outfitters a taste of what it feels like to be hunted. Especially if one or both of you can spring for an advertising budget to boost the videos on social media until they go viral."

"I'll give you whatever you need, dear. Is there anything else?"

"I hate to ask, but can you upgrade my room to a suite? The extra space will make it easier for me to work."

"I'll take care of that," Barry said.

"And we're gonna have to extend our stay for five or six days. This isn't something I can do overnight."

Barry grabbed the car keys from the corner of the desk and tossed them to Beth. "I think you two have some shopping to do. While you're gone, Gertrude and I will extend our stay and try to switch us to side-by-side suites." He held out a hand to Jenny. "I need your keycard."

Jenny raised a palm and said, "Whoa. I doubt management will have any rooms available until after checkout time. Plus, I wanna have some breakfast before leaving. Let me eat and pack up my stuff first. When I'm ready to go, I'll bring over my travel bag and keycard."

* * *

Jenny and Beth spent the entire day shopping. Barry, on the other hand, completed his tasks quickly and was even able to indulge in an afternoon nap. He was sitting on the couch, contemplating having to eat dinner by himself, when the two women showed up carrying much more than just a new laptop and smartphone.

Beth set an armful of packages on a side chair and grinned. "We needed new outfits and makeup. If we're gonna be in videos, we have to look our best." She tossed a bag to Barry. "I bought you a shirt."

"Gee, thanks," he said sarcastically.

"Nice suite!" Beth said.

"Nothing but the best for the Silver Squad," he replied.

"The two of us shopped with the same philosophy."

Jenny waved her new smartphone in front of Barry's face. "Isn't this great? It'll do everything I need it to do. I was even able to trade in that old phone I didn't dare turn on and open a new account that Joe will never find."

Barry tried to look impressed. "That's just wonderful, Jenny. Is anyone hungry?"

"I'm famished," Beth said.

Jenny tapped her smartphone screen a few times before slowly raising her head. "Why don't you two go out for a nice, intimate dinner? I'm too excited about getting my phone and computer set up to even think about eating. If I get hungry later, I'll grab something downstairs in the bar."

Barry handed Jenny her new keycard. "For some reason, side-by-side rooms are hard to come by in this hotel. Your suite is straight across the hall, and your travel bag is waiting for you on the couch."

"Awesome!" She loaded up her arms with the items Beth bought her, flashed a wide smile, and strutted out the door.

CHAPTER 27

Both Places at Once

By the following day, Jenny had her new smartphone and computer set up just the way she wanted them to be and had even rearranged her suite to make it more conducive for production work. When she met up with Barry and Beth for lunch in the hotel restaurant, she explained, "On the technical side, I'm ready to go. But we should still watch more of the videos the outfitters have posted on their websites, and it wouldn't hurt for us to drive by some of their storefronts and hunting lodges."

Barry looked up from his menu and asked, "Why is that necessary?"

Jenny pushed her menu aside and said, "Because our next step is writing a script—actually several scripts—and the more personal this feels for us, the better those scripts will be."

"I have lots of writing experience from working at universities," Beth said. "I'm happy to take everyone's ideas and condense them into scripts."

"Wait a minute," Barry said. "I've worked at radio stations for most of my adult life, and when I sold advertising, I also wrote the commercials. So—"

Beth reached over to squeeze Barry's hand as she interrupted,

"We'll write them together, dear."

"Um. . . . That's exactly what I was going to suggest," he said.

"Okay then," said Jenny. "We'll head up to my suite for a video session after we eat. Then, if it's not too late, we'll do an outfitter drive-by."

* * *

Jenny sat between Barry and Beth on the couch in her suite. She opened her laptop computer and waited until everyone was ready. Then she clicked the icon to start the first video. When it ended, she clicked the next one. The video review session was painful to watch, with macho hunters attempting to depict the alligators as the bad guys by calling them "mean," "sons of bitches," and worse.

"What do those hunters expect the alligators to do when they snag them with huge treble hooks?" Barry asked. "Fighting for survival doesn't make any animal mean!"

"Can you imagine how much it would hurt to have one of those hooks yank you through the water?" Jenny added. "That an alligator can even put up a fight is amazing. If someone did that to me, I'd scream and do anything I could to prevent the hook from ripping my flesh."

"So do alligators feel pain the same way humans do?" Beth asked.

Jenny nodded. "I've always assumed all animals feel pain, but just to be sure, I read up on the subject before falling asleep last night. Alligators definitely feel pain. In fact, despite their armor, some parts of their body are more sensitive than a human fingertip. They're also quite intelligent."

Jenny clicked on another video. This one featured a father with his young son, presented in a way that made alligator hunting appear to be a heartwarming bonding activity.

Beth pointed at the screen. "That asshole is teaching his son that cruelty is acceptable if you disguise it as hunting."

"He reminds me of Joe," said Jenny. "It's one of the reasons I stayed on the pill when he thought we were trying to have a baby. If we'd had a son together, he would've used a similar activity to teach him cruelty."

Beth shook her head. "I know from years of working with students that not every child becomes their parent. Even so, violent and hate-filled minds rarely become that way in a vacuum. That poor boy is only seven or eight, and the cards are already stacked against him."

Jenny grimaced. "Poor boy? I'm more worried about his poor future wife!"

"We really need to stop watching these videos," Barry said. "Each one inches me closer to believing that our blaze of glory fantasy is a fitting solution."

Beth leaned around Jenny for a better view of Barry and said, "Your face looks red. When was the last time you checked your blood pressure?"

"Since before we left Minnesota, obviously. I'll be fine. When I realized I was running low on my blood pressure meds, I switched to taking them every other day."

"You did what!"

He looked down. "I didn't think we'd be gone this long."

Beth grabbed Barry's hand as she stood. "Come on."

"Where are we going?"

"You know *exactly* where we're going, old man."

Barry looked at Jenny and flashed an innocent smile. "I guess it's either to the pharmacy or to the doghouse."

"Who says you can't go to both places at once?" Beth hissed. She pulled Barry all the way to the door before glancing back at Jenny and rolling her eyes. "We'll be back in an hour or so."

CHAPTER 28

SPAM and Coke

Barry felt vindicated when the pharmacist informed him and Beth that a spike in blood pressure likely wasn't the cause of his flushed face. Instead, it was probably something temporary, such as a strong emotion. Considering the videos they had been watching, that made perfect sense.

No matter what the cause, the pharmacist's assistant checked Barry's blood pressure and confirmed it was well above normal. "Your wife was right to be concerned about you!" she scolded. "You must take your medication every day."

Barry smiled at the notion of Beth being mistaken for his wife, and when he looked up at Beth from the chair he was sitting in, she was smiling too.

Despite their smiles—or perhaps because of them—Beth refused to allow Barry to leave the pharmacy parking lot until he'd swallowed a day's worth of pills. He didn't resist, and by the time they returned to the hotel, he was looking less like a sunburn victim and more like an eccentric old man. For him, that was a good thing.

Before going into their own suite, Barry and Beth knocked on Jenny's door to let her know they'd returned. She promptly answered and said, "I found an alligator hunting outfitter less than an hour from here and already have the address programmed into my phone. If we hurry, and don't hit too much traffic, we might be able to make it before they close for the day."

* * *

Their trip east took longer than expected, and they passed right by the outfitter's inconspicuous collection of metal buildings before Jenny realized what happened and instructed Barry to turn around.

He stopped the car on the gravel road in front of the main building and let the engine idle. "Are you sure this is it?"

"Yes. My guess is that the outfitter wishes to remain anonymous to everyone except their clients. Because . . . Well, you never know when vigilantes armed with canned meat might come by to muck up their day."

Barry pulled forward a few feet and turned into the driveway, which widened into a parking lot several car-lengths later.

"What are you thinking?" Beth asked. "Knock on the door and ask for a tour?"

Barry pointed to a door sign with the hands of a clock on it. "See that? We're too late. They're already closed."

Jenny squinted. "It looks like they'll be back at seven. They must have a nighttime hunt scheduled. That gives us plenty of time to snoop around."

Barry drove all the way into the parking lot and switched off the car. He sat there for a moment before stepping outside, gravel popping under his feet as he walked to the main door. He rang the bell, just to be sure. When no one answered, he shaded each side of his head with his hands and peered through the glass at the top of the door. Inside, he saw a reception counter and a sitting area—the latter packed with taxidermy mounts of alligators, wild hogs, deer, ducks, and other animals.

Beth stepped onto the gravel and walked only as far as the front of the Mustang. She looked around and said, "This place gives me the creeps."

Jenny glided over next to her and sat on the edge of the hood. She swiveled on her butt as she pointed and said, "Everything here was confusing when I looked at it using Google Earth. From above, all I could see were treetops. That building and that building and that building were hidden under the foliage. Whether or not it was intentional, I can't say, but all these trees certainly give the outfitter privacy from satellite snoopers like me."

When Jenny swiveled back toward the main building, Barry blocked her view. He cleared his throat at an exaggerated volume.

She shot off the hood. "Sorry!"

"Someday this car, or at least this model of car, will be a collector's item."

Jenny crouched down and used the bottom edge of her T-shirt to buff the paint where she had been sitting.

"That's enough," he said in a gentle voice. "You're forgiven."

"Let's split up and check out all these buildings," Beth suggested.

While Barry and Jenny headed in opposite directions, Beth walked over to the closest metal outbuilding. She ignored the large sectional garage door and instead tried the smaller side door. It was locked. She continued along the wall to a dusty window. When she stood on tiptoes to look inside, she saw a disassembled airboat and an outboard motor mounted on a stand.

"This must be the repair shop," she muttered to herself.

When she stepped back, she grew curious about a two-track road that ran alongside the shop and curved around behind it. She followed the road around the corner and disappeared for a moment before returning to yell, "Bingo! Barry, Jenny, come back to the car!"

As soon as everyone reached the Mustang, Beth commanded, "Barry, pop open the trunk! I found an aboveground fuel tank. It's gotta be for refueling the boats. If we squeeze some SPAM inside it, we might be able to shut down this entire operation for days."

"That would certainly be easier than SPAMing individual boats," Barry said. "How many cans do you think it'll take?"

"It's a fairly big tank," Beth said. "I don't know. Maybe ten?"

Jenny reached into the Mustang and pulled out a mostly full two-liter bottle of Coke. "This has been jammed behind Beth's seat since our first day in Florida. When it got too warm to drink, I forgot all about it. If you pour it into the fuel tank, it'll probably do even more damage than the SPAM."

She handed the bottle to Barry, and he handed her the car keys. "Beth and I will take care of the tank. Stay here on lookout."

As soon as Beth finished loading one of their cloth shopping bags with SPAM, she and Barry hurried back to the tank.

"Where's the filler-cap?" Barry asked.

"I didn't think to look for it." She retreated a few steps before pointing. "There it is. Are you tall enough to reach it?"

"I don't think so. There must be something here I can stand on." He set the bottle of Coke on the ground and walked around the tank, inspecting the discarded junk strewn about, which included boat parts, a broken chair, a table with a missing leg, a cracked motor oil drain pan, and a couple of old-fashioned milk cans. "These will work," he said, carrying the milk cans to the front of the tank and setting them side by side.

"Don't fall!" Beth said.

Barry resisted a snarky retort to her obvious statement and carefully raised himself up with one foot on each can. He hoped Beth didn't notice his shaking legs.

Until that moment, Barry hadn't thought about fingerprints. But if they were going to make videos attacking the alligator hunting industry, it was important not to leave any physical evidence that they were the ones who contaminated the fuel.

He pulled out his handkerchief and covered his hand before

twisting off the filler cap. Glancing down at Beth, he asked, "Have you touched this tank?"

"No."

"Good. Give me the first can of SPAM."

She opened a can and handed it to him.

He turned it upside-down over the fuel tank inlet.

The SPAM remained inside.

He shook the can.

Nothing happened.

He shook it harder.

Same result.

He tried to pull the meat out with his fingers but couldn't get a grip.

"Do you have a knife?" he asked.

"Why would I have a knife?" she replied.

"Because you seem to have everything else in that purse of yours."

"My purse is in the car."

He sighed. "I know that. Do you have a knife in your purse, which is in the car?"

"No, the only knife I have is in our vigilante toolkit, which is back at the hotel."

"Why did you leave the toolkit there?"

"We drove out here to do some reconnaissance, not vigilante stuff."

"How 'bout the fork? Is that still in your purse?"

"Sure, but why risk bending my fork when this will work just as well?" She smiled and handed him a thick piece of metal strapping she'd found sticking out of the weeds next to the building.

Once again, Barry resisted a snarky retort. Focusing on the task at hand, he jammed the strap into the SPAM and extracted the meat, which he broke into small pieces and tossed through the inlet.

After doing the same with five more cans, Barry grew tired of the tedious project. "We're assuming the fuel will dissolve the SPAM enough to muck up the engines, but for all we know, it'll just drop to the bottom of the tank and sit there harmlessly intact for eternity. Hand me the Coke. I agree with Jenny that it's our best bet to stop the boats."

She handed him the bottle. He poured in most of the Coke before screwing the tank cap back on. Then, while he was still up there, he poured the remaining liquid onto his handkerchief and used it to wipe off all traces of SPAM and every surface he might have touched.

He jumped down, put the milk cans back where he found them, and re-wiped the side of the gas tank.

"Now it looks too clean," Beth said.

"It's better than leaving any fingerprints on it."

Beth pulled one of the empty SPAM cans out of her bag and used it to scrape up some dirt. When she flung the dirt at the tank, just enough of it stuck to make Barry's cleanup appear less obvious.

Barry dropped his filthy handkerchief into Beth's bag, and they hurried to the Mustang. They had just enough time to clean their hands and shut the trunk before a silver Dodge pickup, pulling a boat, turned into the driveway.

The driver steered alongside them and lowered his window. "Are you here for the night hunt?"

"Oh, no. We're . . ." Barry put his hands into his front pockets and rocked on his heels as he tried to come up with a plausible reason for them being there.

Jenny stepped beside him and announced, "Dad wants to kill an alligator, but he's worried he might be too old to do so."

The driver laughed, his bushy eyebrows reaching for the brim of his baseball cap. "You picked the right place to come to today." He pointed to the far side of the parking lot and said, "I'm gonna park my rig over there. Walk across. Boy, do I have a surprise for you!"

As the man pulled forward, Barry looked at his companions and asked, "Do we stay or make a run for it?"

"We have to stay," Beth said. "If we run, we'll make him suspicious and ruin everything."

Jenny added, "I know it may be difficult for *some* of us, but we need to act normal. We can't give the man any reason to jot down Barry's license plate number."

Barry shot the women his best deranged-old-man-look before conjuring up a dignified expression and escorting them to the truck.

Even though the tinted glass had concealed the rear seat occupants, it surprised no one when the doors opened and two men climbed out who looked older than Barry did. Website videos had prepared them for that. Besides the father-and-son alligator hunting videos they'd watched, common themes of other videos included young men showing how macho they could be, young women showing they could be just as ruthless as the men were, and old men—like the ones in front of them—showing they weren't yet ready to be put out to pasture.

The driver approached with his hand extended. "I'm Larry, one of the guides here, and this is Beau and Emmett."

Barry shook his hand and replied, "Nice to meet you. I'm Bart, and this is my wife Bertha, and our daughter . . . Birdie."

"The three Bs!" said Larry.

"Oh, that's funny! No one's ever called us that before."

Beth discreetly elbowed Barry in the side.

Larry turned to his clients and said, "Hey Beau, Emmett. Let's show these three nice people what a successful gator hunt looks like!" He walked back to the boat and waited until everyone gathered around. Then, with the flair of a magician twirling a cape, he yanked back the tarp.

Beth gasped and retreated a step.

"Don't worry," Larry said. "They can't hurt you. They're all dead!"

As Jenny used her phone to shoot a video that panned across the alligators, Barry grinned at Beau and Emmett and said, "I'm impressed! You two killed all four of these?"

Emmett puffed out his bulky chest. "Larry had to help with the two biggest ones, but Beau and I dispatched the smaller ones without any help."

Barry looked down and shook his head. "Were ya scared, Beau?"

"For the first big one, I was terrified. I was yellin' and swearin' like a nigga at a robe party and—"

"Beau!" Emmett shouted. "Dial it back. All these years I've known you, and you still don't know how to talk around the ladies."

Beau's bony shoulders tightened as he grabbed the brim of his baseball cap. "My apologies, ma'ams."

"It's okay," Jenny said. "My husband sometimes talks like that too. Are ya married, Beau?"

"No."

"Ya got a woman?"

"Yeah."

"I bet yer not gonna need any Viagra tonight. Am I right?" She winked.

His face flushed.

"Well!" Larry blurted. "I need to settle things up with Beau and Emmett and get these gators on ice." He stepped back to the truck and reached into the cab to pull out a business card. He handed it to Barry. "Call my office tomorrow and tell Betty I sent you. She can go over all the options with you. I'm not sure, but I think we have one opening left for next week. The gators have been puttin' up *real* good fights these last few days. So if ya wanna have the ultimate hunting experience, now's the time!"

"Thank you, Larry. I'll check my schedule tonight to see how next week looks. Oh, wait! I'm retired. Every day looks good! Ha! Ha! H—"

Beth cut Barry's exaggerated laugh short with another discreet elbow.

With nothing left to do but get away, Barry shook hands with all the men and led Beth and Jenny back to the Mustang. As he turned the car around in the parking lot, the women smiled and waved through Beth's open window, doing their best to draw attention to themselves rather than the car or its license plate.

Beth waited until they were well out of sight before wiping her brow and declaring, "I *so* need a drink right now."

"Oh, yeah!" Jenny agreed.

Barry looked into the rearview mirror. "Well, don't just sit there. Use that fancy new phone of yours to lead us to a watering hole."

"I'm on it, Dad!"

CHAPTER 29

The AI Copywriter

Upon returning to the hotel, the Silver Squad gathered in Jenny's suite and wasted no time getting to work on writing and planning their videos. Their motivation lasted for all of twenty minutes.

Barry placed a pillow on the arm of the couch and tipped onto it like a fallen domino. "I'm tired," he groaned.

Beth yawned and tipped onto Barry, like a second fallen domino. "Me too."

From the chair opposite the couch, Jenny stared at her friends for a moment before shutting the lid on her computer, padding over to the cushion next to Beth, and becoming the third domino. "Well," she said. "This has been productive. Don't wake me when you leave."

* * *

The Silver Squad writing and planning meeting resumed the following morning, after breakfast. Once again, Barry and Beth sat next to each other on the couch, and Jenny sat opposite them, with her computer on her lap and her feet on the coffee table.

Jenny spoke first. "After yesterday's adventure with Larry,

Beau, and Emmett, and a night to think about it, do we still dare do this?"

Beth leaned back and steepled her fingers. "I highly doubt the police in Florida would try to extradite any of us for vandalizing a gas tank. And even if they did, Barry wiped off all his fingerprints, making the case tough to prove."

"Rest assured that should the police come after us, we'll keep you out of it," Barry added. "And since we're eventually heading to Des Moines to pay Joe Asshole a visit, the chances are good that any crimes we've committed before we get there will be legally insignificant compared to whatever happens after we arrive."

"What about you, Jenny?" Beth asked. "Are you having second thoughts?"

"Hell no. I just wanted to make sure we're all on the same page before proceeding."

"We are," Beth said.

"Then let's get to work. To inspire our thinking, I set up a ChatGPT account when I woke up this morning and asked it to write a thirty-second commercial opposing alligator hunting in Florida. I saved it as a PDF file."

"What is ChatGPT?" Barry asked.

"An artificial intelligence chatbot."

"Huh?"

"A computer program you can have a conversation with."

He wrinkled his nose. "Um . . . Okay."

She opened the file, set her computer on the coffee table, and turned the screen toward Barry and Beth.

* * *

[Upbeat music playing]

Narrator: Attention, nature lovers and conservationists! Are you concerned about the future of Florida's unique wildlife? Then listen up!

[Scenic shots of Florida's wetlands and alligators]

Narrator: Imagine a world without the awe-inspiring beauty of Florida's alligators. These magnificent creatures have called this land home for centuries, and now they need our help.

[Close-up shots of alligator hatchlings]

Narrator: Alligator hunting poses a serious threat to the delicate balance of our ecosystem. It disrupts their natural habitats, disturbs their breeding patterns, and jeopardizes their very existence.

[Images of families enjoying outdoor activities in Florida]

Narrator: Florida's wetlands are not just a home for alligators; they're a sanctuary for countless species of birds, fish, and plants. By preserving this ecosystem, we ensure a vibrant and diverse environment for future generations.

[Text on screen: Protect Florida's Wildlife. Say NO to Alligator Hunting!]

Narrator: Together, we can make a difference. Join us in advocating for the protection of Florida's alligators and the preservation of our natural heritage.

[Text on screen: Stand up for Nature. Protect Florida's Alligators.]

Narrator: Let's celebrate these incredible creatures, not hunt them down. Together, we can create a future where alligators thrive and Florida's natural wonders continue to inspire us all.

[Upbeat music fades out]

[Text on screen: Protect Florida's Alligators. Visit www.protectfloridasgators.com for more information.]

* * *

"That's not bad!" Beth said.

"It gets better," said Jenny. "Obviously, a simple generic commercial won't do. We need something that will take advantage of our celebrity status. Let me show you what happened when I gave ChatGPT more specific instructions." She took the computer back, opened another PDF file, and returned the computer to the coffee table.

* * *

Instructions: Write a thirty-second commercial opposing alligator hunting in Florida. Make it sarcastic, and have it feature Barry and Beth, two elderly celebrities who defeated a mass shooter in Kansas City.

[Cheerful music playing]

Narrator: Ladies and gentlemen, gather 'round for a tale of heroism and an urgent cause! Meet Barry and Beth, the unstoppable duo who triumphed over a mass shooter in Kansas City.

[Clip of Barry and Beth receiving medals]

Narrator: They've faced danger head-on, but now they have a new mission: saving the alligators of Florida from the treacherous clutches of hunting.

[Barry and Beth posing with alligator plush toys]

Barry: (sarcastically) You know, Beth, after dodging bullets, taking on alligator hunters seems like a walk in the park!

Beth: (laughs) Oh, Barry, I've had my fair share of adrenaline-pumping adventures, but fighting for our scaly friends in the Sunshine State? Now that's what retirement dreams are made of!

[Close-up shots of alligators with exaggerated, comical expressions]

Narrator: These wise reptiles have been around since the dinosaurs, folks! Who needs dinosaurs when we have alligators?

Barry: (leaning in with a smirk) That's right, folks. Forget about thrill-seeking hunts. Let's make sure Florida's alligators keep the thrill alive for generations to come!

Beth: (holding up a sign that reads "Allies for Alligators!") It's time to embrace the scales, people! Together, we can protect our ancient friends and preserve the wild beauty of Florida!

[Text on screen: Protect Our Scaly Friends. Say NO to Alligator Hunting!]

Narrator: So, join Barry and Beth on their epic mission to save the day once again! Let's keep Florida's alligators sassy, snappy, and strictly off the hunting list!

[Text on screen: Stand with Barry and Beth. Say NO to Alligator Hunting!]

Barry: (with a wink) Remember, folks, heroes can be found in the most unexpected places. Let's be heroes for the alligators!

[Upbeat music fades out]

[Text on screen: Support Our Heroes. Visit www.protectfloridasgators.com for more information.]

* * *

"That's hilarious!" Beth said as she swiveled the computer back to face Jenny. "But you were as much of a hero as any of us, and you're not in it."

"For the ChatGPT examples, I didn't want to overdo it on the instructions. That's why I didn't add my name or separate private land hunting from public land hunting either. Besides, I'm going to have to run the camera when we film. You two will be the on-screen stars, not me."

Barry jotted something on a pad of paper before looking across the coffee table to Jenny and saying, "Both commercials cited a website address. Is that an actual website, and if not, do we need to get one?"

"It's just a fake placeholder address, and no, I don't think we need to get one. If I understand this project correctly, our goals are to educate people about the cruelty involved in private land alligator hunting and to make life more difficult for alligator hunting outfitters. For now, at least, what we're doing doesn't require people to visit a website to interact with us or seek additional information."

"If we're forgoing a website, how 'bout asking people to call the governor of Florida instead?" Beth suggested.

"That's a great idea," said Jenny. "Although, as the governor has made clear at his rallies, 'Florida is where compassion goes to die.'"

"Well, he doesn't speak for everyone in Florida," Beth said.

CHAPTER 30

Social Media Influencers

Inspired by the ChatGPT commercials, Barry and Beth got to work on writing the actual scripts they would use for their project. Once they felt comfortable with the words, everyone agreed that filming outdoors would be more effective than filming inside Jenny's suite. Besides, it was a fine excuse for all of them to indulge in more bird and alligator watching. With that in mind, they returned to the Loop Road and Fakahatchee Strand Preserve State Park for two days of video shooting.

That gave them enough footage for four videos, which Jenny edited on the third day. Since Jenny was also responsible for planning the social media posts and advertising buys, Barry and Beth helped out by making sure she had everything she needed, whether it be food or drink, looking up instructions whenever she screamed she was out of her league, or searching the internet for alligator-killing videos she could copy to use as B-roll.

Everyone worked late into the night, and on the morning of the fourth day, Jenny uploaded the first video.

* * *

[The camera pans from a serene pond of alligators to Barry and Beth in the foreground. Music reminiscent of "Dueling Banjos" plays softly.]

Barry: Hello. I'm Barry.

Beth: And I'm Beth.

Barry: You may recognize us as the seniors who used a simple can of SPAM to subdue a vicious mass murderer armed with an assault rifle, at Benny's Country Dancehall in Kansas City.

Beth: Today we're in Florida to take on another form of mass killing—private land alligator hunting.

Barry: You may think it's *only* an alligator, but alligators are intelligent beings that feel pain just like we do.

Beth: For private land alligator hunts, pretty much anything goes. You can hunt year-around, and unlike on public lands, where you have to use a bang stick for the death blow, on private lands you can kill with a rifle, a muzzle-loader, a pistol, a crossbow, or even a spear.

Barry: Can you kill with a can of SPAM?

Beth: Sure, technically. But private land alligator hunts aren't for people interested in a fair chase. Instead, they're for insecure cowards who only want to give the appearance of being brave. Typically, a guide will take those cowards to a spot where he's previously confirmed the presence of alligators. Sometimes the gators will be lured in with bait, for easy killing from a stand high above. Other times the gators will be snagged with a large treble hook, for killing from a boat. Whatever method they use, it's all about delivering the death blow. Or, more accurately, the money shot.

Barry (holds up a huge treble hook): Imagine going out for a swim, minding your own business, and someone snags you with one of these. Then, before you realize what's happening, that someone yanks the line as hard as they can to embed the hook deep into your flesh. Would that be humane or resemble anything close to a fair chase?

Beth: Cruelty doesn't make you brave. It makes you pathetic. Please call the number on your screen and ask Governor Ritchie to end private land alligator hunting in Florida!

[Music volume increases]

[Text on screen: Call Governor Ritchie today! (850) 717-9337]

* * *

After some debate over whether a snarky and demeaning video would help their cause, Jenny uploaded the second video to social media sites:

[Rapid-fire video clips of people killing alligators, accompanied by ominous-sounding music. After several seconds, Barry and Beth fade in. They're standing in front of a serene alligator pond, with birds singing in the background.]

Barry: Hello. I'm Barry.

Beth: And I'm Beth.

Barry: You may recognize us as the resourceful senior citizens who used a can of SPAM to subdue a mass murderer armed with an assault rifle, at Benny's Country Dancehall in Kansas City.

Beth: Today we're in Florida to use our resourcefulness to take on private land alligator hunting.

Barry: Often practiced by microphallused incels who only feel important when they're dominating someone, private land alligator hunters partake in a sadistic blood sport that slaughters animals that feel pain just like we do.

Beth: Did you know that Florida has two sets of alligator hunting regulations—one for public lands and another for private lands? On private lands, pretty much anything goes. You can hunt year-around and kill with almost anything, including an assault rifle, a muzzleloader, a pistol, a crossbow, or even a spear.

Barry: Can you kill with a can of SPAM?

Beth: Sure, technically. But private land alligator hunts aren't for people interested in a fair chase. Instead, they're for cowards who only want to present the illusion of being brave. Once an alligator has been snagged or lured in with bait, even an old lady like me could do the actual killing.

Barry: So this is nothing like the late naturalist Steve Irwin, who used his bare hands to catch and release crocodiles for scientific or relocation purposes?

Beth: Oh, hell no. Most private land alligator hunters would crap their panties if they got anywhere close to an alligator without a weapon in their hands.

Barry: But they're still proud of their trophy.

Beth: That's the whole idea. A wild animal trophy is simply a prop to make pathetic people feel important.

Barry: So please, be a wildlife hero, not a microphallused incel. Call the number on your screen and ask Governor

Ritchie to end private land alligator hunting in Florida!

[Volume of singing birds increases]

[Text on screen: Call Governor Ritchie today! (850) 717-9337]

* * *

By lunchtime, Jenny had uploaded the final two videos.

The first one was longer, showing a medley of clips she had lifted from alligator hunting websites. The creators of the original videos had intended to put a positive spin on their services, but when Jenny sequenced the kill shots one after the other, those videos portrayed the brutality of alligator hunting in a much darker light.

The second one featured Barry's camerawork, which allowed Jenny to star with Beth.

All four videos began generating views within minutes of posting, and as the three vigilantes-turned-social-media-influencers resumed their travels northward, Jenny planned to monitor the progress of each video and more vigorously promote the ones that attained the most action.

CHAPTER 31

And Now, a Musical Number

Jenny checked an internet travel site and learned that their drive from Naples, Florida, to Des Moines, Iowa, would cover roughly fifteen hundred miles and take twenty-one hours. For them, of course, those twenty-one hours could end up being divided into short segments over days or even weeks.

After all, why rush to complete a road trip for the aged and abused, when a dangerous encounter with Joe loomed as the grand finale? Therefore, Barry, Beth, and Jenny ate a leisurely breakfast before they checked out of their hotel in Naples, indulged in a little beach time along the way, and ultimately traveled only as far north as Sarasota. At that point, Barry complained that he had a sore back and suggested they check into another hotel. Beth and Jenny agreed, and neither said anything when Barry's hunched posture straightened out the moment the front desk clerk handed him the keycards.

* * *

At breakfast the following morning, Jenny suggested that they at least get out of Florida. Two of their videos were going viral, increasing the chances of someone recognizing them and alerting an ambitious police officer or a furious hunting outfitter of their whereabouts.

They made it as far as Valdosta, Georgia.

Given that the time was already four in the afternoon, the trio checked into a chain hotel and walked across the street to one of the many chain restaurants that stick to such hotels like remoras.

They slid into the red plastic booth seats, with Barry and Beth on one side and Jenny on the other.

Beth waited until everyone ordered and the waiter was out of earshot before announcing, "It's time to rediscover our helping-people-purpose."

"Our helping-people-purpose?" Barry asked.

"Yes. Southern states have the highest poverty rate in America. There are certainly many people here who would appreciate a can or two of SPAM."

"How do you wanna steal it this time?" Jenny asked.

Beth flicked a limp-wristed hand forward. "Stealing SPAM is so yesterday. When we paid for all the cans we acquired in New Orleans and Naples, the SPAM gods seemed to be okay with it. Sure, it spoils the Robin Hoodness of it, but this entire adventure has challenged us to be flexible."

Barry twirled a sugar packet on his placemat. "In that spirit, I suggest we expand our delivery menu beyond SPAM. Perhaps we could add something nutritious, like fresh fruit."

"How 'bout bananas?" Jenny proposed.

"Bananas would be perfect. We can store them without refrigeration, and the peels could come in handy if we ever need to make a quick getaway."

Beth laughed. "I don't think banana peels work as well in real life as they do in slapstick skits or cartoons. But sure. Why not? We'll give each homeless person some bananas with their SPAM."

Armed with a plan to rediscover their helping-people-purpose, the Silver Squad lingered over their chain restaurant meals for the minimum acceptable amount of time and hit a large supermarket immediately thereafter. This time, however, *hit* took on a different meaning. Instead of hitting the store like a band of petty thieves, they hit it with a wad of cash and a grandfather's care to make sure only the finest bunches of bananas made it into the shopping cart.

Disciplined teamwork and a minimum amount of bickering allowed Barry, Beth, and Jenny to complete their shopping trip without drawing attention to themselves. That is, until the cashier rang them up for sixteen cans of SPAM, ten bunches of bananas, three bottles of soft drinks, and one roll of Tums—all of which Beth paid for with assorted bills.

If there was one thing no one in the Silver Squad should've forgotten, it was that Barry's Mustang wasn't built to accommodate comfortable cross-country travel by more than two adults at a time. Even with Gertrude back at the hotel, getting all the items—which Barry insisted weren't bagged properly—into the car was a challenge. Then the humans had to get in too.

Jenny shifted in her seat, trying to figure out the best position to feel the fewest number of cans digging into her legs. "I know it's late, but we need to get rid of some of this food tonight."

"Tonight?" Barry whined. "I just wanna head back to the hotel and get a good night's sleep."

"And leave all these bananas in the car? Remember, we're still in the South. If we don't take them up to our cool rooms tonight, they'll spoil."

"No, they won't!"

Beth pulled a bunch of bananas from the bag she was holding in the front seat and said, "I wouldn't doubt Jenny. Imagine how much spoiled bananas would stink up your car." She replaced the bananas and made an obvious show of looking inside the bag. "The bag boy really didn't do a good job. Did he? We're gonna need to re-bag before carrying everything up to our rooms."

Barry raised his hands in surrender. "All right! I know you ladies are just playing me, but I recognize a no-win situation when I see it. Where to?"

"I'm not sure," Beth said before looking over her shoulder and asking, "Jenny?"

Before Jenny could reach for her phone, she spotted a smartly dressed middle-aged woman pushing a shopping cart toward a blue BMW, which was taking up two spaces, one row beyond the Mustang. "Barry, slide your seat forward and lower your window." As soon as the window stopped, Jenny craned her head out and tried not to smirk when the low-in-the-sky sunlight caught the woman's dangling diamond earrings, making them sparkle like a disco ball. That's when she called out in a snooty voice, "Excuse me! Can you tell me where I can find the homeless people?"

The wealthy woman appeared to be amused rather than offended by Jenny's attempt at humor. She even pulled three twenty-dollar bills out of her purse to contribute to the cause after learning the reason for the request.

More importantly, the woman gave Jenny directions to a place in the woods where numerous homeless people camped. "I haven't been there personally," she said. "But I read in the newspaper that the people who live there can't stay at a shelter because they either have pets or mental issues that make it difficult for them to live close to others."

"Thank you," Jenny said.

"Be careful," said the woman. "It'll be dark soon, and not every homeless person will be gracious." She waved and continued to her car.

Jenny reassessed the space around her and tapped the back of Barry's seat. "Let me out."

"Where are you going?" he asked.

"To put the sixty dollars she gave me to good use. It'll be tight back here, but since we don't have to travel far, I can find enough room to jam in a few small bags of cat and dog food."

Barry reached into the center console and handed Jenny a twenty-dollar bill. Opening his door, he said, "Pick up a flashlight while you're in there."

"And some more cloth grocery bags too," Beth added.

* * *

When the Silver Squad reached the woods, they didn't see any homeless encampments. Only when they spotted the smoke from a campfire were they confident they'd followed the wealthy woman's instructions correctly.

Barry pulled onto the shoulder and turned off the car. When he cracked open his door, Beth flashed him a palm. "Just a moment," she said. "We need to get organized." She transferred items to the sturdy cloth grocery bags before declaring that she and Jenny would each carry a bag containing human food, and Barry would carry a bag containing pet food. He'd also lead with the flashlight, switching it on when the sky grew dark enough for it to be effective.

Once they were ready to go, Barry said, "Remember. We stick together. And if anyone gets aggressive toward us, we simply set the bags on the ground and back off." He scanned the side of the road, located a path leading into the woods, took several steps down it, and paused. "Oh, and if anyone comes across a roll of Tums while handing out food, don't give it away. It's mine!"

Their first stop was a tent, nestled between two white oak trees, not far from the road.

"Hello!" Beth called out as they approached.

"Go away!" a woman's voice shouted from inside.

"Don't worry. We're not cops, and were not from any shelter or government agency."

Silence.

A cat meowed.

Beth reached into her bag. "That's okay. I don't blame you for not trusting us. We're gonna leave some food for you outside your tent. And something for your cat too."

They continued on to the next shelter, where they received a similar response. Perhaps it was because of the darkening sky, or perhaps it was because they were first-time visitors, but the predominant greeting they received was one of frosty distrust.

The warmest response came from a man who was cooking something over the smoky campfire they'd spotted from the road. "Thanks, man," he grunted.

Barry, Beth, and Jenny didn't fret over the cool reception they were given. They hadn't entered the woods to be heroes and only wanted to add a positive moment to the lives of those who could use all the positive moments they could get.

In all, they found three tents, plus three makeshift shelters that the occupants had constructed from scraps of cardboard, plywood, and sheet metal. At least one shelter had multiple people living inside it—perhaps a family. They left SPAM and bananas in front of each tent and shelter, and if they saw or heard a cat or a dog, they left some pet food too.

After emptying their bags, everyone agreed that there was no reason to save anything for anyone they might meet down the road. So when they returned to the Mustang, instead of leaving, they refilled their bags and made a second delivery to each location.

The forest was dark by the time they completed their last drop-off, making everyone appreciate the new flashlight. That the flashlight had also helped Beth find Barry's Tums while they were purging the Mustang added value to the purchase.

The trio was almost back to the car when a deep male voice began singing. At first, they couldn't make out the words. Then another voice, closer to the car, joined in, "SPAM, SPAM, SPAM, SPAM, SPAM, SPAM, SPAM . . ."

Barry and Beth burst into laughter.

Jenny's expression grew confused. "What's so funny?"

"It's Monty Python," Beth said.

"Who is he?" Jenny asked.

Beth forced herself to respond as seriously as she could. "Monty Python isn't a person, dear. They were a British comedy troupe that was popular when Barry and I were much younger."

Barry wiped a giggle-tear from the corner of his eye and said, "Monty Python's SPAM skit and song are classics. Look them up on the internet tonight in your hotel room."

Beth nodded along for a few bars before joining the homeless choir. Barry jumped in shortly thereafter, "SPAM, SPAM, SPAM, SPAM, SPAM, SPAM, SPAM . . ."

Jenny shook her head, as if she were a teenager embarrassed by her parents' behavior, and climbed into the back seat.

Barry and Beth were still singing as the Mustang veered back onto the road and rumbled toward the hotel.

CHAPTER 32

Ambulance Chaser

As the days rolled on, the Silver Squad traveled from town to town, grocery store to grocery store, and homeless encampment to homeless encampment. Deep down, everyone knew that their giveaways were now as much for the three of them as they were for the homeless people. In exchange for each morning they devoted to giving the homeless enough food to make it through the day, Barry, Beth, and Jenny got to delay their Des Moines arrival by a day while simultaneously banking that day as another when they felt good about themselves. Because if things went wrong—or right, depending on how they looked at it—at Jenny's house, times when they felt good about themselves were going to be in short supply.

At the same time, the Silver Squad was back in the news. First, Florida's Governor Ritchie held a press conference to express his outrage over their anti-alligator hunting videos and promised to have his attorney general look into any crimes the trio may have committed. Then, an organization representing alligator hunting outfitters claimed that the kill shots featured in the videos were deep-fakes and that alligators felt no more pain than a fish on a hook did.

Even though Jenny had expected the outfitters to respond, she still rolled her eyes when she learned that the organization representing them had trotted out the old falsity that fish couldn't feel pain. What she hadn't expected were the threats. Most of her social media ads and posts allowed comments, but since those comments were public, the negative ones tended to be nasty rather than violent. That changed when the email address she had set up for advertising and social media account registrations became public. All it took was the mistake of providing the address in the comments when someone asked for it in order to send a donation via PayPal. From that point on, omitting the email address from all her ads and posts no longer mattered, since any internet savvy person could find it with minimal effort.

Threats arriving in the Silver Squad email inbox included the following:

> "Your going to end up like a allygator if u don't deleet that videyo."
>
> "Watch yur back!"
>
> "Antihunting commies like you dezerve 2 die!"
>
> "I no wear you live."
>
> "Greetings Barry, Beth, and Jenny: I must say that your videos have inspired me! I had no idea there were so many ways to kill an alligator. Do you think those same methods would work on humans? I'm pretty sure at least three of them would be effective. I'm such a fan. See you soon!"

At first, Jenny decided not to tell Barry or Beth about the threatening emails. After all, the chances were slim that any of the writers would follow through with their threats. Later, she changed her mind and read to them some of the milder ones. Choosing the middle ground, she reasoned, satisfied her obligation to alert her senior friends to the possibility of danger without unnecessarily worrying them.

On the bright side, the fan who had originally asked for the email address really did use it to send in a donation. And several other fans did the same thing. Knowing there were people out there who supported their cause inspired Jenny to set up a GoFundMe page and add a donation request to all the Silver Squad ads and posts.

So while threats and nasty comments frequented the Silver Squad email account, donation notifications sent to the same account made checking emails a task she looked forward to.

At Jenny's suggestion, most of the money coming in from their campaign against private land alligator hunting went right back into funding more internet ads. And since all the ad accounts were already billing to Beth's credit card, Jenny arranged to have all direct and GoFundMe donations deposited straight into Beth's bank account. She also proposed that Beth keep 15 percent of whatever came in as an administrative fee. Naturally, Beth objected to keeping any of the money. Instead, she agreed to let that 15 percent help cover what she was paying out for SPAM, bananas, pet food, and travel expenses.

Without realizing it, Beth had fallen for Jenny's surreptitious plan to reimburse her for her generosity in supporting the Silver Squad and its causes. Now, at least Beth wouldn't return to Minnesota with an empty bank account.

That wasn't Jenny's only scheme to help fund the founding members of the Silver Squad. Barry was also draining his bank account to keep them on the road. She wasn't sure how to help him until someone set up a website to track their current appearances and predict their next ones. Now, wherever they stopped, their fans would already be waiting for them or show up within minutes of their arrival.

All that attention made everyone feel uneasy. After all, lingering among the fans could be one of the threat-makers, or even Joe. That is, if Joe hadn't already figured out that their path was pointing them toward Des Moines, and all he had to do was stay where he was and wait.

Apprehension aside, Jenny started collecting five-dollar donations from everyone wishing to pose for selfies with the Silver Squad. While some of that money bought food for the homeless, most of it went to cover what Barry had been paying for hotel rooms, gas, and other items.

Jenny also learned that if she called ahead to a supermarket in the next town on their route, not only would that store have SPAM, bananas, and pet food ready for them when they arrived, but sometimes they'd even donate the goods or sell them at a discount.

Now that they had help with their expenses, the Silver Squad stopped more frequently, working their way through small towns in Alabama, Mississippi, and Arkansas. Each stop moved them a little closer to Des Moines, and each time they'd grant at least one interview to a local newspaper, radio, or television reporter. Those interviews would inevitably begin with questions about how they were able to subdue a mass shooter before Barry, Beth, or Jenny deftly pivoted to their causes of feeding the homeless and ending private land alligator hunting in Florida.

With so many interviews, everyone took their turn as the primary spokesperson. While Barry felt uncomfortable with any interview that involved a camera—be it a still camera for a newspaper or a video camera for a television station—he allowed himself to enjoy the radio interviews. Whether they were with a seasoned announcer who had been the voice of the town for decades or some nervous rookie who was just learning the business, Barry felt waves of nostalgia for his own radio career during those interviews.

It was during a radio interview in the parking lot of a Jonesboro, Arkansas, supermarket that Barry collapsed. At first Beth laughed, thinking he was pulling a stunt, like he had done while robbing the church in Minnesota, but when she reached down to feel his forehead, his clammy skin told her his condition was very real.

She grabbed her cell phone and dialed 911.

A woman's voice answered, "Nine-one-one. Fire, police, or ambulance?"

"Ambulance! My companion, he . . . he just collapsed. I think he could be having a heart attack!"

"What's the address, ma'am?"

"I . . . I don't know." She thrust her phone toward the reporter's face. "Tell nine-one-one where we are!"

As the reporter took over the call, Beth kneeled beside Barry and said softly, "Don't you die on me, you cranky son of a bitch. Not now, when for some fucking reason I've fallen for you all over again." She reached deep into his front pants pocket.

"Do you really think that'll wake him up?" asked Jenny, who was kneeling on Barry's opposite side.

"Wake him. . . ? *No!"* She pulled her hand out and jangled his ring of keys. "We're gonna need his car, no matter what happens."

The ambulance arrived moments after the reporter returned the phone to Beth. The two women stepped back and squeezed each other's hand as they watched the EMTs work on Barry. From their point of view, they couldn't see much, though both were relieved that neither of the EMTs charged up the defibrillator paddles and yelled, "Clear!"

Instead, the EMTs placed an oxygen mask over Barry's mouth, lifted him onto a gurney, maneuvered him into the ambulance, and raced out of the parking lot with their siren blaring.

"Let's go!" Beth shouted.

They jumped into the Mustang and chased after the ambulance.

CHAPTER 33

One-Shoed Keisha

Upon their arrival at the hospital, Beth identified herself as Barry's wife and Jenny as his daughter. No one challenged their claims. And when the receptionist asked for Barry's Medicare card, Beth simply said, "It's in his wallet. I'll bring it to you after you let me into his room."

The two women settled into seats in the main waiting room, expecting to be there for a long time. That just over an hour passed before a nurse retrieved them suggested a positive outcome. They followed the nurse down a long hallway to just outside of Barry's room, where he told them to wait.

When a gangly doctor stepped out of the room, Beth wondered how someone who looked so young could possibly be anything beyond a first-year resident.

After introductions, the doctor led the women a short distance down the hallway. She towered over them as she said, "I have good news and bad news. The good news is that Mr. Swanson is going to be fine. He has a few minor health problems that are typical for someone his age, but I didn't find any signs of a heart attack or stroke. I spoke with Mr. Swanson after he woke up, and he filled me in on the ambitious schedule the three of you have been maintaining. I believe exhaustion brought on by that schedule caused him to faint. He also hit the back of his head on the pavement when he fell. Based on the size of the hematoma, I'm a little surprised he doesn't have a concussion. Nevertheless, I'm going to keep him here for a few more hours of observation."

"None of that sounds like bad news to me," Beth said.

"The bad news is that if Mr. Swanson continues with the same schedule, he could end up in the hospital again, with symptoms that are more serious. See that he gets a day of bed rest, and then cut back on his activities."

"Thank you."

Once the doctor walked out of earshot, Jenny turned to Beth and said, "First you headbutt a fire hydrant, then Barry tries to leave an impression of his head in the pavement. You two are the hardest-headed people I've ever met!"

Beth rubbed her mostly healed wound. "I'd worry if I were you. You could be next."

* * *

Beth and Jenny waited in the hospital lobby for nearly four hours, spending much of that time answering emails from the national media and speaking in person with those in the local media who had figured out where to find them. Everyone wanted to know the latest on Barry's condition, and the women gave them all the same answer: "He's going to be fine, and we ask that you please respect our privacy for the remainder of the day."

When Barry finally gained his freedom, he burst through the main doors as if nothing had happened and scanned the parking lot. When he spotted his car, he marched toward it with his hand held out. "Which one of you drove my Mustang here?"

"I did," said Beth. "And now I'm gonna drive it to our next destination. So don't think for even a second that I'm giving you the keys."

Barry managed to expel the first syllable of what he foresaw as becoming a brilliant oration before Beth shot him a fire-breathing glare that stopped the next syllable from completing the word. With age comes experience, and all of Barry's experience was warning him of severe danger ahead if he entered the on-ramp for an argument he couldn't win even if he were half his age.

He adjusted the trajectory of his walk to reach the passenger-side door.

Jenny stepped around him and grabbed the door handle.

"I'm not riding in the back!" he barked.

She pulled the door open and swept an arm toward the front seat. "Your Majesty's chariot awaits!"

"Ha!" he laughed, carefully raising his leg over the bag of groceries on the floor and dropping into the seat. Noticing more groceries in the back, he blurted to Beth when she opened her door, "We didn't make today's delivery! People are depending on us."

Beth waited until Jenny squeezed in behind the driver's seat before following her inside and replying, "Don't worry. Only the media is depending on us. And today those people were actually courteous enough to respect our privacy. As for the people at the homeless camp we're heading to, they can't possibly be depending on us, since they don't even know we're coming."

"So we're doing that now?" Jenny asked. "I thought the doctor ordered us to escort Barry straight to bed."

Barry snorted.

Beth hurled a second fiery glare at Barry before starting the car and saying to Jenny, "That was the plan until it occurred to me that we were being sexist toward ourselves. Why do we need a man to accompany us? We can leave Barry in the car and make this a women's only delivery. It'll be easy. We'll simply carry the bags to a central location, yell out an announcement, and hand out the goods as quickly as possible." She unfolded a piece of paper, entered the address she'd written on it into the GPS, and shifted into drive.

"Where are we going?" Barry asked.

"To an abandoned warehouse Jenny found while we were waiting for your release."

"It's amazing what you can find on the internet when you're bored," Jenny added.

A closed-off street and the lack of available parking spaces forced Beth to park two blocks away from the warehouse. That distance only made Barry protest more vigorously as the women packed up three bags of food and left him sitting in the car. They hurried toward their destination, trying to ignore the long shadows created by the approaching sunset and the obstacle course of sidewalk litter that threatened to conceal a demon, or at least a mouse.

According to Jenny's research, the dilapidated brick warehouse was an eyesore for people with jobs and housing in the area, but a favorite for those who had nothing and preferred to avoid the homeless shelters.

Beth flicked on a flashlight as they entered the cavernous building. Neither she nor Jenny saw anything except discarded cans, bags, newspapers, boxes, and rotting who-knows-what that were collectively threatening to birth the virus of the next pandemic. Inhaling once through the nose was all it took to avoid doing so again.

Staying within a short sprint of the entrance, Beth called out, "Hello! We've brought food for anyone who wants some."

When no one answered, the women waited for a moment before nodding to each other to back out of the building.

"Hey chickie, chickie, chickie," a grating male voice taunted from the floor near the far side wall.

Beth cringed before recomposing herself and saying, "Hi there! It's been a long time since anyone has called out to me like that. I'm afraid I'm too old for you, but I do have some food for you, if you're interested."

"Your friend doesn't look too old," he said. "How 'bout I give her a little thank you for whatever is in her bag?"

Up to that point, no homeless person had behaved aggressively toward anyone in the Silver Squad. But people can become homeless for a variety of reasons—from domestic violence to evictions to medical conditions to mental illness to drug or alcohol addictions to low wages to abrupt firings. And just like some people with good jobs and secure housing can behave deplorably, so can the homeless.

Jenny put her hands on her hips and scolded, "Hey, jerk-face! We're just here to help. If you don't want that, we'll move on."

The man stood and kicked a small whiskey bottle out of his path, startling a skinny dog that had been sleeping on some cardboard a few feet away. "I don't need no help from any goody-two-shoes bitches."

"Leave her alone, Jason!" a hoarse male voice called out from a dark corner.

Jason emerged from the shadows with the dog by his side. His black hair was long and matted, a fresh gash marked his right cheek, and he wore a baggy gray sweatshirt and Army surplus fatigue pants. He made eye contact with Jenny and said, "Come on, baby. I may not look like much, but I know how to please the ladies."

"It's not gonna happen," she replied.

Jason stepped close enough that Jenny could smell his rancid breath. When she sidestepped, he mirrored her move.

Beth pointed. "Is that your dog?"

"Yeah."

"What's your dog's name?"

"Buddy."

Beth pulled a small package of dog food out of her bag. "Jason, do you think Buddy would like something to eat?"

He retreated a few steps, and his face softened. "You brought something for Buddy? No one's ever done that before."

"Of course. Dogs can be homeless too." She handed the package to Jason. "Would you also like a can of SPAM?"

"For me or for my dog?"

"It's probably best that you eat it."

"Sure." He took the items, uttered "Thanks," and lumbered back to his space, where he called out in a gentle voice, "Here, Buddy. I have something special for you."

Beth scanned the warehouse floor with her flashlight. Though she didn't see anyone, she knew all the dark corners, half walls, and scattered junk could be hiding more than just Jason and the man who had scolded him. She raised her voice as she announced, "If anyone else has a dog, we have one more package of food."

"We also have bananas, oranges, SPAM, and three cans of cat food," Jenny added.

When no one responded, Beth considered leaving everything on the floor of the warehouse. She changed her mind when it occurred to her that she could be encouraging a fight over the food once they left. "Last chance," she shouted. "We're leaving in thirty seconds and taking everything with us."

"I'll take the cat food," a woman's voice called out.

When a bony woman in her late teens limped into view, carrying a scruffy black cat, Beth noticed that her face was bruised, and she was only wearing one shoe. "What's your name, dear?" she asked.

"Keisha."

"Why do you only have one shoe, Keisha?"

She looked at the floor for a moment before answering, "Had to throw the other one at somebody."

Beth felt the back of her throat burn. She slipped off her shoes and used her toes to push them forward. "I think we're close to the same size."

Keisha stepped into the shoes and smiled. "Thank you."

When Beth looked up, a man and a woman who appeared to

be in their seventies shuffled into view. Even though Beth was used to helping homeless people of all ages, it was always unsettling for her to encounter individuals who were her age or older. "I'll be right with you," she said to the two before making eye contact with Keisha. "I'm gonna put together a special bag, just for you."

Beth and Jenny took a few steps back and whispered to each other as they sorted through the bags they were carrying. Once they felt satisfied with the proportions, Beth handed the heaviest bag to Keisha and said, "The cat food is in here, plus some fruit and SPAM." She returned to a whisper. "We've also included the last package of dog food. If your cat doesn't like it, you can trade it with someone, or give it to Jason if you need to get on his good side."

As Keisha walked away, Jenny handed the two lighter bags to the old man and woman.

With everything distributed and no reason to stick around, Jenny looked at Beth in her stocking feet and leaned over. "Hop onto my back. I'll carry you out of here."

"Don't be ridiculous. Lead the way and try to avoid the broken glass."

Beth followed Jenny outside and walked with her until they reached the spot where the street opened up. There she stopped and handed Jenny the car keys. "I'll wait for you here while you fetch the Mustang. Just be careful not to startle Barry. He's probably sleeping."

* * *

The Silver Squad hung around Jonesboro for two more days to make sure that Barry was back to his old self and ready to resume their journey toward Des Moines. During that time, Beth and Jenny returned to the abandoned warehouse twice. The first time was to bring more food for the people and their pets, and the second time was to bring Keisha a care package that included clothing, a blanket, women's products, a small amount of cash, and a canister of pepper spray.

Des Moines lay five hundred fifty miles to the north—a distance drivable in a single day if they desired. They left early the following morning, wondering if this would be their last day of travels together.

CHAPTER 34

Des Moines

Despite Barry's declaration that he was feeling perfectly fine, Beth and Jenny ganged up and relegated both him and Gertrude to the front passenger seat. For the remainder of their journey, the women planned to take turns driving, switching between the front and back seats after each stop.

Shortly after crossing into Missouri, Beth reached from the back seat to put a hand on Barry's shoulder. "Do you think we should find a town somewhere between here and the Iowa border to spend one more night and make one more delivery?"

He thought for a moment and said, "As good as it feels to help others, I think we need to think of ourselves this time. Right now, as far as we know, the media isn't following us. But if we stop, especially in the state where we became famous, the media could be all over us again. Why risk anything that could alert Joe that we're on our way?"

Jenny flicked on the blinker to pass a car and said, "I agree with Barry. Although I wouldn't count on Joe being oblivious to our approach, no matter how careful we are. He has access to numerous police resources and most likely has been monitoring the website that tracks us and predicts our next destination."

* * *

The trio reached Des Moines late that evening and checked into a hotel a few miles from Jenny and Joe's house. Rather than confront Joe immediately, they planned to spend a few days staking out the house and formulating a strategy.

Before going to bed, Beth invited Jenny to step into hers and Barry's room for a glass of wine. After pouring for everyone, she sat in the desk chair and swiveled to face Barry. "How are we gonna stake out a house in a black Mustang? This entire road trip would've been so much easier and so much more comfortable if you'd only had the sense to buy a no-nonsense, tan, four-door sedan."

Barry sipped his wine, the brittle plastic hotel glass crinkling beneath his fingers, and said, "If you remember, my job was to buy a getaway car. And for that task, the Mustang has served us quite well. You never said to be practical, in case we pick up a stranger on the run from her husband and the three of us become famous for stopping a mass shooter at a country music nightclub."

Jenny held her glass in front of her as she leaned against the open doorframe between their two rooms. "Forget the surveillance! Forget the Mustang too. During our drive today, I did a lot of thinking and have reconsidered allowing either of you to help me with this. It's too dangerous. So tomorrow, after Joe goes to work, I'd like you to drop me off in the alley behind my house and get out of Iowa as fast as you can."

"No!" Barry and Beth shouted in unison.

"Yes!" Jenny shouted back. "If anything happened to either of you, I'd never forgive myself. Confronting Joe is something I need to do alone."

"And what are we to do?" Barry asked. "Go back to the Blue Loon Village and sit in front of the TV, bored to tears, until death puts us out of our misery? Beth and I embarked on this adventure to feel useful—perhaps for the last time."

"Don't take this away from us," Beth added. "I watched my parents and grandparents grow old without a fight. And I suppose, subconsciously, when I moved into the Blue Loon Village, I was ready to do the same thing. I needed this age-defying adventure with the three of us more than I thought I did. You worry about not forgiving yourself if we accompany you when you confront Joe, and something happens to us. The same goes doubly for Barry and me if we *don't* accompany you, and something happens to you. All the good feelings about what we've accomplished together will disappear in an instant."

When Jenny's face softened and she offered a slight nod of agreement, Barry pointed to Gertrude, who was asleep in the clear plastic container on the dresser. "You can totally forgive yourself if something happens to either Beth or me. We're in this willingly and accept the consequences if things go bad. Gertrude, on the other hand, is innocent. If something happens to make her an orphan, all I ask is that you make sure someone takes care of her. A list of all her needs, along with some cash to cover her expenses, is taped to her terrarium in my apartment."

"You have my word that Gertrude will not be abandoned," Jenny said.

"Alright then," said Beth. "Now that we have an understanding, first thing in the morning, let's get to work on giving Joe the level of vigilantism he deserves." She finished her wine, held the bottle to the light, shrugged, and poured the remaining liquid into her glass. It was gone in a single gulp.

* * *

To eliminate the problem of attempting a stakeout with a black Mustang, the Silver Squad began their morning by visiting rental car lots to find an ordinary-looking four-door sedan with tinted windows. Such a car would allow them to sit across the street to observe Jenny and Joe's house if they wanted to. Finding the ideal vehicle took some time, however, because Barry insisted that they rent a vehicle with the darkest window tinting allowed by law. The two women were almost out of patience when Barry found a blue Chevrolet Impala at a lot that specialized in renting used cars.

The rental car, along with using their cell phones to stay in constant contact, would give them some security. Even so, they would attempt to examine each move from the point of view of both a cop and a criminal before going forward.

The trio began their stakeout by working in two-hour shifts, with each person walking from the nearby but out-of-sight Mustang to relieve whoever was in the Impala. After Barry fell asleep on his first shift, the women shortened his future shifts to one hour. And if that failed, they promised to wake him abruptly with a shot of ice water to the crotch.

Jenny remembered Joe's work schedule, so mostly she wanted to make sure nothing had changed and that there were no new complications.

"Oh, that little bitch!" Jenny hissed into her phone when the first new complication showed up shortly after six.

"What are you talking about?" Beth asked from the Mustang.

"I was bracing myself to see Joe at any minute, but Tiffany, one of the dispatchers at the police station, beat him to the house. She had a key and let herself in the front door, confirming my suspicion that Joe is having an affair with her!"

"Did you really expect him to be faithful to you after all that has happened?"

"No. But this goes way back to my final, naïve attempt to salvage our marriage. When I confronted Joe about Tiffany, he assured me that flings with other women were in the past and that lanky, doe-eyed redheads like Tiffany weren't even his type. The second he shows up, I'm gonna hit the gas and run him over!"

"No, you're not! Your shift is done. Barry is walking toward you now. If we're gonna have any chance of succeeding, we have to stick to our plan."

Jenny pounded on the steering wheel and spat, "Fucking, fuckety, fuck!"

As soon as Barry appeared in the rearview mirror, Jenny scanned up and down the street to make sure Joe wasn't approaching too, stepped out of the car, and stormed the opposite way around the block.

* * *

The Silver Squad discontinued their surveillance after two and a half days. When Joe didn't leave for work on Saturday morning, Jenny knew his shift rotation called for two days off, which this time happened on the weekend. Since she needed to get inside the house without Joe around, they could use Saturday and Sunday to refine their plan before implementing it on Monday.

The addition of Tiffany meant their plan now had to accommodate for her showing up at the worst possible moment, and despite Jenny declaring her a little bitch, she didn't deserve the same thing Joe had coming to him. Even Jenny admitted that. Besides, Joe certainly told Tiffany lies about Jenny, and she might already be a victim of his violent temper.

Now Jenny was glad to have Barry and Beth's help. When the time came for her to deal with Joe, one of them could serve as a lookout while the other waylaid Tiffany if necessary.

Even so, as Saturday progressed, self-doubt dominated Jenny's thoughts. As she knew from the times Joe hit her, he was much stronger than she was, and since he was a cop, he also had more experience with weapons and fighting than she did. Her only advantage would be the element of surprise.

And what was she going to do with Joe if she cornered or

captured him? Kill him? No, she wasn't a murderer. Shoot him in the balls or tie him up and shove SPAM up his ass until he begs for mercy? While both ideas appealed to her hunger for revenge, she knew they were unrealistic.

What had seemed so simple and rational, when she was a thousand miles away, now seemed complicated and irrational.

That evening, Jenny propped up the pillows on her bed, leaned back, and closed her eyes to concentrate on her predicament. Could she really use the element of surprise to subdue her husband? And if so, what *was* the realistic and appropriate punishment for a man who hid behind a public persona of an upstanding police officer while unleashing anger and cruelty on his wife and others?

"I've got it," she whispered to herself before falling asleep.

CHAPTER 35

The Gun Safe

Since Joe had parked his car in the driveway behind the house over the weekend, on Monday morning Barry positioned the Impala on the street so he could look down the gap between the houses and see when Joe entered the alley to leave for work. The moment he spotted him, he called Beth, who was sitting with Jenny in the Mustang a few blocks away. "Gray Lady. It's Gecko Man. Tell Blondie that Asshole Man has flown the coop. I repeat. Asshole Man has flown the coop."

Beth facepalmed. "We're using cell phones, not CB radios. No one but me is listening. A simple 'Joe has left for work' would've sufficed."

"I'm just trying to add a little levity to the situation."

"I'll drop Jenny off in the alley in two minutes."

Barry set down his phone and contemplated the coffee in the cup holder. He felt like he should drink some to make sure he stayed awake. On the other hand, drinking any of it was bound to make his bladder strain before he could leave the car. He took a tiny sip and licked his lips. The coffee from the hotel lobby was especially tasty today. He took another sip.

Jenny crossed the backyard to the old, beige, stucco-sided, two-story house she and Joe bought when they moved to Des Moines.

She climbed the back steps, reached into her pocket, and pulled out the house key she'd been carrying since the day she ran. She didn't expect it to work anymore, but decided to try it before attempting to break in through a basement window. The key turned the deadbolt, just as it always had. The alarm system was next. She opened the app she'd downloaded to her smartphone and tapped in her code. That hadn't changed either. "Typical Joe," she muttered to herself as she stepped into the mudroom and verified on the control panel that her code had worked. "Still too lazy to do anything around the house."

She sent a text to Barry and Beth: *I'm inside. Going silent.*

Dropping the phone into her back pocket, she walked from room to room, being careful not to move anything. Had the house belonged to someone else, not moving anything wouldn't have required as much concentration. Here she was in a house that was still half hers. More than once she had to stop herself from instinctively picking up after Joe, whether it was a piece of clothing he'd tossed on the floor or a dirty plate he'd left on a side table.

She worked her way upstairs to the walk-in closet in the master bedroom, where Joe's gun safe was located. When they lived together, she often scolded him for spending so much money on a fancy gun safe and then leaving it open all the time. This time, however, it was locked.

"Damn," she whispered to herself. Her plan for the morning was to make sure she could still get into the house and to grab one of Joe's powerful handguns while she was there. If she couldn't get into the safe, she'd have to get by with the tiny pistol Beth had offered her when she returned to finish the job.

That's when she remembered that Joe kept a handgun in the drawer of the bedside table. She reversed course and opened the drawer. The gun was gone, replaced by a box of condoms and some men's magazines. She returned to the safe and stared at the keypad. She had opened the safe once, many years ago, but couldn't remember the combination. She tried the combination for their alarm system as well as Joe's birthday and the date of their anniversary.

No luck.

She pulled out her smartphone, searched for the website of the store where Joe bought most of his gear, found the make and model of the safe, and clicked over to the manufacturer's website to download the owner's manual. When she opened the PDF, she learned that the safe required a six-digit combination. She began trying six-digit numbers that would be significant to Joe. After the first few failed, she recalled that it had something to do with a cop show that was in reruns.

She went back to her smartphone, entered a search for "cop shows with numbers in the title," and scanned the list: *21 Jump Street, 24, Adam-12, Car 54, Where Are You? Hawaii Five-0, Reno 911!*

None of them were six digits.

She closed her eyes to concentrate. She could see the face of the lead actor in Joe's favorite show, but couldn't remember his name. *Keifer . . . something.* She slapped a palm to her forehead and said to herself, "How did I forget that?" She slid her smartphone into her back pocket and punched in 2-4-2-4-2-4.

The safe unlocked.

When she pulled open the door, her jaw dropped. There was nothing inside, except a note taped at eye-level:

Welcome home, Jenny!

Don't move! There's a gun pointed at you. An unsavory friend owed me a favor and rigged it up to a motion-sensing camera. When you opened the safe, you activated that camera. See you soon!

XXXOOO

Joe

"Fucking, fuckety, fuck, fuck," Jenny whispered to herself.

Did she dare to reach for her cell phone or even turn her head? She had no way of knowing how sensitive the motion-sensing camera was, how precisely it was aimed, or how quickly it would trigger the gun.

Her eyes darted in all directions. She couldn't see any equipment above or to the sides and considered that the note could be a bluff to make sure she didn't leave. Then she noticed the faint reflection of a red light on the inside of the gun safe's black metal door. Whatever was creating the light had to be to her left, since the safe door opened to her right.

She strained her eyes to look as far left as possible. When she spotted the narrow red light, surrounded by blackness, she reasoned it must be coming from either the camera or the device that detected when she opened the safe door. Deciding it was prudent to assume that both pieces of equipment would be next to each other, she contemplated the more crucial issue of gunshot avoidance. If the gun was to either side of her, she might be able to jump back fast enough to make it miss. But if it was hidden behind her, jumping back would just move her closer to the shot.

As she stood frozen, afraid to move, her mind raced onto other thoughts: *How long can I hold this pose until I trip the camera? Did opening the safe notify Joe that I'm here? What if he doesn't find me until he comes home from work? If I survive that long, will he do something to me that's even worse than death? Oh fuck, does he know about the Chevy Impala, or did he spot the Mustang? If so, Barry and Beth's lives are in danger!*

A bead of sweat dripped into Jenny's eye.

When her smartphone chimed to announce the arrival of a text, she had no choice but to ignore it, and when it rang, she prayed that telemarketers had discovered her new number. Realistically, she knew that either Barry or Beth was trying to contact her, and the chances were good that whichever one it was would come looking for her.

Her phone rang again.

"Shit!" she whispered. Now she was certain one or both of her friends would soon enter the house. More thoughts raced through her brain: *Can I yell without tripping the motion sensor? What if they tiptoe up the stairs and I can't hear them? I might not know they're here until it's too late!*

Even if it killed her, she had to make a move—and do it soon.

Jenny envisioned the layout of the bedroom. Had Joe moved anything since she'd lived here? She didn't think so. Certainly, the safe and the bedside table were in the same place, but until she read Joe's note, she'd been concentrating on finding a gun, not the positioning of the furniture. She was confident a dresser was directly behind her. A handgun or short-barreled rifle could be rigged up in one of the drawers, pointed at her back. That was the most logical location.

Assuming the gun was in the dresser, would dropping to the floor be her best option? She attempted to think like her husband: *If he really wants to kill me, he'll aim the gun low, anticipating that I'll most likely drop.*

A stair creaked.

"Barry? Beth?" she called out. "Don't come in here! There's a gun aimed at me."

A second stair creaked.

"Don't come in here!" she repeated louder, tensing in anticipation of a gunshot.

Another thought: *If the motion-sensing camera is to my left, my body is blocking it from seeing my right hand.*

She inched her hand over, just enough to grab the edge of the safe's door.

A floorboard on the landing creaked.

With her brain screaming, *Fuuuck!* Jenny moved faster than she'd ever moved before, ducking into the safe; yanking the door shut as the room exploded with a thunderous boom!

She felt a moment of ecstasy before panic hammered it to pieces. Had she just locked herself inside?

Her cramped position made getting any leverage difficult. If she could just turn her shoulder, she could . . . The door popped open!

She goggled at the sight before her. It was Barry—covered in confetti!

CHAPTER 36

Cleanup

Jenny collapsed.

Barry dropped beside her. "Are you okay?"

From the hardwood floor, she looked up at Barry's too-close face and blew some confetti off his cheek. "Hmm. . . . Physically, I'm fine. But I'm gonna kill that motherfucker!"

Beth rushed into the room. "Oh, my God! What happened? I was at the bottom of the stairs when I heard what sounded like a cannon blast."

Jenny sat up. "Joe didn't think it was satisfying enough to kill me. He wanted me to suffer."

"I don't understand," Beth said.

Jenny held up a finger. "Give me a second to clear my head." She blinked several times before standing, walking over to the bed, and plopping down on the mattress. "Okay, long story short. When I opened the gun safe, there was nothing inside except a note from Joe, warning that I had activated a motion-sensing camera rigged to trigger a gun he had aimed at me. I stood frozen for a long time, afraid to move. When I heard the floorboard at the top of the stairs creak, I couldn't risk either of you entering the room and tripping the camera. So I tripped it myself by jumping into the safe."

"Why didn't you just yell to us?" Barry asked as he stood. "We might have been able to disarm the gun, or at least stay in the hallway."

"I raised my voice as much as I dared, but it's difficult to yell without moving. And since I was facing into the safe, you couldn't hear me."

Beth brushed off Barry's back. "So the bullet was loaded with confetti, not lead?"

"There's way too much confetti for that. We'll have to look around. My guess is that it was a confetti bomb, and no gun was involved. Joe was probably hoping to come home and find me sweating up a storm, struggling to stay still. Then he'd mock me for a while before throwing something that would force me to move and give him the pleasure of yukking it up when the explosion covered me with confetti."

"Well, you have to admit he was creative," Barry said.

"Oh, his creativity would've only been getting started. I can't stress enough that Joe gets off on the power he feels when he makes people suffer."

"So what do we do now?" Beth asked.

Jenny looked from one side of the room to the other before straightening her shoulders. "There's a change of plans. Since Joe hasn't shown up already, I don't think his motion-sensing system was sophisticated enough to notify him that I'd opened the safe. That means he'll likely keep to his regular schedule. We need to work fast to clean up the room and re-create the scene. I want Joe to believe he won."

* * *

While Barry returned to the Impala to resume his lookout duties, Jenny found the remains of the confetti bomb nestled between the dresser and the bed. There was no way to rearm it, but that was okay. As long as Joe didn't see any confetti when he entered the bedroom, he'd assume the bomb was still armed.

"How can I help?" Beth asked.

"The vacuum cleaner is in the closet, down the hall. If you can vacuum up all the confetti, that'll give me time to search the house for guns."

"I'm on it."

Jenny found most of the guns under a pile of blankets in the spare bedroom closet. She also found two rifles hidden in the basement. She considered removing them all, but Joe would be coming home armed anyway, and she didn't want to risk tipping him off that he was being played. It was better just to know where the guns were in case she had to grab one on the run. The only gun she took was Joe's old Glock 19, which was with the other guns in the spare bedroom closet. Before their marriage went bad, Joe had insisted she learn how to shoot, and that was the handgun she used at the shooting range.

The two women had everything in place an hour and a half before Joe's probable arrival. Now they had to wait.

While Jenny rechecked everything—including making sure her gun was properly loaded and her smartphone was fully charged—Beth relieved Barry in the Impala. He toddled into the house and yelled up the stairs, "It's Barry. I'm gonna use your bathroom and then head over to the Mustang."

"Okay," Jenny yelled back. "Be careful!"

Time passed slowly. Jenny attempted to speed up the wait by mentally rehearsing her plan, but all that did was make her sweat more, sending her into the upstairs bathroom to towel off her hands and face.

Finally, at ten past six, her smartphone rang. "Blondie. It's Gecko Man. Asshole Man is in the alley. I repeat. Asshole Man is in the alley."

She tapped the screen, slipped her smartphone into her back pocket, inserted the Glock under the front waistband of her jeans, wiped off her hands one more time, and assumed the position.

CHAPTER 37

Scene One, Take Two

Since Joe typically entered the house through the rear, Jenny had left the back door unlocked and a light on in the mudroom. She wanted him to know she was inside and hoped to route him directly to the bedroom. She listened intently as he stepped through the mudroom and walked from room to room on the main floor. She expected him to climb the stairs next, but instead she heard the unmistakable sound of his boots clomping down the wooden basement steps.

She heard nothing for a few minutes. Then the clomping returned to the main floor.

Finally, he called out in a sarcastic voice, "Honey, I'm home!" and started up the stairs to the second floor.

Jenny took a deep breath and made a slight adjustment to her position in front of the open gun safe.

Joe whistled as he entered the room. He leaned back against the near bedroom wall and shimmied halfway to Jenny. "Look at that ass! I used to love that ass. Hmm. . . . It looks like it's gained some weight. I'd come closer to give it a squeeze test, but you've always complained I never spend enough time on foreplay. We'll hold off on giving you the big bang for a while."

"You haven't given me a big bang since the night before our wedding night," Jenny replied, her voice echoing ever so slightly.

"I knew you couldn't resist coming home, but I wasn't sure if you'd remember the combination to the safe. I'm glad you did. If I had to resort to Plan B, it wouldn't have been nearly as much fun." He shimmied back to the door. "I'm gonna pour myself a drink and have a smoke. Keep holding that ass up, nice and tight. I won't be long."

Jenny maintained her position while allowing her limbs to relax a little. Facing into the safe had made it impossible for her to see if Joe had his gun holstered or pointed at her back the entire time. Despite the risk, she had been tempted to turn and fire a bullet at Joe's forehead. Now she was glad she'd had the willpower to stay put, because once Joe satisfied his addictions, the chances would increase that he'd drop his guard and make a mistake.

She glanced over her shoulder and debated whether to cut the game short and shoot Joe the moment he reappeared in the doorway. That seemed like a solid plan—unless he walked in with his gun ready. She was a good shot, but had no doubt he was faster and more competent with a gun than she was. When the floorboard outside the bedroom creaked, she faced back into the safe and stiffened her limbs.

"Getting tired yet?" Joe asked as he shimmied along the wall.

"What do *you* think?" she spat.

"How long have you been standing there?"

"Maybe three hours. I don't know. I haven't been able to look at a clock."

"Impressive. Where are your friends?"

"If you ever used even a fraction of that tiny brain of yours, you'd know exactly where they are!"

"I asked you a question!" he bellowed.

She expelled a drawn-out hiss. "Fine. . . . They dropped me off this morning and continued north."

"You better not be lying." He slid something metallic across the floor. It clinked against the inside of her foot and stopped between her shoes. "Put those on."

"If I move, the gun will go off."

"Do ya trust me?"

"Hell no!"

"Well, you're gonna have to trust me now. The motion sensor is aimed directly at that beautiful, albeit fatter, ass of yours. As long as you keep it still, you can pick up the present at your feet."

She looked down at the handcuffs. "I can't bend like that!"

"Oh, I think you can."

"Are you crazy? I haven't been that limber since high school."

"If you can't do it, I'll throw something at you that'll make your entire body move."

Jenny put on a show of struggling to pick up the handcuffs. Once she had them, she knew what Joe's next command would be.

"Put them on. Nice . . . and . . . tight."

She clicked the handcuffs.

"Now. Turn around. We're gonna have a party!"

"No! The gun will go off."

"Turn around!" he demanded.

"No!" she shouted.

"You fucking bitch!" He pounced, and in one violent move, grabbed Jenny by the neck and slammed the muzzle of his handgun against her temple. He looked up. "Hey! Where's the confet—"

"Surprise!" She pulled the gun from the front of her jeans and shot him in the thigh!

Joe fell to the floor, dropping his gun as he screamed, "Fuuuck!"

Jenny kicked his gun under the bed and stood over him with her Glock pointed at his forehead. "Oh, don't be such a baby! If I really wanted to hurt you, I would've aimed a few inches higher." She waited until he stopped screaming before dropping the handcuffs on his uninjured leg. "Put these on. We're *still* gonna have a party."

"I'm . . . gonna bleed to death," he whined.

"No, you're not. If I'd hit your femoral artery, there'd be a lot more blood. Put on the handcuffs and apologize for insulting my *perfect* ass. Once you do that, I'll get something to stop the bleeding."

He put on the handcuffs.

She glared at him.

He squeezed them, nice and tight. "Now, will you please get something to stop the bleeding?"

"I didn't hear an apology."

He cringed. "I'm sorry about insulting your ass."

"My *what* ass?"

"Your *perfect* ass."

"That's better." She pulled the phone out of her back pocket, tapped the screen until Barry's name appeared, then tapped one more time. When he picked up, she said, "Gecko Man. It's Perfect Ass Girl. Asshole Man has been neutralized. I repeat. Asshole Man has been neutralized."

"You killed him?"

"No! He's in handcuffs and bleeding all over the place."

Barry's phone beeped. "Hold on. It's Beth."

Jenny kept her ear to the phone as she retreated to the doorway, contemplating the proper first aid for Joe's leg.

Barry clicked back in. "I told Beth what happened, but we have a problem."

"Oh?"

"She says a tall redheaded woman is crossing the lawn to your front door right now."

"Shit! . . . Okay. We can't let Tiffany get away. After she enters the house, you and Beth follow. If she doesn't come to the bedroom on her own, escort her up here." She dropped the phone back into her pocket and said to Joe, "Well, well. It looks like we're gonna have a bigger party than I thought."

CHAPTER 38

Tiffany Attempts a Field Goal

While still holding her gun on Joe, Jenny sidestepped to the bedside table and took the receiver off the landline phone. She stood there for a moment, with her free hand massaging the back of her exhausted legs, before plopping onto the bed to wait for the rest of the party to arrive.

Soon Tiffany called from the bottom of the stairs, "Joe, are you up there?"

Jenny stiffened her aim on Joe and nodded.

"I'm in the bedroom!" he shouted.

Tiffany ascended the stairs and, upon stepping into the bedroom, her face twisted in confusion as her eyes grappled with the sight before her. "What the hell's going on in here?"

Jenny stood with her gun pointed at the floor and her empty hand held out. "You'll find out soon enough. Your cell phone, please."

After Jenny set Tiffany's phone on the bedside table, she swung her gun back to Joe. "Where's your cell?"

"On the kitchen counter. Dial it if you want. You'll hear it ring."

Jenny retrieved her smartphone from her back pocket and

made a test call. She disconnected after the first ring and waved her phone at Tiffany. "Move over next to my husband."

Tiffany tilted her head and said slowly, "Don't you mean *ex*-husband?"

Jenny snorted. "Nope. I purposely called him that to observe your reaction. I've stuck with Joe for almost thirteen years of wedded misery, going through all the self-blaming and rationalization bullshit. But don't worry, that's all about to end."

"He told me your divorce was finalized!"

"Yeah, he's not exactly the poster boy for an honest cop."

Tiffany positioned herself beside Joe, scorching him with her gaze the entire way.

The floorboard on the landing creaked twice, announcing Barry and Beth's arrival.

"Oh, my!" Beth said. "That's a lot of blood. What can we do to help?"

"There should be a first aid kit in the closet, where the vacuum cleaner lives. Look on the second shelf. You'll find some towels there too."

Jenny leaned sideways to pick up Tiffany's phone and held it out to Barry. "You're in charge of cell phones. This one's Tiffany's, and Joe's is downstairs on the kitchen counter. Turn both of them off and hide them somewhere in the house."

Beth returned and said to Jenny, "I found everything you asked for. Is there anything I should know before bandaging him up?"

"Taking care of Joe is Tiffany's job. I'm pretty sure she had to complete an advanced first aid class before becoming a police dispatcher."

Tiffany nodded and muttered, "I did," as she took the supplies.

Beth held out her empty hands to Jenny. "How else can I help?"

"Did you bring your gun?"

She leaned over and pulled the pistol out of her sock. "It's right here."

"Good." Jenny reached behind herself to wedge her Glock under the waistband of her jeans. "This is a time when two guns are better than one. Wherever I move, stay on the opposite side of the room from me."

Barry returned and announced, "I'm done!"

Jenny pointed to the bed. "Take a seat for now. We'll get started after Tiffany gets Joe all patched up."

Barry did as she said, and when Jenny sat next to him, Beth adjusted her position to lean against the safe.

As Jenny watched Tiffany clean Joe's wound, she noticed a lack of tenderness. At first, she assumed Tiffany was just upset that Joe wasn't actually divorced. Her assumption changed when Tiffany switched positions to wrap his leg, and the back of her shirt pulled up when she leaned over.

"How many of those do you have?" Jenny asked.

Tiffany looked over her shoulder. "How many what?"

"Cigarette burns."

"I don't know what you're talking about."

"On your lower back."

"Oh, that?" She scoffed. "It's just a birthmark."

Jenny pulled up the front of her shirt. "Isn't that amazing! I have a complete set—front and back—that looks just like yours. Mine are from Joe's cigarettes. And this . . ." she pointed to a narrow scar on her side, "I got when Joe's knife *slipped* while he was reminding me that he was the head of our household, and I was to obey. But he was *so, so sorry* afterwards! Do you wanna hear about the time he dislocated my shoulder?"

Tiffany didn't answer. Instead, she told Jenny all she needed to know when she yanked the wrap around Joe's leg so tight he screamed.

Jenny continued. "Assuming Joe survives the night, you can

have him for all I care. Just know that you can't fix him. Oh, he may treat you like a queen for a few weeks—even months—but his addiction to cruelty always returns. It's who he is."

"Joe Asshole," Barry added.

"If only he was just an asshole," Jenny replied.

"Can I say something?" Joe asked from the floor.

"No!" Jenny and Tiffany shouted in unison.

He continued anyway. "Then you better pray you kill me tonight. Because if you don't I will—"

"Shut the fuck up!" Tiffany shouted, giving his leg-wrap one last yank.

Jenny bounced off the bed and towered over her husband. "You may talk tough, but I know you better than anyone else. Unless you're in charge, you're a coward. Hmm. . . . I wonder if we can find any of the men you beat to the ground and arrested for the crime of being black. We could invite them over for a real honest to goodness intervention!"

Tiffany stood. "I know of someone who recently got out of prison on appeal."

Jenny looked Tiffany in the eyes and smiled wryly. "My, you sure switched sides easily."

"You wouldn't believe how often I have to dispatch officers on domestic violence calls. Joe's only hurt me once. But seeing what he did to you . . . well, I know you're right. If I stuck with him, sooner or later one of my coworkers would be dispatching an officer to help me."

"Welcome to the club. Though forgive me if I don't totally trust you."

Tiffany brushed a red lock out of her eye. "I don't blame you. Battered women frequently defend their tormentors. I could be pretending to switch sides, only to help Joe escape when you let your guard down."

Jenny grinned. "Well, a swift kick to his balls would help to prove your loyalty."

Tiffany craned back her neck, unsure if Jenny was serious. "Sure. . . . I guess. . . . If it would really help you to trust me."

"It would." Jenny reached behind and pulled the Glock from her waistband. She pointed it at Joe and nodded.

Tiffany nervously circled around a pool of half-dried blood and positioned herself at Joe's feet. She gave one of his feet a little kick to open some room between his legs. Then she backed up, gathered her courage, and sprang forward with her leg cocked!

"Stop!" Jenny shouted. She thrust out an arm to catch her, but it was too late. Tiffany's forward motion carried them both, and when Jenny's foot slipped on the bloody wood floor, they tumbled awkwardly onto Joe's chest.

The tangle of women gave Joe the opening he was waiting for. He twisted his body sideways, liberating his bound wrists from under the women, and clasped his hands together, transforming his arms into a makeshift nightstick. His first blow struck Tiffany on the shoulder. When Jenny jerked back to avoid his second blow, he seized the opening created by her evasive maneuver and lunged for her gun.

Bang!

Plaster dust rained down from the ceiling above Beth's little pistol.

Jenny and Tiffany scrambled to their feet.

After waiting a moment for the air to clear, Jenny looked up at the hole and smirked. "Joe, I have a chore for you once we're done here." Her expression turned serious as she glared down at her husband and pointed her gun at his chest. "You're not in charge anymore, and it's going to remain that way."

Tiffany rubbed her shoulder before gently grasping Jenny's arm and pulling her off to the side. "I don't understand."

"I just wanted to see the look on Joe's face when he realized you were really going to kick him. I missed it when I had to grab you, but I'm pretty sure it was priceless. That's okay. You now have my trust. Besides, a swift kick to his balls would only lower us to his level." She looked at Joe with a slight tilt of her head. "And he deserves *so* much more than that!"

CHAPTER 39

Revenge of the Wife

Later that evening, the bedroom is ready. All the blood has been cleaned up, and lamps brought in from other rooms illuminate the shadows. Joe is sitting six feet in front of the safe, secured to a chair, with duct tape over his mouth. Barry stands partway across the room, holding Jenny's smartphone [Its camera takes in a wide view of the scene]. When Jenny signals from her position to the left of Joe, Barry presses the record icon.

"Hello world. I'm Jenny Callahan. Many of you have been following the travels and adventures of the Silver Squad. While I'm not old enough to have silver hair, my new friends Barry and Beth [The camera switches to selfie mode to show Barry and Beth standing together] took me in as an honorary member and virtual daughter after my husband, Joe Callahan, [The camera returns to the main lens and focuses on Joe] hurt me more times than I could endure."

Joe grunts and struggles against his restraints.

[The camera view widens to include Jenny]

"When I first met Barry and Beth, I had nothing other than what I was wearing. They gave me food, clothing, shelter, and one hell of a ride. And they did it all while expecting nothing in return.

Our adventures included two high-speed escapes from my husband, subduing a mass-shooter in Kansas City, rescuing dumped kittens in Missouri, saving alligators from cruelty in Florida, and helping homeless people in towns across America."

Jenny strolls over to stand behind Joe.

[The camera view tightens slightly]

"Today might be my last day as an honorary Silver Squad member. My goal is simple: to tell the world about my husband, and, hopefully, make sure he never hurts anyone again."

Joe continues to struggle.

Jenny puts her hands on his shoulders. "I'm sure Joe would love to personally confess to you how he used his power as a man and a police officer to abuse me, other women, and people he's arrested under false pretenses. I'll give him that opportunity now."

She rips the tape off his mouth.

"My name is Officer Joe Callahan. My wife has shot and kidnapped me. I'm at one-two-two-one twenty-e—"

She slaps the tape back over his mouth. "Unfortunately, he's tied up at the moment. But that's okay. His handiwork will speak for him."

Jenny steps around Joe and halves her distance to Barry. She lifts her shirt until it's just below her breasts and points. "Here's where Joe put out a cigarette. And here and here and here. This is from his knife. And if I were to lift my shirt higher . . . well, you'll just have to imagine."

Using her index finger, Jenny beckons Tiffany into the shot. [The camera view widens] "This is Tiffany, one of Joe's coworkers. She was in a relationship with Joe until she found out he lied to her about divorcing me. Please turn around and pull up your shirt."

Tiffany follows her instructions.

[The camera view tightens briefly, then widens]

"Who did this to you, Tiffany?"

When she turns back to face the camera, tears are streaming

down her cheeks. She points at Joe and says, "He did."

"Thank you. I know that was difficult. Are you aware of anyone else Joe has abused?"

Tiffany steps sideways to face Jenny. "Not from his personal life. His professional life, I suspect, has many more victims. Recently, his conduct as a police officer allowed one of his victims to appeal a conviction successfully, and sometimes, at dinner, he'd rant to me about various ethnic groups—especially blacks—that angered him. And when he did so, he didn't use the polite word. I wouldn't want to be a black man pulled over by Joe when he's having a bad day. That's fer sure."

Jenny circles back behind Joe [The camera view tightens] and says, "Tell us, Joe. Do you use extra force when arresting black men?"

"Mmm, mmm, mmm," he whimpers behind the tape.

"What's that?" Jenny lowers her ear to his mouth before straightening and nodding vigorously. "He says 'yes.'"

She rests her forefinger against her cheek and looks directly into the camera. "Now, you're probably wondering how Joe ended up tied to a chair with his leg wrapped in a bandage. He claims I kidnapped him. Is he right? Or are appearances deceiving?"

Jenny waves Barry closer to the safe. "We're standing in Joe's and my bedroom, and you're looking at the gun safe in our closet." She pulls open the door with game show host flair. "This note greeted me this morning."

[The camera zooms in until the note fills the screen]

"A professional handwriting analyst will be able to confirm that Joe wrote it. That note forced me to stand, facing into the safe, too terrified to move even an inch. I resisted the mental and physical stay-still-or-die pain until I heard Barry entering the bedroom to check on me. I couldn't risk him walking into gunfire, so I tried to save us both by grabbing the door and diving into the safe. The gun Joe wanted me to fear turned out to be a confetti bomb, but the anguish it produced was real."

[The camera shot widens to include Jenny]

"At that point, I knew my only chance to stop my husband permanently, short of killing him, was to record him confessing. Beth helped me clean up the confetti and reset the room. Then she and Barry moved outside so they could keep watch. When Barry notified me that Joe was about to enter the house, I set my smartphone on record, placed it into my back pocket with the camera facing out, and stood in front of the safe, as if I'd been there the entire time."

Jenny reaches out, and Barry hands her the smartphone. [The camera switches to selfie mode] Looking into the lens, she says, "I just figured out how to do this, so forgive the clunkiness of the transition."

[The screen goes blank for a moment before the video recorded from Jenny's back pocket begins]

"Getting tired yet?"

"What do *you* think?"

"How long have you been standing there?"

"Maybe three hours. I don't know. I haven't been able to look at a clock."

"Impressive. Where are your friends?"

"If you ever used even a fraction of that tiny brain of yours, you'd know exactly where they are!"

"I asked you a question!"

"Fine. . . . They dropped me off this morning and continued north."

"You better not be lying. . . . Put those on."

"If I move, the gun will go off."

"Do ya trust me?"

"Hell no!"

"Well, you're gonna have to trust me now. The motion sensor is aimed directly at that beautiful, albeit fatter, ass of yours. As long as you keep it still, you can pick up the present at your feet."

"I can't bend like that!"

"Oh, I think you can."

"Are you crazy? I haven't been that limber since high school."

"If you can't do it, I'll throw something at you that'll make your entire body move. . . . Put them on. Nice . . . and . . . tight. . . . Now. Turn around. We're gonna have a party!"

"No! The gun will go off."

"Turn around!"

"No!"

"You fucking bitch! . . . Hey! Where's the confet—"

"Surprise!"

Bang!

"Fuuuck!"

[A live shot returns, with the camera still in selfie mode]

"Well, I think that's enough for now. As the video you've just watched clearly shows, I shot Joe in self-defense. That allowed me to secure him with his own handcuffs and wrap him up as he appears to you now. Tiffany knows a police officer we can trust. Once this video begins streaming on multiple sites, she'll call her and have Joe arrested."

Jenny looks away from the camera. "Would anyone like to add anything?"

Beth raises a finger [The camera switches to the main lens and focuses on Beth]. "I'd just like to say that I witnessed Joe's temper, when he stalked and chased us all the way from Des Moines to Kansas City. Jenny wasn't an escaped criminal. She was an abused wife, trying to escape her violent husband. I imagine she broke a few laws today, but what other choice did she have? Her husband is a cop, and cops like him stick together. If she'd dialed nine-one-one, the very cops responding to her call could've been his drinking buddies! What she did here today is a victory for battered wives everywhere."

Tiffany waves to get Jenny's attention [The camera pans to Tiffany] and adds, "Not just battered wives, but all battered women."

Barry waves too [The camera pans to Barry] and says, "Along the same lines, I think I can speak for all the good men and all the good police officers out there when I say to the bad ones: what the fuck is wrong with you? Right now, I'd like nothing better than to hurl cans of SPAM at Jenny's husband until he's black-and-blue from head to toe. But because I'm an adult, with self-control, I can refrain from violence. Instead, I look forward to testifying on Jenny's behalf if she faces any legal consequences for what happened today."

[The camera switches to selfie mode and focuses on Jenny's face]

"Thank you all for watching. If you'd like to help the Silver Squad feed the homeless, protect alligators from unethical hunting, and perhaps even hire a skilled attorney, please visit our GoFundMe page. I'm Jenny Callahan, and this has been a Silver Squad production."

EPILOGUE

One Year Later

Des Moines is a three-and-a-half-hour drive from the Blue Loon Village in Minneapolis. Barry and Beth traveled there to watch and testify at Joe Callahan's trial. As expected, multiple cops testified on Joe's behalf, swearing that he was a non-violent man who had been seduced into consensual discipline and bondage sex as part of his manipulative wife's elaborate scheme to fleece him out of everything in their divorce.

The judge also appeared to favor Joe, confirming Jenny's earlier worries of her husband's cozy relationship with numerous Des Moines judges. And whether it is right or wrong, juries in America tend to be more trusting of police officers than they are of everyday people.

In the end, much of the prosecution's case, including the felony kidnaping charge, was either disallowed on technicalities or judged by the jury as not reaching the standard of beyond a reasonable doubt. Instead, Joe was sentenced to six months for the misdemeanor of false imprisonment and nine months for the serious misdemeanor of domestic violence, both to be served consecutively in a county jail.

Jenny also faced a trial for her actions, with the most serious charge being false imprisonment. Ultimately, she escaped Joe's fate by reaching a plea agreement that included nine months of house arrest. And since the judge didn't consider her a high-risk offender, she only had to wear an ankle bracelet for the first five months.

That was all fine with Jenny, since a separate judge had awarded her sole ownership of the house in the final decree of divorce. She found having the house to herself an exhilarating experience. When she had lived with Joe, the house often felt like a prison. Now it was her sanctuary, providing her with newfound freedom. And as part of that freedom, she adopted three cats from an animal shelter, in honor of the three kittens they had to give up in Jackson, Mississippi.

The experience of creating and distributing the videos to protect alligators, along with the viral "Joe in Bondage" video—now with over 100 million views—had sparked Jenny's interest in pursuing a career in a related field. She wasn't yet sure what that would be, but she was taking on-line college courses that would prepare her for whatever she ultimately decided to do.

In the meantime, Jenny grew her fame with streamed appearances on most of the major television talk shows. While the hosts of those shows always wanted to talk about her experiences of overcoming a mass shooter in Kansas City and an abusive husband in her own home, Jenny would give them what they wanted and then veer off into her causes of supporting battered women and protecting alligators.

While helping battered women was far more important to Jenny than protecting alligators, she kept up the latter out of respect for Barry. And despite being a lower priority for her, she learned that she could be effective at promoting more than one cause at a time.

Her work maintaining the ad and social media campaign she started back in Florida, along with her, Barry, and Beth mentioning the plight of alligators in interviews, had produced tangible results. Outfitters who specialized in private land alligator hunts were now having to offer deep discounts to fill their schedules, and a coalition of Democrats and Republicans in the Florida legislature were even discussing a bill that would subject private land hunts to the stricter regulations of public land hunts.

Jenny also asked Barry and Beth to move in with her. "My extra bedroom does me no good sitting here empty," she declared.

They both declined, knowing that they moved into the Blue Loon Village for a reason. Old age always wins, and each new day would push them a little closer to losing their independence. Saddling Jenny with the responsibility of eventually becoming their nurse or having to agonize over putting them into a nursing home was something neither of them would consider, no matter how much she argued that doing so would only be repaying them for the kindness they showed to her.

Even so, Jenny always had her extra bedroom waiting for them whenever they visited Des Moines, which, as it turned out, happened frequently. Jenny had become the daughter Barry and Beth might have made together if they hadn't broken up after high school.

Back in Minnesota, Barry and Beth narrowly avoided legal problems of their own. Only a little selective forgetfulness by the Hormel Foods truck driver saved them from having to face a trial for their armed robbery in Albert Lea. It didn't take much work for a detective to figure out who had committed the crime. After all, Barry had yelled, "You've been robbed by the sometimes tired, always inspired, Silver Squad!" at the scene. Nevertheless, when they stood in a police lineup, the truck driver—who had reported the crime and later became a fan—shook his head and claimed he didn't see anyone who matched his memory.

One more trial was on the horizon. The trial of the Benny's Country Dancehall Shooter would have been a huge spectacle. That is, if the defendant hadn't choked to death when country music fan inmates force-fed him an entire unsliced can of a certain jalapeño flavored processed meat, just days before Barry, Beth, and Jenny were to travel to Kansas City to testify.

All the while, Barry and Beth continued their work to feed the homeless. Enough money was coming in via the Silver Squad GoFundMe page to run a homeless shelter, but that was incompatible with their efforts to help those who, because of pets, mental illness, or some other reason, lived on their own. So instead of a shelter, they improved their in-person deliveries with a few modifications.

Included among their modifications was Beth trading in her old Honda Civic toward the purchase of a brand-new Subaru Forester. The new SUV would give them more room for transporting food, and the all-wheel drive would help them get to where they needed to go during Minnesota's snowy winters.

Another modification was in the quality of food they delivered. As Beth pointed out to Barry over drinks in the Silver Squad lair, "Handing out SPAM was a fun novelty, but now we need to get serious about nutrition."

Without anticipating how one change could lead to another, Beth's nutritional goal spurred on the growth of the Silver Squad—with actual silver-haired seniors.

Since creating healthy meals would require the use of a kitchen—preferably a certified commercial kitchen—Beth approached the Blue Loon Village's director, Samantha, with a proposal to use the kitchen there and involve its residents too.

Although Samantha didn't immediately say yes, she eventually succumbed to Beth's persistence and gave the Silver Squad permission to use the Blue Loon Village's kitchen. Her primary requirements for use were that they only used it after hours, provided all their own ingredients, and left everything spotless when they finished. Soon the Silver Squad expanded into a rotating team of three shoppers, three cooks, four clean-up crew, four delivery assistants, and three drivers with reliable automobiles.

As Samantha said, when a reporter from a local television

station interviewed her about the project, "At first, I was reluctant to give the Silver Squad permission to use our kitchen. After all, many of our residents are physically unable to participate. But after observing for several months now, I'm convinced that the residents who can participate have benefited as much, if not more, from this project than the homeless people they're helping. People are happier and healthier when they feel useful, and that doesn't change when someone moves into a retirement facility."

Samantha's words led to even more participation, as another Blue Loon Village resident started up a knitting group for seniors who weren't mobile enough to help with other tasks. Soon their knitted hats, scarves, and mittens became cherished additions to the food deliveries.

With trips to Des Moines and helping the homeless keeping Barry and Beth active in their retirement, they let Jenny be the primary talk show star. The few times they agreed to make television appearances, they limited them to only the biggest shows and refused to discuss any of their adventures, unless they were also guaranteed sufficient airtime to discuss their pet projects of feeding the homeless and ending unethical alligator hunting.

As for Gertrude, she couldn't have cared less about saving alligators, feeding the homeless, supporting battered women, or appearing on television talk shows. She did, however, enjoy the rides.

ABOUT THE AUTHOR

The author on stage at Northwestern Michigan College

Marty Essen grew up in Minnesota and lives in Montana. In addition to being an author, he is also a talent agent and a college speaker. Since 2007, Marty has been performing *Around the World in 90 Minutes* on college campuses from coast to coast. *Around the World in 90 Minutes* is based on his first book, *Cool Creatures, Hot Planet: Exploring the Seven Continents,* and it has become one of the most popular slide shows of all-time.

Please enjoy all of Marty Essen's books:

Cool Creatures, Hot Planet: Exploring the Seven Continents
Six-Time Award Winner. Features 86 photographs.

Endangered Edens: Exploring the Arctic National Wildlife Refuge, Costa Rica, the Everglades, and Puerto Rico
Four-Time Award Winner. Features 180 photographs.

Time Is Irreverent
An irreverent, liberal, twisty, time travel comedy.

Time Is Irreverent 2: Jesus Christ, Not Again!
Another irreverent, liberal, twisty, time travel comedy.

Time Is Irreverent 3: Gone for 16 Seconds
Yet another irreverent, liberal, twisty, time travel comedy.

Time Is Irreverent: Ooh, It's a Trilogy! (Books 1-3)
The entire beloved series in a single e-book.

Hits, Heathens, and Hippos: Stories from an Agent, Activist, and Adventurer
A humorous memoir, with rock 'n' roll, headhunters, a demon-possessed watch, and a hippo attack.

Doctor Refurb
An unconventional, satirical, controversial, time travel comedy.

For information on Marty Essen's speaking engagements, please visit www.MartyEssen.com. For beautiful nature photography and biting political commentary, please visit www.Marty-Essen.com. To purchase signed copies of Marty Essen's books, please email Books@EncantePress.com.

Special Thanks To:

Deb Essen
and
Nellie

PLEASE REVIEW THIS BOOK:

Reviews are important! If you enjoyed *The Silver Squad: Rebels With Wrinkles,* please post a review on the website of the retailer where you purchased this book. Thank you.

Made in the USA
Middletown, DE
04 February 2025

70099468R00167